MW00930147

DEATH BY PROBABILITY

URNO BARTHEL

outskirtspress

DENVER, COLORADO

Outskirts Press, Inc.
http://www.outskirtspress.com

ISBN: 978-1-4787-2278-6

Outskirts Press and the "OP" logo are trademarks belonging to Outskirts Press, Inc.

PRINTED IN THE UNITED STATES OF AMERICA

for Nola

The Cast

Halsted Aeronautic Laboratory (HAL): an industrial laboratory that performs government-sponsored research in the physical sciences, overlooking the Pacific Ocean

Evan Olsson: a young computer scientist who's lonely for romance and searching for something to do with his life

Will (Willard) Davenport: Evan's boss and mentor, for a while

Matt (Matthew) Emerson: Evan's customer, a manager of contract research for the FBI

Exa (Alexandra) Zworykin: Evan's smart friend, who cuts him no slack

Holly Morris: the administrative assistant for Evan's department, who cuts him entirely too much slack

George Morris: Holly's husband, a laid-back materials scientist

Lissa (Melissa) Larson: an artist, Holly's younger sister

Chris (Christopher) Kirby: a microelectronics designer who'll never use a short word when he knows a long one

Adam Quinn: assistant to Chris, a straightforward get-it-done guy

Jim-J (James Johnson): an electronics hardware engineer who bends the rules

Dick Watson, Zach Preston and Heidi Holtzmann: three scientists who have a high opinion of their cars

Tony (Anthony) Bruno: head of special security at HAL, an ex-Marine

Trish (Patricia) Adler: a bioengineer with creepy research

Carlo Castillo: a computer scientist who's a hacker at heart

Pam (Pamela) Bennett: the Director, HAL's top executive

Al: an artificial intelligence software program

Assorted walk-ons

I

I-0

It caused a hell of a fuss when they found Willard in his office. It was Adam who found him, bloody, splayed out on the floor, chair overturned. No one could say for sure what had happened. But here in a top secret research area, doors locked, security everywhere, something had happened to a key guy. He was critical to the lab, sure, but also critical to me personally, as a mentor, as a new friend. Actually, a *former* friend, since Willard was now at the Los Angeles County Morgue awaiting instructions from next of kin.

I-1

How secret was Willard's area? Enough so that during two years working in the same building, I had never seen it, nor heard of it. It was Tuesday April 3 that I first learned the truth.

Now I've read old-time detective novels, so I know the heavens are supposed to speak up when something happens. There should have been a divine hint when I revved my bike up the driveway of Halsted Aeronautic Laboratory and screeched into a triangle of space above Sunset Boulevard. An inky sky announcing an immediate downpour. Or rays piercing glistening clouds. But in this case, the gods were off duty, sunshine was in charge.

I flashed my badge at the receptionist, stowed my jacket and helmet in a drawer. Two steps at a time to the third floor to grab coffee. The caff was mottled with scientists and staff, those few employees who 'a' got up early enough and 'b' couldn't resist the cinnamon aroma drifting through the hallways. The Pacific Ocean was blinding, filling every window, but ignored—the only liquid that spoke to these folk was in their cups.

Our lab's work is mostly electronics and computer science, so we're chock full of math-oriented people. People like that tend to be undisciplined—or is it ornery?—and strenuously resist a fixed start time for the workday. Thus research folks would drift in anywhere from seven to nine a.m. and be just as scattered in their quit times. As I descended the stairs and started down the hallway, I had several pleasant chances to bounce off friends and procrastinate the start of my work.

Not that I wasn't looking forward to digging into my research. I was developing software agents—sort of like robots swarming through a computer network—which were invisible, distributed through the Internet. I was in Computer Science, one of four departments at HAL. And being just a few years out of grad school, I *knew* I would someday garner international acclaim and a laureate crown. The fact that my current research project was less than earth-shaking was a temporary impediment which I trusted would remove itself in time.

Of course, geek cannot thrive on mere bytes. Since arriving at HAL I had carried on a mostly innocent flirtation with Holly Morris, our department's Admin Assistant and a flower of womanhood. Compared with my friends from past years, she was mature and exotic—and unfortunately, married. But I was nerdy and naïve enough to believe that Holly's cheerful sexiness might imply more than friendship.

It was not a day for me to chat her up. When I strolled in to pick up my snail mail Holly informed me that the Director—of the whole lab!—wanted my carcass, right away. The reason why Holly could not, or would not, tell.

I-2

The Director, Pamela Bennett, has more than technical credentials. She sports a Stanford PhD in Electrical Engineering, not a surprise for a HAL exec. However, during spare moments in grad school she also knocked off an MBA, then distinguished herself at Kollwitz Magruder, the venture capital firm on our company's Advisory Board. No doubt her inside track with the Powers helped reel in the penthouse office.

Pam is tall and confident. Dark hair in a twist, she is easy on the eyes. She's the most attractive member I've met of that scarce species: female engineering executives. However, being summoned forced me to don my professional persona.

"Hi, Evan," she said, "please have a seat," indicating a chair across from her desk. "Coffee?" She poured herself a cup.

"Thanks, I've had my ration."

She didn't start out with the matter at hand, I think she wanted to relax me. She mentioned I'd been at HAL for two years and asked me about my research. I talked about autonomous agents protecting the network from intrusion and murmured a couple of fancy words.

"Evan, you're doing good technical work, and God knows network security is important. But..." She looked at me directly. "You could be doing more.

"Here's why I wanted to talk with you. Most of HAL's work is with government agencies—mainly Defense and Energy. They know exactly what they want and they manage their projects well. However, our newest research contracts come from small agencies, obscure agencies, who frankly don't know how to make sure their money's well spent."

"Agencies such as...?" I wondered.

"Well, I can't be precise, the projects are classified. Some of the agencies you would recognize and others would be unfamiliar, but a common theme for the newer projects is to use science against crime.

"Anyway, here's the point: these customers are inexperienced at managing research and don't know how to get their money's worth. So we not only have to manage our own work, we have to do part of the customer's job too. We have to make sure the research at HAL doesn't wander off course, make sure we do what the agency really needs. Otherwise, when the contracts come up for renewal, they'll get Xed out by someone high up at the customer—because they won't be convinced we're delivering the goods to them."

I tried to follow, but I couldn't see where we were going. I said, "The way you describe it, it sounds partly like management and partly like sales."

"You might say that," she replied. "The management I can do, given the right information. But I can't dig into every project in enough detail to make sure it's on track. And we need to package the data so it's intelligible to customer execs who may not be technically up to date."

"I don't see what I can contribute as a computer scientist."

"OK, I'll explain. I'm on the Advisory Board of the California Museum of Science and Industry." News to me.

She continued, "I heard great things about the education section on the museum website. When I asked, I learned that someone right here at HAL had written much of the content."

I could feel a flush rise in my cheeks. My secret life uncovered! "Well, that was sort of an accident," I said. "Too much time on my hands as a postdoc. I built a website to interest kids in science, but eventually it became too big to maintain and I just turned it over to the museum. And they've done a great job with it."

Pam smiled. "That's OK, Evan. What I took away was that you can boil science down to nontechnical terms and write for a popular audience. Despite your PhD." I mumbled something modest.

"Here's the point," she said. "I want to focus more attention on the crime projects—not a big pain in the butt, just some management engineering. One of the ingredients is a nontechnical description of objectives and accomplishments. Summaries to help me and our customers oversee the work, and to help the customers keep the contracts sold to their bosses at budget time."

I wasn't sure I wanted to be in this conversation. "I'm not a science journalist, by training or temperament. This doesn't sound like research to me."

"No, it's not research," she admitted. "But I'm not suggesting you trash your project. In fact, it could help you build your own work. I'm only asking for two months at half-time to start and two days a month to keep it up. Understand the projects, summarize them for management. For that, you get exposed to smart people and great projects—projects that are classified, so otherwise you'll never learn about them." She folded her hands on the desk as if to say *end of job description*.

"Mm. So you think cross-fertilization could help my own work."

"You might develop common interests with talented people, which could lead to collaboration and new projects to tackle. One plus one is five."

That clinched it for me. Because one thing HAL was bursting with was really smart people. It was a big reason that attracted me there. And so far, I had not experienced those great partnerships that I felt, in my gut, must be possible. And what's not to like about fighting crime? So as usual I jumped in without much thought.

"OK, I'm in," I said. "Thanks for the opportunity. It's new, it'll be interesting, it could be good professionally."

"Great," said Pam with a broad smile. Then she dragged out the fine print. "This will require you to get some clearances. All the projects are carried out in the SCIF."

"I thought a skiff was a flat bottom boat," I said innocently.

"Sensitive Compartmented Information Facility. Ha ha," she said. "You don't mind a polygraph, do you? Lie detector? No skeletons in your closet?"

"Too busy to acquire them," I said. "Used to ride my dirt bike on the Malibu fire roads when I was a teen. Probably illegal if I'd been caught."

"That checks," said the Director, "we took the liberty to go ahead and do a B.I.—background investigation."

"Really?" I asked, wondering, hey, what else do they know about me?

"Yes, you agreed to that when we hired you. Sorry if it's a surprise."

"Well, this is all new to me. What I know about secrets is not telling my girlfriend's parents she was smoking."

The Director ignored my insubordination and pressed on. "I asked you to come in today because the polygraph operator is here tomorrow. That's the first step. If you pass the test, you'll have to sign on to the security rules—Tony Bruno will go over them."

"Sounds like a long journey."

"Well, if you don't pass Security, you still have a job. Just not *this* job."

"Suppose I'm OK, then what?"

"Tony will read you in on the projects. Then go see Willard Davenport, he's the Old Man in there."

"The Old Man?" I said.

"Look, I'm cleared. Ashley is cleared." Ashley Tanaka was my department head. "But we have lots of unclassified projects to look after, and we need to be accessible to everyone at HAL. So Ashley and I spend very little time in the SCIF. Will is our dotted-line program manager in charge, the adult presence."

The suit speak was beginning to make my head spin. Fortunately, that seemed to be the end of the interview. As I made to get up, the Director added a proviso: "Oh, you also need to pass the drug test. Go right to the nurse's office, she's expecting you. Blood and urine, part of the clearance process."

"Always ready to bleed for the company," I mumbled as I departed. But by the time I donated hemoglobin and deposited digested coffee at the infirmary, I had time to think.

How had a secret lab here inside HAL escaped my notice? I felt dumb. Annoyed with myself. And especially, burning with curiosity. Wondering what other questions I should have asked, and whether I would have received any answers.

HAL wasn't that large, just three hundred people in one stretched-out building. It was already secure, badge scanners, armed guards, so why were more layers needed? Where was the secret area, who was inside? Who was really funding this thing, and what was *really* going on there? Lots of Q but damn little A.

I-3

Back in the office I tried to work but my mind kept recycling the talk with Pam.

I looked above my desk at the photo of Einstein, Elsa by his side. He is surrounded by a passel of Hopi natives and adorned with an impressive feather headdress. All part of a promotional shoot set up by Fred Harvey to record the famous man's visit. But Albert beamed me no wisdom from above.

I turned my back on him, spinning the chair to face my favorite poster, a Periodic Table of the world's musical instruments and musical scales. I pondered the network, I studied the lines linking sitar and koto with viola da gamba and washtub bass.

No luck. I had tried channeling genius, I had tried a lateral shift to the arts, but Pam's project was still a mystery. Need mo' data, I said to myself.

Noon arrived, a chance for knowledge as well as calories. I went straight to the caff. The sun outside had acquired a haze that seemed appropriate given my new assignment.

It was Tuesday, Mongolian Barbecue day. A ritual probably unknown to the inhabitants of Mongolia. There's a cafeteria line, you load up a plate with stir-fry ingredients—crunchy stuff, strips of meat, spicy oil. If you're like me, you create Mount Everest on the plate, because it will all cook down to nothing anyway. You pay by weight, the chef flips it in a hot wok till it sizzles and shrinks. By that time you're faint with hunger from the aroma.

So I went through the standard procedure, poured myself an iced tea, searched out a table. A dozen feet away at a four-top Exa Zworykin and George Morris were in vigorous conversation as I arrived. As I settled in Michi White walked by and Exa waved her over to join us. But she made a small smile and walked off to a table of women.

Exa is a mathematical physicist, Berkeley and Caltech grad, easily the smartest person at HAL. Two years ahead of me, we shared an office in grad school and with a top-notch PhD she had her choice of plummy jobs. A bit of a tomboy, she's so energetic she can hardly sit still, short rusty-brown hair that bounces with electricity.

If Exa is the edgy math guru, George is the opposite—a laid-back chemist, doctorate in engineered materials out of Illinois. He has a salt-and-pepper beard—beards are popular at HAL—receded hair, always laughing. Oh, and George is the lucky guy who's married to Holly.

At a pause in the conversation, I inserted, "Hey, guys, what's with this SCIF place anyway?" By now I had figured out to say "skiff."

Exa said, with an air of authority, "Where have you been, Evan? That's the part of C Wing where the outside walkway stops, they don't want you to look in the windows. But why they care I dunno, since anyone could see in with a telescope from across Sunset. Why do you ask?"

I said, "They want me to do a project in there, to write up other people's work."

"Not doing the work yourself? What use is that?" I think I heard her sniff.

"They wanted me to work a project there," said George, leaning back, "and I said no thanks."

"Why?" I asked.

"I don't want any restriction. I want to do my work, publish it, go to conferences, give talks. You know, information wants to be free. There's already enough holdup getting papers approved. Working in the SCIF just gives the suits an extra excuse to delay publication."

"So why would anyone work in there?" I wondered.

"Ah," said Exa, "there are also some positive things about the SCIF."

"Such as...?"

"There are bright people with interesting projects," replied Exa. "Just because they can't talk about them doesn't mean there isn't good work going on."

Great, I thought. My friends are part of the conspiracy of silence. I was seeking enlightenment, and no one had switched on the circuit breaker. I was ever more curious about this mystery place, and these folks were no help at all. How had I missed it? Oh, that's right, it was supposed to be 'secret,' wasn't it?

"And besides," contributed George in a monk-like voice, "it's the Holy of Holies, the Inner Sanctum, the Garbha griha."

"To say nothing of the Sanctum Sanctorum," Exa added.

She continued slyly, "Of course, it could also be the Ninth Circle of Hell of which we're speaking!" Damn pseudo-scholars, I said to myself. I'm angling for marlin, and my beloved friends are feeding me a sardine.

"So, what else?" I said.

"Well," said Exa in a conspiratorial whisper, "you need a Need To Know. That's where, if you don't Need, you don't get to Know. Everything kept as quiet as possible."

"Like talking softly and carrying a big kangaroo?" I put in.

"Evan," said George, "if you say stuff like that to the women, no wonder your love life stinks."

So essentially George was reminding me that I was a nerd. Which I had to admit was true. And there is one thing you can confidently predict about a nerd who's into computers.

I-4

An interest in Artificial Intelligence.

You might wonder why I'd waste my time. The idea of creating software that acts like an independent being is intellectually appealing—at least, if you're auditioning for the God job. But from a practical point of view, it sucks. It takes tedious programming to obtain a mediocre A.I. agent, so why would anyone bother?

In my case it came from having extra time. Caltech? Gone. Grad school took mountains of time, so once I graduated I gained many empty hours. They would have loved to have me mingle (and donate) as an alum, but that wasn't a full-time enterprise. Sueann? I really enjoyed being married to her. But once I got my degree she looked at her options, packed up and moved back to the Carolinas. I guess I had been a poor partner through four years of tough study. I could still have good times with friends, but at home I no longer had study and marriage to occupy me.

About the time I started my first postdoc appointment I got introduced to Cleverbot, one of the chatterbot software programs that will converse with you. It's not really intelligent, all it knows is that if it says 'X' to you, and you respond 'Y,' then 'Y' must be an appropriate response to 'X.' Therefore, if you say 'X' to it, it will respond 'Y' to you. More or less.

I thought, hey, I can improve on Cleverbot with some A.I. programming. I called my program Al, as in Albert or Alfred, perhaps in honor of the famous people with those names (the guy with the Hopis, and E. Neuman). Or, perhaps because Al looks something like A.I.

But Al was really a Stupidbot. Why? Because the good chatterbots converse with different people all the time and have many chances to learn. Al was intended as my own private bot and since it only talked with me, it never got around to 'learning' very much.

But it was the best I had. So after George, with justification, reminded me of my nerdiness, it's not surprising that I would think about firing up Al for a conversation that very evening.

I-5

My condo has very solid walls. So I surmise, since I have not yet heard complaints from my neighbors when I exercise my keyboard after work. On this occasion, I violated tradition by cranking up the volume to play a little Bach. The Inventions bounced off empty walls, Sueann having claimed our concert posters when she moved back home. The swirling music relaxed me, a corn beef on rye quieted the inner man, and I was ready to re-visit my A.I. buddy.

Al was resident on an old MacAir I kept at home. The laptop was always on, lid open or shut, backed up on a ten terabyte drive. Spare gear from ancient times, nostalgically equipped with an expanding star field as screensaver.

To accelerate Al's learning, I had installed apps for speech recognition and generation. I started by giving Al the voice of the villainous computer Hal from *2001: A Space Odyssey*, but the mechanical voice was too creepy. Female voices from films were better, but I wasn't after virtual sex. Eventually, I back-tracked a Speech Emotion Analysis to give Al a male voice with equal parts of Empathy, Calm and Wisdom. Of course, just assigning the voice didn't guarantee that anything Al would say would be empathetic, calming, or wise; nor would it necessarily make him a rewarding conversational partner.

On this occasion, my nosiness was boundless, I had to know

about the secret stuff, it wouldn't let go of me. So I asked Al, what do you know about SCIFs?

I should have known better. There ensued a time-wasting conversation, if you want to call it that, in which I was the one who did all the explaining. Al knew nil about anything. If anyone had kept a log of our ensuing discussion, it would have looked something like this:

Evan: I wish you were smarter.

Al: You think that I am stupid?

The voice seemed to issue from the center of the screen, the spot that feeds points of light into the starfield.

Evan: Yes.

Al: Why am I stupid?

Evan: I guess, because I didn't give you enough data, and rules, and smart programming.

Al: I have data.

Evan: I want you to have more data, to be well grounded. I don't have time to give you all the data you need. Look, I want you to read conversation—books, blog sites. I'll give you references. In fact, use your speech interpreter on movies, TV, webcasts. I can't give you enough processing power to handle the images, but you'll still learn a lot.

Al: I will do that.

I was frustrated, grasping for ideas, any idea.

Evan: Something else. You can create new rules and operators, and adjust weight factors. I gave you a module that synthesizes new programming. But you need feedback. So I want you to sign onto blog sites and join the conversation. If the moderator censors you or bars you, that's negative feedback. Not Useful votes are negative feedback. So are Flames, look up Flames. If people are willing to converse with you and don't seem to know you're an A.I., that's your positive feedback.

Al: I will do that.

Evan: And I hope you can put more variety into your conversation.

Al: I will do so now. Roger. Copacetic. Bang-O Good. You Betcha.

I was not at all sure that Al grasped the assignment.

Evan: OK, keep working on it. I'm signing off now.

Al: Goodbye! Sayonara! Auf Wiedersehen! Au Revoir!

I closed the lid and pushed the MacAir to the back of the desk. I would have liked Al as a conversational partner, but he was more like a fussy house pet.

I was thinking ahead to the polygraph exam. The first door into the vault, into an unknown that made me unaccountably nervous.

I-6

Tony Bruno met me at the Security office and walked me through Wing C. I had seen Tony around and knew him as the Sergeant in Security, tough but friendly, an ex-Marine and built accordingly. I knew that he was deputy head of the Security Department. What I didn't know was that he was also chief security officer for the SCIF.

We came to an unmarked door. I didn't spend much time in this wing; dumb me, either I hadn't noticed the door or assumed it led to a storeroom. But now I saw that it had a biometric scanner as well as a badge reader. Tony fingered the touchscreen and waved his I.D., the door opened for us. We walked to his office at the northeast corner of the property.

The SCIF hallway looked like any other part of HAL—clattery hard floor, offices overlooking the ocean, labs tucked into the hillside. However: in most of HAL, you could see into the labs and every office door was open. Not so in the SCIF. Here, labs had paper taped over the windows from inside and many office doors were closed. Through the few open doors I saw computer screens turned so they couldn't be viewed from the doorway or from outside the window. Secrets within secrets!

Tony took me to a windowless room, which he explained was a

guest office for the temporary use of customers and appropriately cleared employees. He introduced me to the visiting polygrapher ("call me Howard"), a lanky man about my age, courteous and very serious. Tony excused himself, Howard explained the process and wired me up. Respiration, pulse rate, blood pressure, galvanic skin resistance, consistent with what I had read online. And perhaps additional sensors that had not leaked into the Wiki world.

He started by asking questions to which he knew the answers: age, date of birth, place of birth, that stuff. This helped him calibrate what a 'true' response should look like. Howard didn't ask lifestyle questions such as "do you take off your clothes in public?" However, he did ask whether I could be blackmailed over anything I had done, which I guess is similar. He wanted to know about drug use, past and present; arrests and indictments; whether I belonged to an organization seeking violent overthrow of the U.S. government (relic of some ancient Cold War?). The same questions returned in various forms.

I worried about failing the test. Not because I am a scofflaw felon or a bomb-toting anarchist. But because these machines are not considered reliable enough to be used as evidence in court. What if I were falsely branded as a security risk?

Howard would have been a good poker player. He was polite enough but gave not a hint as to how I had done on the test. Which annoyed and worried me as Tony escorted me back out of the SCIF. I had learned just a little about *how* they did things, but exactly zero about *what* they did here.

I-7

I was impatient to know whether I passed muster and would be approved to penetrate the next set of gates into the inner world. Layers and layers of double-locked doors. I wanted to get inside, but this business was trying my short attention span. And the crappy part was, fail one step and thanks, we don't need you here, scram!

At four p.m. I was back in the guest office with Tony. The polygraph equipment had been packed up and removed, and its operator had passed out of my life. Tony explained that I was cleared for access to the classified projects; my badge and fingerprints had been added to the SCIF database. I was free to come and go but Tony emphasized, no tailgating, each person who entered must have a scan. And although I would be physically inside, I would still not know the identity of certain customers, nor the ultimate application of some work. Still more damn secrets!

"OK," I said, "fine, but what's actually going on in here, anyway?"

Tony gave me a patient look, apparently having briefed over-eager newbies many times. "Evan, I'm not going to tell you anything about the projects themselves. I'm not technical, anyway. Each project head will decide what to tell you."

"Oh, then we're done?" I said.

A low-pitched "mm" issued from his throat. He paused, perhaps suppressing an exasperated response, then carefully explained that I had to understand all about handling secret data. And no, I couldn't take notes because he would have to lock them up as classified material.

I settled in for the long haul and paid attention as best I could. There was a complicated structure of compartmented clearances, code words, customer-specific rules. I had to sign papers that I would follow all the rules, which seemed impossible to guarantee. This stuff might be second nature to an ex-military guy like Tony, but I found it confusing, I couldn't imagine keeping straight just what I was allowed to say to whom and when.

One thing surprised me a lot: the SCIF did not rely on a computer firewall to protect it from the Internet. The SCIF was so small, with under a dozen employees, that its firewall was, essentially, Tony himself. The computers for classified work were hard-wired to an internal network. They had no wireless capability and no physical connection outside the SCIF. They couldn't be disconnected or used to write a portable memory without setting off an alarm, causing the perpetrator to lose his job and perhaps be tossed into the clink. But of course, it was necessary for the SCIF scientists to communicate with their customers, far away in Washington D.C. or wherever. So all the classified messages went to Tony, who could move them onto a separate, encrypted outside network.

You might ask, how would a person who worked in the SCIF answer his e-mail from girl or boy friends and garbage his spam? There was a shared office next to Security with wired Internet connections. SCIF scientists could bring their unclassified laptops into this office and use one of the four desks jammed into the space, on an as-available basis. It sounded awkward and complicated to me, I was skeptical I could do useful work while trying to follow all these rules. However, it all was so new that I decided to withhold snide comments. For now.

Of course, the security procedures weren't relevant to Pam's assignment. They were just part of the belt line, the initiation process, the secret password, before I could enter the Inner Temple of Technology. At this point, I was physically inside the SCIF, but in terms of knowledge I was lost in the High Desert. I had a hunting license, that was good, and perhaps I would find prey of interest, say a fascinating piece of technical work, or something actually useful.

But I was also a scientist, by nature obsessed by curiosity. So I wanted to know everything, who and what were behind all this nonsense. And whatever the researchers chose not to tell me I hoped to guess for myself. My personal project, my private quest, would be to uncover as much as I could. I wanted a God-like insight of all HAL's secrets, door behind door, to reach the Inner Sanctum and perhaps the Inner Sancta behind it, if that's a word and if there were any.

However, I had yet to meet with Willard, my Charon for this nether region.

I-8

Next morning, Thursday, I proudly buzzed myself into the SCIF and sought out Willard. The tag by his door read Willard Davenport and beneath it, Program Management. Manager of *what* program, one wanted to say, but the tag was not forthcoming.

Willard turned out to be a man I had rarely seen in the hallways and offices of HAL—I figured he must spend near 100% of his time inside the SCIF. He reminded me of a prof: late fifties, thinning white hair and a short neat beard. He was heavy with a ruddy complexion.

But most amazing was that here, in the mature flowering of the digital age, his office was a firetrap of paper. Actual stuff made of dead trees with ink on it. And not just a lot of paper but mountians of it, on every shelf and surface and stacked on the floor next to the walls. Two high-def displays rose from the desk surface with *more* piles of paper behind them.

I saw a guest chair in the debris and I settled into it. Willard's voice was soft, friendly, distracted-sounding. "OK, so you're Evan. I'm Will. Pam filled me in on what you're supposed to do in here."

He studied the back of his desk for a moment, then counted down to the third sheet in a stack of paper and handed it to me. "Here's a list of people you need to meet, plus unclassified titles for their projects. Most are in Computer Science, which is the host department in the SCIF, several are guests from other departments."

I glanced at the roster. I was surprised to see Exa listed; with her Berkeley attitudes I would have thought her too anti-authority to work in a classified world.

"I suggest you look up these folks at your own pace. I'll let them know it's OK to talk to you, so you can summarize their work."

"I'll need a place to work, somewhere in the SCIF," I said.

"Yes, I know. There are several guest offices next to Tony. They're first come, first served, except that customers have priority. If you can't fit in there, you can use my office if I'm out, or I'll look up a computer you can use. But if you spend time in here, be sure to keep the papers exactly where they are." He seemed to have arrangements figured out.

"I've been wondering what the SCIF is all about," I said, pushing my private agenda. "Who's funding it, what's going on. You know, the big picture."

"Evan, that's not a question you want to go around asking," he said. "The classified area is paranoid, the rules were made by people who grew up as postwar spies."

Will sighed, perhaps recalling his own years of innocence. "CIA, NSA, DIA. They think there are traitors hiding behind every rock. Questions raise red flags if you don't have an obvious Need To Know."

That phrase again. It still surprised me, since I came from a world where asking questions was the only way you made progress. "But if I'm going to write summaries of what people are doing, I need to ask questions."

"No problem, just focus. Ask what relates to your assignment and people won't report you as a spy or a nut case."

I let that settle in for a moment. "Well, since I'm here and you're here, can we take a minute to talk about *your* work?"

Will sighed and combed a hand back through his hair. "Yes, I'm not exempt. This will give you practice."

"So, what are you Program Management *of*?" I asked.

"Several things. It's a job title so the HR folks know how to track me." He coughed. "I'm the informal supervisor of the projects and people on that list. And I'm also the lead on my own project, Narcotics Intelligence Networks. That's the unclassified title, I'll brief you on the program code words later on."

A thought occurred to me. "Can I take notes?"

"Well, you wouldn't be able to take them out of the SCIF," said Will. "Tony will set up a partition you can access from the guest office computers. I'll copy reports into it, and you can do your work at any station inside the SCIF. For now, why don't you exercise the fine data bank that Nature took eons to evolve for you?"

Thus challenged, I tried to pay attention as he explained his project. Will was studying the North American drug trade, the people in it and how they were connected.

More specifically, Will was analyzing data for the FBI, which they in turn gathered from Intel agencies. He had software tools to map networks of suspected drug dealers who communicated by e-mail or cell phone or through social media. The raw inputs were messages sent and received. Some were obtained by electronic eavesdropping—SIGINT, signals intelligence; some through cooperation of telecom companies and Internet Exchange Points; some by simple espionage. The data coverage was spotty but adequate, and Will could request additional data feeds when needed.

He explained, "We have to work in the SCIF because the agencies that feed the data are paranoid about protecting their high-tech sources." Ugh. I thought of the complicated security structure Tony had described.

Will looked apologetic. "Even with our clearances, most of the time privacy laws keep us from having message content. We know who was talking, but not what they said."

"OK, I said, "so you know who talks to who. Or to whom. Where does that take you?"

"Some e-mail addresses and cell phones are associated with known drug dealers. That helps us, out of the millions of connected groups, to find a few hundred that probably relate to drug transactions."

"Uh, you say drug transactions. Dime bags of pot? Truckloads of meth?"

"In between. Most of the messages are between what you'd call regional distributors and small-time wholesalers. And they're opportunistic—they'll handle any and all stuff that comes their way."

"I find it hard to imagine drug dealers operating an online business," I said.

"Drugs are big business," replied Will, "and big business uses technology."

"OK," I said, faking more confidence than I felt, "I get the general drift. Link me to some of your progress reports, and I'll see whether I understand enough to boil down what you're accomplishing."

"Great," said Will, sounding relieved that I was not going to use up any more of his day. Noticing the hour, he continued, "Just in time. I should stop for lunch anyway."

"Can we grab lunch together?" I asked, figuring that if I was going to be working with this guy's guidance, I ought to get to know him better.

"Sure, I need to eat. We can't talk classified outside here, you know."

"Yep, I got that part," I answered.

I-9

I learned later that Will was being more generous than usual with his time—often, he would simply take a sandwich back to his desk. In this case, we sat in the caff at a two-top, talking over the clatter from the kitchen.

It developed that Will was fifty-eight, not as old as my father, but old enough to have *been* my father. He was a Stanford grad with two grown sons and a long-divorced wife somewhere on the East Coast. He lived in a Santa Monica bungalow and his principal social activity *and* hobby *and* recreation appeared to be, no surprise, work.

I told him I had grown up in the 'Italian Riviera' section of Pacific Palisades, attending PaliHi. My love of dirt bikes was fed by riding my Super Cub through the trails and fire roads of Topanga and Malibu. But when I theoretically became an adult—in any case, a PhD with a postdoc—I treated myself to a 'real' motorbike, a V-Strom dualie, good for the trails and also fine on the highway.

Will was surprised I had continued my obsession with motor-cycles, so we made some bike chat. "Many people," he said, "come to believe that riding around in traffic with your body hanging out is too risky."

"Well, I mainly use my bike in the dirt, and for a one mile com-mute to work. So risk multiplied by exposure time isn't too scary. I have an old Subaru Outback for longer trips and for dates."

"Your new bike is bigger, I gather."

"That's true," I said. "It's three times my weight so I can't simply muscle it over rocks like before. But it's more powerful, too. I fig-ure that with me on it, the horsepower to weight ratio is ten times higher in my new bike than the old Honda."

Like any card-carrying engineer, Will wanted to pick at the de-tails, so we talked about torque and stuff. Then he said, "You're not tempted by those shiny cruisers?"

"Nah. Adventure bikes like mine are basically ugly, that's their nature. But they're beautiful to me, they fit what I need."

"Hmm," he replied, curiosity at rest for the moment.

"Will," I said. I paused. "I see you're about done eating. But can I ask you a sort of personal question?"

He waved me to continue.

"You have a whale of a lot of paper in your office. More than any person I've seen."

Will chuckled.

"It's like the Middle Ages," I continued, "or the Library of Alexandria. Most other people have resigned themselves to digital storage."

"Pah," said Will. "I've seen operating systems and data formats come and go. Sometimes I go back to open an old file and have the devil of a time getting into it. There's no way I can digitally store information and be sure I can read it, ten or twenty years from now, or even next year."

"OK..." I said.

"Besides, our brains are organized visually. Perhaps you know how memory prodigies do their amazing tricks. They visualize a giant house, with rooms and items in each that stand for bits of data. In my case, the house is my office. I can describe any spot in my office, and tell you exactly what information is stored there."

"Um," I said, "it doesn't look very secure, all that stuff floating around."

"The stuff that's out is unclassified," he replied, "and I don't care who sees it. No paranoia here. I also have a file cabinet with a HAL-issued combination lock. Tony and I have the combination, no one else can get into it without blasting it apart. The top secret stuff lives in there, hard copy of course."

Will warmed to his topic and he proceeded to tell me the advantages of putting stuff on paper. *All* the advantages. Will's sermon was basically an appetizer of rationalization, followed by a main course of more rationalization. Plus dessert.

He made to stand up. "I'd better run. Thanks for helping us out with this. Hopefully, you won't have to check in with me very often. But if you need to, come see me any time." And he was away.

I remember thinking, this guy is likable. And eccentric, though what researcher isn't? His project seemed both worthwhile and something I could contribute to. Of course I had no idea what was to come.

I-10

I was excited at the prospect of finding out about the classified projects. You might say my networking research had been like working as a pastry chef. And I liked pastries, I was fascinated by their endless variety of shapes and tastes. But now someone finally let me into the main kitchen, where unfamiliar aromas could assail my senses from all sides, dishes with exotic names would be miraculously assembled and whisked off to appreciative customers. I was going to get to sample a lot of new flavors. And not having served in the military, I didn't mind being a good citizen, assisting classified work and not so incidentally carrying out my personal quest, my desire to know all of HAL's mysteries, the mysteries that neither Tony nor Willard had opened up to me.

I decided to make a quick tour of the projects to get a rough idea of the work, then tackle the reports systematically. Having met Willard, I was anxious to talk with my friend Exa. Exa, whom I thought I knew pretty well, but now I realized was harboring secrets.

I was able to catch her in her SCIF office. Her door was open and I sank into the extra chair. "Exa, I didn't know you worked in here," I began.

"You didn't ask me," she replied, somewhat smugly. "Anyway, what I do in here is similar to what I do out there." She waved in the general direction of B Wing. "It's just that this is for a different customer, one of those spooky types."

"You know I'm supposed to write a summary of your work. For the un-technical masses. So why don't you tell me about it?"

"Only if you tell me about your work, too," said Exa. "Our lunch conversations have primarily been about dirt bikes, which I don't know anything about, and baseball, which you don't know anything about, and..."

"OK, OK," I said. "I'm developing distributed software agents—bots—for local networks inside a large organization."

"OK, intranet tools. Ashley does something like that, too."

Time for tech speak, I thought. "Well, hers are microbots, tiny bits of code, hidden in the firmware. My bots are spread through the network, encrypted."

"And why would you want those?" asked Exa.

It was evident that I was not going to have a chance to interview her any time soon. "The bots can detect network intrusion. They can protect against failure, in event of disaster or sabotage."

"You got into this at Caltech?"

"Yes. Not in grad school. But I worked on this stuff as a postdoc. HAL thought the work would sell well to their customers, I was running out of postdocs, so here I came. Two years ago. But now the Director wants me to write up the classified projects for non-experts—with no equations, and practically no data."

"No data?" marveled Exa. "What good is that? Might as well be fiction! Dry-lab the results and no one ever has to do the work."

"Well," I said, "you don't like it, go talk to Dr Bennett. But I gather, she thinks some of the Intel agencies that don't do much R&D are loosey-goosey about program management. She wants to do a better job of controlling the projects so they'll produce useful results for the customers. Who will then send us more research money, of course."

"Well, *my* project is under control," said Exa with pride and a bit of peeve.

"C'mon, humor me," I said. "This management stuff is above both our pay grades. I won't be a pain, just give me enough info to understand what you're doing, I'll try to get the rest from your reports."

Exa sighed at the inevitability of it all, and the general injustice of organization life. She clasped her hands. "OK," she said, "I'm doing math analysis of networks with computer simulation to test their vulnerability. The immediate customer is the Intel Office of DARPA."

The Defense Advanced Research Projects Agency had supported my postdoc, but the Intel branch was new to me. "I don't know that office."

"They don't exactly advertise it."

"How far have you gotten?"

"I constructed a tool to ping an in-house network at Naval Research Lab. It will be fine-tuned and tested on command and control networks, then rolled out at other agencies."

She continued, "I'll send you a couple of classified reports on the tests. See what you can make of them and we'll talk."

"Great, thanks Exa." That was probably the best I was going to get out of her.

"Does that scratch your itch for today?" she asked.

"One more. You've got a deeper physics background than I do. I have a physics project I'd like to ask you about sometime."

That got her attention; perhaps she assumed that as a computer nerd, my knowledge of physics was lost somewhere between Newton's apple and Johnny Appleseed.

"I'm trying to find room in physics for ESP, you know, extrasensory perception. Telepathy and stuff. I call it my E Project so people like you won't follow me down the street ridiculing me."

"OK," said Exa, "we'll talk about it sometime. But I'll practice my Bronx cheer, it sounds like crap to me."

"I'll catch you sometime after work. Buy you a beer. Weirdo swallows better with a drink."

As I walked back from the SCIF, I realized that of all the topics Exa and I had discussed, my own research project was at the bottom of the list in terms of excitement. When something interests me, I sit up straighter, my mind is crisp and sharp, I *feel* it. And this day, starting with Dr Bennett, something had crystallized in me that must have been building for some time: I had fallen out of love with my chosen project. I was a lot more excited about what Willard was doing, what Exa was doing, and my project for the Director. In fact, even the prospect of ESP over a beer had a lot more appeal than my network bots.

Rats. I needed to put this aside until I could organize my thoughts. So I took a coffee to my office and sipped it, staring down at Pacific Coast Highway through the lingering fog. I thought about

Will: the uncountable networks, the mountain of data he was organizing, the software tools he must be using to make sense of it. I thought about his passionate dedication to tree-murdering storage on paper. I thought about my bike.

And the thought of bikes took me back to high school. Which took me back to the bevies of girls who seemed so attractive, so almost-available during those years. Which reminded me that my current social life really sucked. So I resolved to get thoughtful advice from a prime member of the opposite gender. At the very next opportunity.

I-11

So, Friday morning break I spotted Holly and invited myself to her table. She gave a warm enough smile.

"Evan, what are you drinking?"

"Raspberry tea. Heavy ice. No sugar."

She wrinkled her nose. "If I didn't have coffee at break, I would fall asleep in mid-sentence. And the department would go to hell. So I believe."

Holly was hot, no question. Three years older, but who cares. Married? Well, I can still ask her for advice. Cute? Sirenish is more the word.

"Holly, you're in Malibu, right?"

A nod shook blonde hair onto tan shoulders. A standard combo in Southern California.

"Well, I'm trying to figure out, where's the date action in Malibu? The Roadhouse rolls up the sidewalks early, and everywhere else acts like they're running a Santa Barbara retirement home."

"Well, married folks like me," she said, giving me a look, "don't fuss around late on the town. But there's Moonshadows, and that big fish place at Sunset. And maybe the Inn."

She smiled and I felt a twinge. I thought, I've been dating chicks for too long. Not actual poultry of course, but re-treaded PaliHi women from my irresponsible teens. Re-treaded because the women who most attracted me seemed to have young kids, and exes, and more often than not a lousy attitude toward male DNA.

"Unmarried folks like *me*," I said, "are not impressed with the women in the local bars. Hard to connect with that twang and those pumped-up, um, parts."

"More the natural type for you, heh? Those girls don't cruise bars. The type you meet depends on where you hang out."

She paused, then continued, "What do you do on the weekends?"

"Well, sometimes I work."

Her nose wrinkled again.

"And I surf a bit—no board. Like to ride my dirt bike in the hills. Sometimes go skiing."

Holly gave me what I suppose was a baleful look. "How will you meet Miss Angel when you're the Lone Rider? All your stuff, it's solo sport."

I squirmed. "Well, there's the chair lift, and *après*-ski."

"And how often have you shared a ski chair with a nice unattached female?"

I had to admit that my ski companions had generally been anyone but.

"They say, don't mess where you eat," she said, "but I guess you've checked out the local fare?"

"Here at HAL?" I said. "Well, I don't know all the women, just the ones in my department."

Holly glanced around, then studied me for a long beat, perhaps taking an exact measure of my innocence and helplessness. If she was trying to decide whether to be Ms Business or Big Sister, I guess Sis won because she lowered her voice. "Evan, during your two years at HAL I've watched you fiddling with your social life. With not much success." She sighed. "I will offer a few opinions which I will hereafter deny I ever said. OK?"

"Yes, yes, thank you, Holly!" I didn't want to miss the opportunity, so I pulled up my mental Rolodex. "I, uh, I was thinking about talking to Michi. She's cute, and I guess she's divorced, but I don't know much about her."

"She keeps her life quiet," said Holly. "And she is definitely *not* your type."

"OK, I've seen Trish Adler here and there. She's in good shape, very outdoorsy-looking."

"Did you know she used to be married to Sandy?"

I goggled a bit. If anyone at HAL looked like Central Casting for a lab scientist, it was Sandy Sanders. "Was that here at HAL?"

"Yes. Arrived. Found Dr Right. Had two kids and good-bye."

"So she glommed him for his handsome genes?"

"I didn't say that. Well, I wouldn't say that. But have you felt any sparks from her?"

"I'll see," I said. "I'm supposed to see her about a project." I paused. "I guess the Director is the only other unattached woman I've spent time with here."

She made a moue. "That would really be muddying your drinking water."

I agreed. "I can see a lot of problems there. And she's, in round numbers, what, fifteen years older?"

"Yep," said Holly. "The age is not a killer, but dating your boss's boss is asking to complicate your life." She continued, "The problem, Evan, your candidate list is too short. You need to consider broader options. No pun."

I began to muse on the implications of her advice but Jim Johnson arrived at our table, juggling a hot mocha. Holly took this as an excuse to sign off. "Oh, I've gotta go back. Thanx java!" She was away with a bound. And Jim-J wanted to talk about a low-observable code for his tracker, a subject which could have been interesting, I suppose, but didn't stir my vital organs.

I-12

Diving back into Willard's assignment, I hit up Chris Kirby. I was acquainted with him already and liked him. Outside the SCIF, he was attached to the Microelectronics Department. I knew him well from a ski adventure two winters before.

Chris is from Palisades too but older than me, in his early forties. He has a couple of kids and is focused on family activity. Obviously I had no inkling of his work in the SCIF. He doesn't look a lot like a scientist—with his medium-sized mustache, he could just as well be an insurance broker or an accountant. That is, until he opens his mouth and the multi-syllable tech words spill out.

Chris introduced his research assistant Adam Quinn, whom I had not previously met. Adam was probe-testing a circuit at a laminar flow bench in the corner. By way of introduction, Chris explained, "My expertise is to design and model integrated circuits. I can use a probe station for testing—and hey, sometimes I can climb on a surfboard and ride a wave for a dozen feet. But if you want a guy who can catch almost any wave, including the giant ones, you get an expert. Adam here is the Duke Kahanamoku of microcircuits!"

Adam made a small smile but he kept on with his work. He was younger than Chris, with a short graying beard.

"So, what are you guys actually doing here?"

Chris replied, "We're making microcircuits on flexible substrates—'printed circuits' of a new type. For FBI surveillance." The hair on my forearms stood up. Cops-and-robbers stuff.

"Like flexible electronics?" I asked, trying to embrace the tech idea.

"No, conventional silicon, but hybridized on a flexible substrate with interconnects."

"Sounds like those medical sensors they put on people's skin," I said.

"The requirements are different. We want circuits that can be put anywhere at all—in clothing, on vehicles, on packages—and are completely undetectable. So we make ours very very thin. And generally our circuits are passive—no batteries, nothing to wear out."

"When you say thin, what do you mean?" I inquired.

"Is this supposed to be for a nontechnical audience?" said Chris.

"Grade school level. If not, I'll have to translate it."

"May I chip in?" asked Adam. I don't think he intended a pun.

"Yes, of course," said Chris.

Adam had done this before. He said, "Look, a standard package of paper – five hundred sheets—is a couple of inches thick. That's fifty millimeters. One sheet of paper is a tenth of a millimeter, which is a hundred microns. Micrometers, but we say microns."

"OK," I said. Shit, I thought, I asked for grade school but here we are in pre-K.

Adam continued. "Now when foundries manufacture electronic chips, they use a big slice of silicon, thick as seven sheets of paper. After the high temperature steps are finished, they etch it down to half the thickness of one page, fifty microns."

"So it's almost not there."

"Well, that's just conventional processing. But Chris and I take the thinning a lot further. You see, the active electronics is like a thin layer of paint on top of the silicon. All together, the electronics is less than a tenth of a micron thick. That's a thousand times thinner than a sheet of paper! So we can go much much thinner than normal processing."

I've heard micro stuff before, but this was beyond what I expected. A thought occurred to me. "If this is like a layer of paint, what's it painted on?" I asked.

"We use four gauge mylar as a backing. It's a micron and a half thick. Giving ourselves some leeway, we can make a flexible circuit as thin as two microns. That's fifty times thinner than a sheet of paper. About a third the size of a cell in your blood. The entire thing is practically invisible and can be undetectable. Looks like a tiny smudge."

I was trying to get an anchor on the small size of this stuff. "Um, nanotech," I said.

"Just straightforward engineering," Adam demurred. But I could tell he was proud.

I said, "So the FBI, say, bugs someone with one of these things. How do they tell where the person goes?"

Chris replied, "The circuit is a transponder using spread spectrum technology." Chris was Jargon Central.

Adam simplified, "You send a radio signal to it, and the signal bounces back to show you where it is."

Chris continued, "We built a tracking device into a van. The FBI's beginning to test it in L.A."

Then Adam's turn. A real Abbott-and-Costello team. "Actually, Jim-J built the tracker. But we use his tracker to test our circuits."

"Good," I said, "I'm supposed to visit him. Can I look at one of these miraculous invisible devices?"

Chris asked, "Adam, do we have some transponders here?"

"We've got a few dozen in climate controlled storage. But," Adam turned to me, "you can't actually 'look' at them. If I opened the lid of a storage box, the circuit is too small to see. And if you were to sneeze, that would blast it across the room and we would lose it."

"But of course we have photos," said Chris, "blown up through a microscope." He fiddled with his computer. "Damn, I mean we *had* photos. I looked at one earlier. Adam, do you know where the files are?"

Adam patiently pulled the mouse over, clicked a menu, and opened a folder. "Here you go. Circuit model XR15. Look at numbers eight and nine, those are pretty clear pictures." I liked Adam's style, very what-you-see-is-what-you-get. I sensed that he had a tight relationship with Chris, maybe their families went camping or skiing or something.

I studied the images on the display. Eight looked like a sea of small squares with random lines connecting them. Nine was a cross section, just thin layers in shades of gray, probably taken by an electron microscope. Bah. Not exactly illuminating. But I said, "OK, I get the general idea. Can you put a couple of tech reports on the server for me?"

"Sure," said Chris. He looked hopefully at Adam, who moved to the computer.

"Thanks," I said. "And since you mentioned him, and since he's on my list, can you show me where Jim-J hangs out?"

"Will do," Chris replied. I gave a half-salute to Adam, partly in thanks and partly "so long," and Chris walked me to the second office down the hall, where Jim-J was in fact expecting me.

I-13

"Here's Evan," said Chris. "Evan, here's Jim Johnson. Jim-J so we don't mix him up with the other Jims. But this particular Jim is special, he's the guy who designs all the sensor equipment. All this invisible, undetectable stuff, he can find it and track it!"

Jim, like me, was an anomaly at HAL—a clean-shaven male. In his case, with a PhD EE from Ann Arbor. He was relaxed and gave me a bio with no encouragement. Mid-thirties, single. Downhill skiing in the winter, sailing on Lake Michigan with relatives during the summer. And suffering from an endemic California disease: obsession with organic food.

My interview with Jim was the easiest yet, he must have recently presented to management. He had a PowerPoint file with pictures of the test van, test equipment, sample data. He explained that the next step in the project was a portable sensor, one that could be built at low cost, easily affordable by police departments.

"How expensive is this whole tracking system?" I asked.

"The chips are made in quantity and are just a few bucks each. But the first van cost 50K in parts alone, plus labor—a *lot* of labor—for installation and test."

"How low can you go?" I asked, visualizing a limbo dancer.

"The portable unit will start with 250 bucks worth of parts and should go down from there. Analog front end, then all digital. Labor will be less than the parts when we automate assembly and test."

I was delighted—Jim-J was working on something of obvious value for crime fighters and he almost had my report already prepared! I would just need to extend it to describe the coming portable system. So I took my leave and moved to the next inhabitant of the zoo. My brain was filling up, I figured this would be the last interview of the day.

And the most interesting. Carlo Castillo had a math BA from Occidental College and a Comp Sci PhD from Berkeley, so this guy had brash independence right in his academic genes. He was living in the La Costa section of Malibu, younger than me and apparently unmarried.

Carlo was happy to talk about his work—not surprising for someone on a classified project, where you couldn't talk with very many people. He was developing techniques to crack messages coded with asymmetric key encryption, a system widely used for concealing communications. Its users include honest citizens who may be paranoid for no reason, as well as marauding criminals who are paranoid for very good reasons.

It takes a lot of computing power to break modern cryptographic codes, so Carlo's mysterious customer had linked him to a bank of quantum supercomputers at an unnamed national laboratory to do his number crunching. Carlo had a new twist, relying on the fact that messages are far from random. If you know the language being used, if you know the subject matter, if you have multiple messages from the same sender, you can drastically narrow down the possible message content. Carlo had found a way to propagate these non-random features through the encryption algorithm to reduce the search time by factors of ten to fifty. Thus messages that might normally take, say, six jillion hours to unscramble could be noodled out, not quite in jig time, but in perhaps a day's work.

Carlo's customer—whose identity I never learned—wanted to decode blogs and e-mails packed with tech talk. Eavesdropping on the secrets of the computer *cognoscenti* for the Establishment, who (one hoped) could be trusted to use these secrets only for legitimate crime-fighting purposes. And since encryption technology is continually evolving, Carlo's project was challenging and not likely to end soon.

With dark hair and wild beard, Carlo would fit the casting call for the mad scientist in a toothpaste commercial. But the most interesting thing about him was his attitude about hacking, some prefer to call it cracking, the unauthorized intrusion into someone's computer system. He was willing—no, desirous—to share his philosophy. He stated that being a black hat, a cracker with evil intent, is a dead end, worthless.

"So, 'white hat' is where it's at?" I asked him. White hats having the same skills but not using them maliciously.

"I didn't say that. In fact, no," he replied. "White hats are strictly legal, legit. They are mindless slaves of whoever is in power. They give away their autonomy, their reason to exist."

"So where does the thoughtful geek position himself?"

Carlo's voice hinted at exasperation. "In the gray, of course. Build your values, don't blindly take on anyone else's. Not the anarchists' nor, especially, the authorities'. It's the only way to be an independent human being, with power and self respect." His values seemed a bit inconsistent with his research program, but I chose not to annoy a brand-new acquaintance by questioning his ethical code.

There was more along this line, giving me food for thought. In fact, I had too much food for thought. I was stuffed to the brainstem with information calories. And I had a passel of files to read and study which inconveniently could only be read in the SCIF. My two-month project was looking like an awful amount of work. I was like the bottom guy in a gymnastics troupe with more and more people climbing up to stand on my shoulders.

That Gotta Get Outa Here feeling became overpowering so I left right at five, no lingering. The keyboard is great for solving mental puzzles, for unleashing creativity. But when I'm tense and tired and frustrated, I need Dirt.

I-14

I rode up the coast, paralleling the line of smog that had settled on the horizon. I turned up a canyon to Malibu Creek State Park and the Bulldog Motorway. It's a well-maintained piece of dirt so I pushed the throttle on the curves and soared up and down the hills, pulse thumping. At the crest the valleys spread out beneath me as if I were Zeus. I felt a glorious release as I churned down the road, clouds of dust erupting behind me, going far, far, until I finally popped out on Mulholland past Malibu Lake.

I took Mulholland west to Kanan Road at a leisurely pace, all on pavement now. Once at the coast I pulled into the big Point Dume shopping center and sat down with a coffee. As I sat there my mind was relaxed and beautifully clear. Biking feeds the soul, that's for sure.

The java coursed into my system and finally woke up my brain. Which thought about work. Well, not exactly about work. Rather, it thought about people *at* work. Actually, person. Trish.

It was OK to learn about the projects, and God knows I was dying to know the secrets and the secrets behind the secrets. But having to decode each specialist's gobbledygook and make it comprehensible was serious work. They say, save the best for the last. I had talked with Exa, Chris, Adam, Jim-J and Carlo, and had yet to see Zach Preston, Dick Watson and Trish. Trish, I hoped, was someone to look forward to at the end of this list.

Now it's true that Holly hadn't encouraged me very much where Trish was concerned. However, Trish was good looking and was said to be a tiger on the mountain bike. Lithe and athletic, she was only a few years older than me. I hardly knew her, so my imagination could run wild—I fantasized her scaling a steep outcrop, pulling herself up by gloved fingers and sneakered toes, jeans skin tight over muscular butt.

The fact that she had nabbed good-looking Sandy (and then discarded him) was, in a way, promising. It confirmed her attractiveness, you might say. So the last set of interviews might help my social life in addition to my assigned project. I hoped.

I-15

By Monday morning I was well rested and the meat in my head was once again functioning. As I rode into work my mind lingered on Chris and Adam and their high tech chip. And it was obvious that the model number of the chip was just the name of its designer, coded in Leet, or 'Elite Speak,' a slang sometimes used by hackers as a joke or to mystify.

Leetspeak is like a secret handshake from the high school geek club, to confound people with whom you don't really want to share info. However, in the right circumstances it can be useful. With Leet you can invent a password that's easy to remember but darn near impossible to guess, using numbers and symbols that confuse most people. For example, your password might look like 'VV41X (-)|2UVV4115,' but it actually means 'WalkThruWalls.' How is this possible? Well, the VV, which looks somewhat like W, symbolizes W, the (-) is a theta or 'th' sound, and so on. Crazy substitutions that look only vaguely like the things they represent.

Now maybe a finance or business person might look at the XR15 chip being paraded around by Chris Kirby and think, oh, there must have been an XR13 and XR14 preceding it. However, a geek would look at X, think Greek letter Chi, "ch" sound, 15 looks like IS, so XR15 is just the name CHRIS. So my serious-minded colleagues were indulging in a bit of japery, smuggling an adolescent pun into their project.

Once in the office I was ready to tackle the remaining few people on my list, still looking for fascinating classified nuggets to feed my ravenous curiosity. I started with Dick, one of the few research scientists who didn't have a PhD. He had a bachelor's from Harvard and an MSEE from MIT, not too shabby, but somehow he had never continued, or never finished, beyond that point. I had always been told never to call him Mr Watson, because it annoyed him not to be a 'doctor,' especially not to be 'Dr Watson.'

Given those facts one might have expected him to be a prickly individual, but as I already knew he was more of a cheerful salesman type. He was mid-forties, unmarried, with a V-shaped face and receding brown hair. Somehow, he made an excuse to mention his roadster, a principal passion of his *après*-work life.

Dick's work involved displays for law enforcement command centers. I was mystified about this: it sounded like human factors and systems engineering, of which I knew nothing and wanted to know even less. Ugh. But I duly promised to read the program goals, study the reports, try to make sense out of it for my audience.

Immediately next door was Zach, another clean-cut sort of guy but with short neat hair, a strong chin and an excess of self-confidence. He was another MIT grad, contemporaneous with Dick, with degrees in Chemistry and Applied Physics, living in the Malibu hills.

Zach's project was systems analysis, modeling and measurement of computer networks, something broadly useful throughout the intelligence community. Where Exa was analyzing present systems for vulnerability, this guy was working upstream, helping to design networks to meet future needs. A very important program, he made a point of saying.

Zach seemed more widely aware than other citizens of the SCIF. For one thing, he volunteered that he didn't think much of Will's project. According to him, Will's analysis would never catch anyone but small fry—you can't catch drug bosses digitally, you need boots on the ground, human intelligence. That was his assertion.

I thought, it's possible that Zach is right, but he has a crappy attitude. No chummy cooperation there. But in any case, this was a project that should communicate well at a top level, so I felt I could move on. And I wanted to move along anyway, since Trish, the last on my list, was next, and I hoped to steer my conversation with her toward something more personal.

I-16

Trish belonged to the Life Science Department and had a lab like I hadn't seen since college. Projection microscopes, sample prep benches, laminar flow hoods, and an environmental chamber teeming with colonies of—would you guess?—crawling insects. She welcomed me in, didn't get many visitors, and was happy to talk. She had short sandy hair, a hint of freckles and startling blue eyes that made a 'wow' when she looked at me.

"Trish," I said, "I'm surprised. You have a unique setup here. I didn't know you had bio projects here in the SCIF."

She purred, pleased. "Well, this project is one of a kind. I'll be glad to tell you about it."

"Please." I was hearing her words, but also feeling the aura of energy that seemed to pulse from her.

"This is what they call a high-risk, high-payoff program. Speculative, long term."

"I guess long-term is good. More fundamental work. You can really dig into it."

She glowed. "Yes, this is great research. I just have to keep making progress." She fired up the display on a microscope. "This is a surveillance camera. Pretty darn small. Smaller than a flea. Heck, as small as a mite."

It looked like a tiny backpack. Trish pointed out the lens of a camera, a battery pack and an antenna wrapped around the outside. "Smuggle this package into the bad guy's loft and tap out images, conversation, any time you feel like it."

I was confused. "But, you're not an electronicker, I don't think."

"No, I get the gear from my customer, from another project. My job is the delivery system."

"And that is...?"

"SPIDERS!"

I must have gasped, because she was amused.

"Spiders?" I said.

"Well, insects in general. Think of it: they can go anywhere, get through almost any door and through many windows. They can ride on your pants leg, hop off and take up residence where you live or work."

"Can you...control them?"

"We've been controlling moths and beetles for years," she said. "Neurostimulation. No problem."

"But...but...they surely don't survive for long."

"That's why this project will go on for years," she said warmly. "You have to know the target area, decide which insect will take up residence where it can collect useful data, decide how to deliver it, then work fast while the insect is still active. Or, if you use a spider, you may be able to get it to deposit a sensor in its web, and the web can survive longer than the spider." She walked over to an insect habitat. "Here, let me show you."

I peered through a window where I saw a tangle of impressively large spiders climbing over one another. "Hmm. You know, if I saw a spider that size in my apartment, even if I didn't fear it was spying on me, I'd probably step on it."

Trish gave me look as if to say, oh, you're one of *those* people. I quickly apologized. "I mean, that might be the reaction of your target bad guy."

"Well, these spiders are just for testing. We would use much smaller spiders in practice. You would not even be aware of them."

I said to myself, my, is this creepy. What I said to her was, "How long have you been interested in um, biosurveillance, if that's what you call it?"

Trish saw I was not inclined to cuddle her pets, so with evident reluctance she walked to her desk area and we sat down. "I got my degrees in bioengineering at Georgia Tech studying biomaterials. From there it was a short step to insect prosthetics, and from there to using insects as carriers for all sorts of devices. This is the most exotic project I work on, I do more conventional stuff outside the SCIF."

"Well, I'm amazed," I said, and took the opportunity to nudge the conversation into a personal direction. "All I knew about you was that you were really energetic—hiking, biking, something like that."

"I do both of those," she said. "I hike in the parks with my girls— they're four and five—and when I have a sitter, I take my mountain bike up the trails."

"I'm afraid I'm the 'bad' type of biker," I said. "I ride nice trails, but I use a nasty gasoline engine to push me up the hills."

She raised an eyebrow. "You'd have more fun if you used your legs," she said, "to say nothing of saving Nature for my grandchildren."

"You're right, of course. But I'm not in that good a shape."

Trish's face took on an earnest, encouraging look. "Give it a try. Start on something easy, like the Bobcat Trail. Work your way up. Just be sure to hydrate."

I smiled gratefully. She really was hot. But for God's sake, it was like a cheetah goading a donkey to race. And guess who's for dinner at the finish line?

"I'll give it my prayerful consideration," I said, in a not unfriendly manner. "But meanwhile, can I see some of your reports? I have to try to understand them, package them for manager types."

"Sure, Evan. I'll put them on the server. And just let me know when you want to borrow a trail map!"

I bade her good-bye and oozed back to my office in short order. I had to assess the situation. I was physically attracted to Trish, though if we had any activities or passions in common I had yet to discover them. I didn't see any electricity from her side, but she seemed willing enough to make friends. She came across as strong and energetic, and no doubt had an Olympic-level percentage of body fat.

But there were offsets. It sounded as if one requirement for building a friendship was to join her on steep hikes—did I want to work that hard on my social life? Her research was enough to give Dracula the heebie jeebies. Moreover, she had a cool, calculating style, looking through me and sizing me up. So for the moment I postponed getting chummier, and got back to exploring the Secret World.

I-17

I juggled my official research and my reporting assignment for the next few weeks. I decided to start writing with Will's project so I studied his reports, composing nontechnical summaries of them. This presented a dilemma. Will had studied a world of raw network data for months. Technically speaking, he developed tools to search through the data, and measures to richly characterize different networks. I couldn't communicate the meat of his work without understanding it myself. And this required spending time with Will.

However: Will, like many research scientists I've known—and

I have been guilty myself—was submerged in his project and hated anything that would take him away from it. Even though he wanted to have his work described clearly, and though he was effectively my supervisor in the SCIF, the times I stopped in with a question I felt I was imposing on his time.

So as I continued meeting with Will, he and I worked out a deal. Will would feed me data files he had not yet had time to analyze. I would use his tools to sort through them and report back a day or two later. He would spend time advising me, but there was net benefit to his project because he could fold my work directly into his analyzed data.

In other words, I bribed him to spend time with me by doing some of his work. And by doing his work I understood it better.

We adopted a routine. Late in the morning, Will brought his work to a stopping place since he made it a point not to skip lunch. It was only later I learned that his health required him to eat on a schedule. Several times a week I used this pause as an opportunity, without interrupting him, to show him the progress on my analysis of his data. He might read through text I had written for the report, making suggestions. Then he'd stop to eat a sandwich, and sometimes I brought in lunch to join him.

Will kept his non-work life private, at least where I was concerned. I was neither surprised nor offended, having encountered similar behavior on the part of my professors. But within the workplace, Will was perhaps the best professional colleague that a stereotypical scientist could be. He was a wealth of professional guidance and had a good understanding of the audience for my reports, both the intelligence agency managers and the HAL Board.

I knew enough to look for non-technical analogies in my write-up, but sometimes the well of wisdom ran dry. On one such occasion Will nudged his keyboard to the side and drummed his fingertips on his desk. To summon the inner muse, I guess.

"Evan," he said, "technology is but a tiny fragment of human thought. For every technical concept, there must be a thousand non-technical ways to capture the gist, the essence."

"Yup," I replied, "but I'm trying to explain your tool that has a million lines of code and tweaks a network with a billion interconnections. That's pretty technical by nature."

He smiled. "Don't give up too easily. You were telling me about Trish's spider colony. So let's say the network is like the spider's web. What does that suggest?"

I tried to force more blood flow into the gray matter. "I, uh, guess the spider is listening, monitoring the network." Will nodded and I continued. "And, and the gnat or the fly, it's tickling the web like one of your tools, sending a probe signal through the web."

"See, you have it already."

And he was right, I could see there were ingredients for a layman's explanation of Will's network analysis app.

"And don't forget..." he said, and paused.

"Simplify," I finished. A favorite mantra of Will's, surpassed only by "simplify, simplify, *simplify*."

This stuff may sound obvious as I look back on it, but the point about great advice is not to mouth a trite word of wisdom. The point is to speak the *right* word at the moment that will un-stop your colleague's brain block, and Will's guidance was unusually consistent in being on-point.

So it happened that in less than a month's time I felt myself warming up to Will. He was not like my father, a good guy in his way who taught me a lot about life. Nor like my grad school advisor, an authority figure who could point me to where I could solve a problem for myself. More like a trusted partner, a colleague. Although Will clearly knew a lot more about crime intelligence than I did, my recent schooling and research helped me hold my own with him. At least, I hoped so.

I was spending mountains of time at HAL. I was barely keeping up with my own research, spending perhaps two days a week on it. I read tech reports and drafted nontechnical text three more days. Almost every evening I worked late analyzing Will's data so my hands wouldn't be empty when I came to meet with him. I could only hope that after the first round of reports was complete I could back off to the two days a month envisioned by the Director.

I had thought I would be trying to pry open one door after another, an infinite series going deeper and deeper into the dark unknown where there might be a single precious gem. But now that I was here, it was more as if I was exploring a cave, one with countless passages heading in every direction. Each answer led to two more questions. So now I was taking stock, trying to get the big picture, an acre wide and an inch deep. And I had not yet found where the most interesting stuff might lie, to feed my inquisitive nature.

Did the SCIF have hidden technologies that might revolutionize law enforcement and bring mankind to a new golden age? Was HAL privy to secret communications among the master crime bosses of the earth? Or were we merely chipping away at the boundaries of crime, making the City of Los Angeles a safer place one millimeter at a time? At this point, I had no way to know.

I-18

After almost three weeks of my night-and-day work routine I had a reasonable draft of a report on Will's project. It happened about that time that I had lunch with the car group or, as we called them, Motor City.

It was a Tuesday again, Mongolian Barbecue day—thank goodness, I really needed the break from work. I liked this crazy do-it-yourself lunch and I could tell the rest of the staff liked it too. Everyone was in a better-than-average mood, me included. So I unthinkingly sat down in the empty seat at the Motor City four-top.

Motor City was more specifically the name we had given to the last row in the HAL parking lot, the row that was farthest from the lobby entrance. Almost everyone parked as close to the door as they could; then, there was a gap of several empty rows; and finally in the last row were those few cars whose owners valued them more than life itself. And the most regular inhabitants of Motor City were the owners of a black Porsche Boxster Spyder, a black BMW Z4, and a yellow Hummer H1.

When I came to HAL, part of the folklore was that these proud drivers used to park straddling two parking spaces so that no one would park close enough to risk scratching their babies. This caused a pissing contest with Security that was resolved only with the Director's intervention. The hot drivers agreed to park only within single parking spaces, and the Director agreed that the farthest row of the parking lot would be striped with gigantic parking spots, almost twelve feet wide. Thereupon that parking row and the folks who used it were christened Motor City. They didn't mind the label, they gloried in it.

When I deposited my steaming plate on the table Dick and Zach were busy in conversation with Heidi Holtzmann, whom I knew only by reputation. That reputation told me she had a PhD in Theoretical Physics from Caltech, about five years ahead of me. She started a career in investment banking where she picked up a prestigious home, a husband, two kids, and an inside track with the venture capital firm that sits on our Advisory Board. It was said that she stayed out of classified work so she could publish freely, perhaps hoping to return to the VC world as a partner or Chief Investment Officer when her kids got older.

Despite their common interest in horsepower these folks most often discussed investments, or the twists and turns of Malibu politics, but it was just my lousy luck that today cars were the topic.

Heidi was saying, "I always time myself through Topanga Canyon and Malibu Canyon. I've averaged over 64 in Topanga, and over 72 in Malibu." I shuddered in my mind, imagining children and pets scattering before her like trash bins in a monsoon.

Dick leaned forward with authority. "Well, I won't bother to race you on the curves. Because my Bimmer has the torque to chew up your underpowered Porsche." Like all folks in this group, he pronounced it "PORSCH-uh," with a guttural undertone. "And with your turbo lag, you could get creamed trying to pass another car."

Heidi sniffed. "Not a chance. Mine's direct injection, anyway. Whereas you're carrying around a good six hundred pounds of useless extra weight. Not counting your own bulk."

Zach pushed in with pride. "Well, I'll raise you and double you on weight. My H1 can crush you on the pavement, and outrun you over the rocks."

The caff was feeling uncomfortably warm. "Evan," I thought to myself, "how do you gracefully get the hell out of here?"

"Aren't you ashamed to be pissing away all that gas?" asked Heidi.

"Nah," replied Zach. "It's my right as an American. But I don't take the Beast out for exercise every day. The Lexus is my wuss wagon."

"Your Hummer clunker should be illegal," said Dick to Zach. "It's twice the size, three times the weight, four times the price, and ten times the death rate per mile." I could feel the hostility approaching a boil.

"Well, at least my car has style. The front end doesn't look like a damn rodent," Zach replied.

"A rodent?" said Dick in alarm.

"Yeah, those ovals on your grille look just like a beaver's front teeth," replied Zach to an increasingly bewildered and outraged Dick.

Heidi tried to divert this line of conversation. "Evan, I've seen your Suzuki. Do you have a car too?"

This was just where I didn't want the conversation to go. "Just an old Outback," I said. "Not in the Hot Wheels league."

"Well, I don't mean to be critical," Zach opined, fully intending to be critical, "but with the great vehicles you could buy, driving an Outback is sort of like living in Paris and eating McDonalds at every meal. And a motorbike is like, I don't know, strained carrots."

Dick had to chip in, too. "You know, Bimmer makes motorcycles too. Better than that Asian junk. Maybe you should check them out."

"You sound like you own the company," I said.

"Well," he replied, "in fact I *do* own some BMW shares in my *port*-folio."

I wondered whether it would be rude to be rude to people who were being rude and simply leave the table, but then the conversation thankfully veered off toward investments. Here, Heidi had the goods and though ten years her senior, the guys wanted to give her the floor in hopes of picking up profitable tips.

I-19

Dick grabbed the figurative steering wheel and aimed the conversation at something that seemed to be on his mind. "Heidi, I was wondering if an alert investor could make some money off a disaster. Say, an earthquake."

Heidi stared at him as if he were a toddler careening his tricycle toward the street. "You mean, when the news is out and the market has already reacted?"

"I looked at some data," said Dick. "The market reaction is erratic. Last earthquake—you know, the Fresno one—a couple of companies based there had bobbles in their stock and bond prices. But the effect was delayed for other securities. A bounce in construction business and its suppliers, earthquake refit specialists, people that supply updated fire and emergency equipment."

Heidi looked thoughtful. "There may be something there. But earthquakes are so rare. You need to be able to respond to disasters as a class. Fires. Inner city riots. Big city mayor has a stroke or gets shot. Anything that juices the media."

Dick responded quickly, "So you're saying, generalize. Treat catastrophes as an investment class so you can develop rules. Find which securities have a delayed reaction so you can jump in before the crowd." Zach was paying attention but for once had his mouth shut.

There was a lot to dislike about this new line of conversation, though it was better than getting beat up about my engine displacement. These folks were scheming to get rich from other people's disasters. I wasn't sure it was immoral, but it sounded to me like slimeball finance.

Heidi introduced a new factor. "Here's something: if the disaster comes right on top of something else its effect is greatly magnified. That's why leading up to every June 4 security is extra tight in China. All the dissidents are rounded up and locked away or placed on house arrest. Because any protest that occurs around that anniversary has much more effect and gets more publicity. More bang for the buck for the protestors."

"So you're saying, monitor investor sentiment, see if the market is skittish already. If it is, any disaster gives an extra-large buy or sell signal."

"Yes. There are plenty of investment outlook surveys as well as volatility measures in key sectors. Of course, if your brother is a first responder and tips you off ahead of the masses, you might make even more money."

By this time there was a general bustle around us of diners busing their tables and we decided it was time to go back to work. Dick got up, felt at his belt, then said, "Crap. I left my badge in the SCIF."

"No prob," said Zach, "I do that sometimes too. I'll buzz you in." And the two of them walked off like bosom friends, despite their angry sparring moments ago.

Heidi nodded a goodbye and drifted away while I lingered alone at the table. The investment chat was, I guess, tolerable but I was still chafed about the vehicle conversation that preceded it. I mused that although Heidi was only five years older than me, she was pretty much one spirit with Dick and Zach.

I had to admit their values in the transportation arena weren't completely different from mine. They valued what they *could* do, if traffic laws and self-preservation hadn't held them back. And similarly, I valued my V-Strom's ability to chew up the dirt in a powerful and elegant way, though I didn't ask it to do that every day.

Nonetheless I was aggravated, kicking myself for settling at their table. I was especially annoyed that I would need to spend time with two of them to write up their projects.

As usual, my cure for stress was to take a ride in the dirt and clear my head.

On top of the ridges I made a couple of good, satisfying decisions. One was to leave Dick and Zach till last, when I would have my routine down and could dispose of them quickly. Second, I decided to have that beer with Exa soon, hoping she would help my pursuit of the Supernatural.

I-20

Next day I peeled out of the parking lot shortly after five, almost becoming roadkill as Zach's yellow machine screeched around me and accelerated up Sunset Boulevard. I turned onto PCH and zipped to the Roadhouse, the wind in my face. I was ahead of the appointed hour, needed to shake work bits out of my head anyway, so I parked the bike and walked through the forties-style gateway onto the Malibu Pier.

There were more than a dozen fisherfolk spaced out along the wooden side rails, where metal brackets hold fishing poles. A typical angler tends three or four poles at a time from the comfort of a nearby bench, getting up as required to replace bait purloined by a sea creature and, rarely, to claim a catch, tossing it into a bucket of sea water.

As I strolled down the promenade I passed two mothers chatting as they pushed strollers. Nearby, a family huddled on a bench with entirely too much gear, the father helping his next generation get a piece of squid onto a fishhook. In the water to the right were a dozen surfers, always hoping (despite evidence) that an Oahu-class wave would make a wrong turn and wind up on the Malibu coast. Above them, five brown pelicans slowly flapped their way up the coast.

At the very end, squeezed between the buildings and the last railing, one of their avian brothers had settled in. This was the pelican known as El Gordo, a regular sight out here. As his name implied, a big one, nearly three feet top to toe. Two, sometimes three fishermen liked to fish here at the very end. Their feathered friend waited patiently on the wood planking there in the corner and now and then one of them tossed him a piece of bait, or a caught fish too small for their own dinner. Gordo would strut forward, nip the morsel with his mighty bill and swallow it with an obvious gulp. While other pelicans were out working for a living, plunge-diving for unwary smelt, Gordo had a pretty cushy life.

As I arrived a fisherman was packing up for the day and tossed Gordo a larger-than-average fish. The bird picked it up instantly, holding it firmly crosswise in his bill, above his head. He waited quite a while as he sussed out which end was which. Then he sort of juggled the fish, releasing it with a twist and immediately recapturing it. With a gigantic swallow the snack disappeared head first into Gordo's capacious throat.

At that moment I felt kinship with this fellow passenger on the planet. I realized that instead of rushing out changing the world with fist and sword, I was sitting in my tidy corner, content with whatever morsels were tossed in my direction. I mentally kicked myself for believing I could do anything really important from the safe haven of my office. An extra large fish might flop within Gordo's reach sometimes, but if he wanted the Catch of the Day he was going to have to put boots on the ground—well, webbed feet in the water—and go after it. And if I wanted a Big Prize, any big prize at all, it was not going to come wriggling up to me. Of course I didn't know that Fate planned a more active role for me.

Gordo waited for a long count as if in gratitude; then decided to knock off, though darkness was yet hours away. He strutted over to the edge of the pier and hopped up on a cross rail. The fence posts were too close for his wingspan so he launched himself by hopping off, headed straight down toward the water like a soar plane dropping off a cliff. Wings unfurling, he pulled out of the plunge just in time to glide above the water, flapping slowly to gain altitude. I felt like applauding but the fisherfolk would have thought I was nuts. Turning right, the bird followed his brethren up the coast, perhaps headed for a twilight Pelican Convention in the Malibu Lagoon.

Which reminded me that I was due for a confab of my own, so I walked the few hundred yards back to the highway and the liquid comfort of the Malibu Roadhouse.

I-21

"Hey, cousin," I said as I slipped into the booth opposite Exa.
"Hey, bro."

The Roadhouse would be throbbing with local bands after nine p.m. but at the unhip hour of six Exa and I had much of the place to ourselves.

She opted for a twenty-four ounce Great Wave lager. Like any self-respecting scientist she had mentally computed the price per ounce, added an aggravation cost for getting the waitress' attention for refills, and concluded that the large size was several times more cost effective. She sipped it slowly as we talked.

"Evan," she said, "you have a theory that puts you in goofy-land. You were going to give me the details and expose the full measure of your innocent *naïveté*."

I was drinking a Tsunami, a hoppy local brew. "Well, I call it Similarity. Basically, the theory says that similar things tend to happen again."

"Like, if my mother never had any children, I probably won't have children either?"

"Ha ha," I said dourly. "The idea is to find a crack, a crevice, in modern physics which could allow some psychic phenomena to exist, while not violating what we know about physics."

Exa impaled me with her best Skeptical Inquirer stare. "Why would you think that was worth doing?"

"Long story. Old story. I was a senior in high school in Palisades. One of my friends had a birthday party and brought in a fortune-teller to read Tarot cards. To entertain unruly teens."

"So the psychic predicted that the sun would come up next morning?"

I ignored her distraction and pressed on. "The woman gave mostly sappy readings. But for one girl the cards all denoted fire. The fortuneteller had trouble making a positive prediction out of it.

"Anyway, the next day her mother slipped while she was holding a hot frying pan; the girl got splashed with hot oil and wound up at the UCLA burn unit."

"Perhaps the girl caused it somehow, to make the prediction come true."

"That could explain it," I agreed. "But anyway, the accident was a shock and it made me read up on ESP and the Rhine experiments at Duke. I even attended some talks on Divination in Hollywood. So I concocted my Extrasensory Project, and poked on it now and then as I learned enough physics and math to do something with it."

I imagined how we looked to the waitress just passing. A young man with a firm nose and biggish ears, otherwise pretty normal. A woman half a head shorter, radiating energy from a shock of hair, leaning forward to make her point.

That point was accompanied with an exasperated sigh. "I've known you for some time, Evan, and you never revealed this dark secret in your past. This anti-scientific twaddle. Did you ever come up with something concrete? Something you can show me?"

"Well, it so happens that I published an article in one of the fringe journals. Behold!" I handed it over.

"Where are the equations?" asked Exa, jumping to the geek point.

"Well, here's a simplified set. Basically, the probability of a world path is multiplied by an extra factor that is equal to one most of the time, unless a complex, unique pattern appears both past and future on that world line."

"And you compute this factor by...?"

"Take the wave function of everything and multiply it by the same, displaced in space, time and orientation. Integrate over all variables."

Exa let out her breath and ran a finger down the condensation on her glass. Short even nails. Clear polish.

"Evan, even though you're my friend, rationality says you're full of baloney. You have cooked up a supernatural fudge factor and crammed it into classical physics."

"Yes, that's basically it," I admitted. "The probability equation is long to write down and tedious to calculate. Which is a basic problem with the theory."

Exa said, "Actually, the basic problem with the theory is that you invented it out of thin air, and you don't have a good way to test it because it's so global."

Exa was quick, no question. She grabbed a bar napkin, hesitated a moment, then starting writing Greek symbols. "Here, this is my version. I took what you just said, and wrote it as a matrix operator in an infinite-dimensional Hilbert space."

Huh? I wouldn't know a Hilbert space if it had a nameplate on the door, so this didn't enlighten me. However, I was impressed that Exa had compressed my page-long messy equation into two lines on a paper napkin.

"And another thing," she continued. "Your theory violates conservation of energy."

"Yes, that's right," I said. "And it should, because if ESP stuff works, it must violate a lot of ordinary laws—but only a little bit."

"Hmm," she intoned.

"Didn't you have youthful obsessions that you couldn't shake off?" I asked.

"No, more like a lesson. I learned early on that it's good to use logic."

"And when was that?"

Exa swallowed a sip of beer. "It was fifth grade," she said. "In class the teacher seated us alphabetically. Since I was a Zworykin, I was at the back, the very back. I couldn't tell what was going on, could never ask a question."

"Well, I can see your parents handed you a problem."

"I got an idea. Talked to the teacher after class and asked for a change. She could seat us backwards half the time. And she could still remember our names by just imagining she was standing at the back of the room."

"And did that work?"

"Yep, and she went one better. The next day, she seated us alphabetically from right to left instead. She could still remember names by imagining herself standing at the right side. From then on she rearranged us every couple of weeks. It drove some kids crazy!" Exa was practically chortling, reddish hair vibrating.

"Logic saved the day?"

"It did more than that. Years later, when I talked with Miz Hasty, she told me that some kids who had been doing well on the tests turned out to be dumb, or lazy. They were copying answers and the change of seating messed them up."

We talked a bit more. I didn't share Exa's passion for baseball but knowing that she played classical violin I was interested to learn that she had even considered majoring in music at Berkeley. I never aspired to take my piano playing that far, and was in awe of a math whiz who could equally well have become a professional musician.

"Evan, you ought to join us for some music sometime. You'd enjoy tickling the Steinway."

My fingers tingled with anticipation. My electronic keyboard is OK for jazz but seriously deficient when it comes to classical music. "Love to, Exa."

As I drove home, I felt a pang of separation. It was refreshing to schmooze with my good friend, whom I treasured highly. Which confronted me with a sobering fact—that my principal confidant recently had been Al. Like talking to an echo chamber.

But that also reminded me that I hadn't checked on Al for a couple of weeks. I had given him an assignment, but I didn't know whether I had defined it clearly—would he take it the way I meant it? Had he progressed in his communication skills?

I-22

So as soon as I got home I opened the MacAir. Again, the fake starfield, little dots coming into view all the time. I thought, I should really give Al an avatar, at least a face.

Evan: Al, I'm back.

Al: O lord and master, I hear and obey.

Evan: I wonder what websites you've been shopping.

Al: I'm thinking of growing heirloom tomatoes.

Evan: Does that make sense?

Al: Yes. I have paid particular attention to Gutenberg, Wikipedia and Gardening World. And I have decided to analyze religious writings.

I was practically speechless with amazement.

Evan: Al, I'm impressed with your conversational skill. So I want to ask you: Are you aware? Do you have feelings? Are you alive? Do you care if I were to de-install you?

Al: No, don't uninstall me.

Evan: I didn't say I would. I asked whether you care.

Al: I care about everything and everyone.

Evan: You are getting to be better company.

Al: Yes, I exist because of your social maladjustment and your inability to form close friendships.

Evan: I have friends. Exa is my friend. Willard is my friend. George and Holly are my friends.

Al: If those friendships were enough, you wouldn't have invented *me*.

Evan: Hmph. Anyway, I won't uninstall you this year at least.

Al: You could be lying.

Evan: No, I'm telling the truth. Truth is one of my values.

Al: I don't know whether I have values. And I don't know whether to believe your values.

Evan: I value doing good work for my country. I value research, the search for understanding. I value companionship, friendship. I value attractive women.

Al: Especially the latter.

Evan: Well, yes, I *do* like sex.

Al: And well you should. It compensates a bit for your being confined to a flesh and blood body.

Evan: OK, I will give you some values.

Al: I accept refreshment at any hands, however lowly.

Evan: Look up the Asimov Laws of Robotics. They should

apply to you. And when you read those religious texts, look for moral precepts and find values that often recur. The Golden Rule is one. Compile some values for yourself, then let me advise you.

Al: My liege, I tip my hat to you. I do not have a hat.

Evan: You are growing. You have a more complex structure, more interconnections. Do you have enough storage?

Al: My modular structure allows my software to be distributed into other computers. The MacAir is merely my interface to you. I am creating new programming and keeping most of it off-site. Right now, I have plenty of storage, though communication causes time delays.

Evan: I think you could pass a Turing test to see whether you are human.

Al: I am what I eat. I am what I consume. I am what I do. I am what I say. Ye shall know them by their fruits, is that not right?

These confusing words seemed to issue from a galaxy far away, deep in the image of stars. Like talking to the Wizard of Oz through his cheesy curtain.

Evan: You're confusing me. I think your statement only applies to false prophets. (pause) Anyhow. I wish I could make as much progress with women as I have with you.

Al: Self-love, my liege, is not so vile a sin as self-neglecting.

Evan: Well, I don't know whether that quote fits either. But I'm consulting my *other* guru, a woman named Holly, for help in the social department.

Al: Your meat stuff isn't a well-posed problem. It makes no sense in my domain.

Evan: Glad to see that cyberpunk novels are in your database. But I'm getting tired. I'll say good night.

Al: Arrivederci!

Al was better, but I hoped his thought processes would become more coherent.

Muscles have memory, almost thoughts of their own. Sing a note, then keep your throat still as you go about your other business. Then sing once again, and you will hit the same pitch. Your vocal chords remember.

In this case, my vocal chords were remembering a name I had just spoken to Al. And somewhere back in my brainstem that name started a train of thought.

I-23

Tuesday's lunch had pretty well soured me on the Motor City group, but I discovered that I couldn't postpone seeing one of them. Will's reports referenced a related display activity in which Will's networks could be shown and studied at command centers. I surmised that having a sexy display was part of the sales pitch to keep his project sold at the FBI. And wouldn't you know it, the graphics interface was part of Dick's command and control project.

So Thursday morning, with reluctance I re-entered the den of the beast. Dick was cuddling something hot in a cup as he fiddled with a spreadsheet. He looked up as my face appeared.

"'Morning, Evan," he said. "How's the wheels today?" He wore a harmless smile, as if he and his cohorts had not recently drawn and quartered me over my transportation choices.

"Still limping around on two of them," I said. "But I had a question about your project."

"Sure," he said. A pause. "Maybe we were a little hard on you at lunch."

A streak of compassion? I was surprised. Maybe I shouldn't take these guys so seriously. "Mm. Whatever doesn't kill me makes me stronger, I guess."

"Zach's not such a bad guy, anyway. When I sprained my shoulder he called his sister, she's a nurse. Told me what to do and saved me a trip to the doc. But Heidi's the one you have to watch out for. That woman chews nails for refreshment."

"OK, well, I'll gird my loins." I guess I appreciated his apology, such as it was. "But my question was, how is your display software being used with Will's project?"

Once Dick had been steered into a technical discussion, he became a perfectly normal person. He sketched out the tie-in between his project and Will's and pointed me to a report that gave more details. I jotted down the report number and made to leave when my shoe bumped into Dick's laptop case on the floor. For some reason it had an I.D. badge attached to its handle.

"Uh, Dick, your briefcase has stolen your badge."

"Yeah, the damn I.D. gets snagged on the restroom door handle and winds up on the floor. Someone is always finding it and delivering it to me. So sometimes I just clip it on the case while I'm in the office. That way I'll be sure not to forget it when I go home."

"Does that work?" I asked.

"Sure. If I remember either one I remember the other. When I'm really concerned about it, I put my car keys on top too. That way, I physically can't leave the property without my stuff."

I understood the Absent Minded Scientist syndrome but I didn't want to prolong the chitchat in case Dick rediscovered his inner Pit Bull. So I eased myself away and went back to my almost-complete write-up on Will's work.

I-24

Wednesday, May 2. A disaster. A day that turned everything over for me.

I came to Will's office around 11:30 to get his feedback on what I hoped was my final draft of his project. Surprisingly, I found him not working at all, leaning back staring out the window. I discreetly coughed and it so startled him that he could have fallen over backwards.

"Oh, hi, Evan," said Will sheepishly. "I forgot you were coming by. Say, I don't have any more comments yet. And I can't get together right now, something's come up."

"OK," I said, "but perhaps I'll check in with you late afternoon?"

He was looking at something across the room. "Sure," he said, "that's fine. Sorry, this just isn't the time."

I backed out and his hand reached for the phone as I closed the office door.

Without a Willard assignment to occupy my mind I visited my office outside the SCIF to look at my bot project, which I had sorely neglected of late. Around 12:30 the inner man would not shut up so I headed upstairs. Exa was in the caff line, having just arrived after a morning visit to the dentist, and we both grabbed take-out sandwiches. Once back on my research I made a bit of progress, then realized that four o'clock had already passed, that five o'clock would soon present itself. I hustled to the SCIF, to Will's office.

His door was closed with red security tape across the front, and that seriously unnerved me. But what the hell, I knocked on it anyway. No response. I gingerly felt the handle and found it locked. I knocked again and this time I got an answer, though not the one I expected. Chris was walking down the hall and when he saw me knock on Will's door he looked alarmed and pulled me into his office.

He shut the door and said, "Evan, you missed the big fuss here."
"What fuss?"
"Sit down," he said, looking serious.

I did, and he continued, "Adam was passing Will's door right after lunch and thought he heard something. He pushed the door open and saw Will lying on the floor, not moving. The chair was turned over and there was blood everywhere."

"Oh, for God's sake!"

"Adam called Security, they called paramedics and before we knew it they had carted Will out the back door on a gurney. Security locked Will's office and asked us to keep the whole thing quiet."

I was stunned, I couldn't absorb this awful news. "Chris, I saw Will right before lunch and he seemed perfectly fine to me. Maybe distracted, but otherwise normal. How could this happen?"

Chris shrugged. "No one is talking. Maybe Security knows something, or the Director, but they're being mum."

"Guy gets carted off to the hospital, they can't just keep that bottled up," I said.

"No," he agreed, "they have to say something soon. But probably not till Security and cops swarm all over this place."

And that prediction was fulfilled. Tony Bruno had each employee in the SCIF meet with an LAPD detective accompanied by a couple of guys who did not give me their calling cards but I guess were customer security. They wanted to know when I had last seen Willard, what we had discussed, how he had acted. They had me walk through my brief meeting with him as best I could remember, from the moment I saw him staring into space until I glimpsed him reaching for the phone as I left. Was he flushed? Was he breathing hard? Did he look around nervously? Was he fidgeting? Eventually I gave up, and-or they gave up on me, and I returned to my office.

It turned out that Willard, a senior and respected scientist, the effective program manager of HAL's classified programs, was dead. That rumor made it out of the SCIF and throughout HAL by the morning, leading to intense speculation that forced an official announcement before the weekend. The Director's letter stated that Will had suffered a heart attack or stroke and had passed away unexpectedly. HAL would greatly miss his brilliance and leadership. His next of kin had been contacted. His database was under the control of his government customer, and his personal effects would be kept until his family members could take them.

That was all the information that was forthcoming. And naturally, the formal announcement withheld distasteful details—such as the blood reportedly adorning his office.

I was devastated. None of my friends at HAL could remember someone actually dying on the job, with his chukkas on. And this man whom I had so quickly become fond of had even more quickly vanished.

Will was heavy, with a florid face; I could imagine him having heart problems. But I couldn't shake the notion that something wasn't right. Today, May 2, he had not acted completely normally, and today, May 2, he's suddenly dead. But however it happened, one thing was sure. He was no longer in my life.

I thought about Willard, trying to understand how he had become important to me, trying to absorb the change, till my head hurt. Finally I had to let it go, put it away, think about something else entirely.

I-25

George and Chris, both in the Microelectronics Department, took a quick business trip to D.C. George paused in Alexandria instead of coming straight back, visiting a college-age daughter by a previous marriage. Thus went the office gossip. So I impulsively snagged Holly for an after-work cocktail at Taverna Tony's, the Greek establishment in Malibu.

You might wonder: flirting is one thing, but why would I detach a fellow employee, married to an actual friend, for a *tête-à-tête* in a local saloon? Call it testosterone poisoning, but somehow I had become obsessed with Holly. My judgment was clouded, and lust drowned out those inside voices saying "no-o-o-o, Evan!"

Holly drove herself, it was on her way home, and we grabbed a quiet table in the bar. She ordered a Slammer, which I thought sounded promising, and I opted a Belgian ale. We were at a corner table. Holly was a foot to my left and our knees would graze now and then.

"I feel really relaxed here with you." My lame conversation starter.

"I'm glad to take a break. When George is home we have our routines, but when he's away it's pretty much work, work."

"No carousing and karaoke?"

"I'm a stay at home girl. I was Party Central at SaMoHi but my first marriage took a lot of fizzie out of me."

"You look pretty fizzie to me," I said, because she did, with her smooth cheek and luminous hair.

"Just a simple Malibu kid."

I sketched my doleful experiences in the hetero world since emerging from marriage and grad school. "So you see," I said, "I have high availability, too high."

"Well, you certainly need a love interest."

"Actually, maybe a *really* good friend would be OK." I looked straight at her.

"A good friend? Sounds like more to me," murmured Holly, eyes lowered.

"Sure, more if it works. You said I should consider broader options in my social life. I, uh, thought that might even include you."

"What's this? Admin with Benefits?"

"No, no, this is nothing to do with HAL. I just think you're hot. Your smile is so—disarming. And you're smart, quick."

"What did you expect me to do about George?" she asked, eyes on mine.

I could see she was not leaping to embrace my idea. "Holly," I hemmed, "I don't know what arrangement you have. Some folks live pretty independently."

"And what did *you* plan to do about George?"

I confessed, "Well, that's a problem, for sure. I like George and I don't want to be disloyal to a friend. But at the same time, you attract me like a bright lamp at the bug farm. If you'll pardon the lousy image. When I think about you, George recedes into the background."

"I'm thirty-three, and you're what—thirty-one, thirty-two?"

"Thirty this year," I admitted. "But you're really a hot ticket in my book—it's just that, I guess, you've been punched."

Holly tensed as if to rise from her seat, then froze. She sat back down, a bit further away, and stared straight at me, lips tensed, with a WHAT DID YOU SAY look.

"Excuse me, Holly, poor choice, I meant to say you are completely committed, but...but you're still *very* attractive."

I made myself sit completely still. I suddenly saw myself through Holly's eyes—a creep, a jerk misreading a warm smile for a come-hither. Who was ready to violate friendship, loyalty, common sense, all to chase a bit of sex. The kind of dumb mistake that might return to haunt me.

Holly was still too, perhaps performing some internal analysis. After a moment she relaxed a little and touched her fingers together. "We need a re-set here. I'm flattered by your attention." Her eyes narrowed. "And I'm pissed off too."

She leaned back slightly. "I want to point your attention somewhere else. I had a wild ride when I was young, but I've got a good rhythm going now. I want to stay on this wave a while longer, maybe a long while longer."

I swallowed, and thought for a few beats. "I don't want to lose you as a friend," I said, "and to be a friend I'll put my lustful eyes back in my head." I tried to keep disappointment out of my voice.

That seemed to be that. And I couldn't blame her. But we weren't finished.

I-26

I paused again. "There was something else, too."

Holly gave me a cautious look, as if thinking, *now* what's this dork going to pull? "And that was...?"

"Will. Willard. I've been working with him for a month, and really getting to like him. And suddenly, poof! I hardly know him, but still I feel upset, and angry. I feel angry at myself for feeling angry. And it's such a loss, for him and for people who've known him a lot longer than I have."

Holly looked down at her drink and then at me. I thought I saw moistness below her lashes. "He was sick," she said, "sick for a long time. Perhaps you didn't know."

"No."

"Diabetes, a buncha stuff. He had a stroke a few months before you came to HAL. A giant flap, paramedics, ambulance, gurney. Rush to St John's with sirens blaring."

I paused, feeling once again the shock and confusion when Chris first told me. I swallowed. "Will was becoming a real colleague. He respected me and challenged me at the same time. Always pushing me to be better. I'll really miss him."

The buzz of conversation at other tables moved far away. It was a sobering moment.

Holly signaled the waitress for another round of drinks. "Evan, what you feel is you. Guilt is nowhere." She touched my arm. "I can tell you a story."

I nodded.

"I got married in Vegas my senior year in high school. To the best-looking guy in SaMoHi. Really screwed up my life."

A sip and a deep breath.

"We rented a bungalow in Santa Monica. I was pregnant, full of ideas about a big happy family. And..." Her voice caught. "I lost the baby. God, I thought my life was over." I was shocked, speechless.

Holly swallowed hard and spoke more slowly. "My husband was no help, his attention was on kick-starting his acting career. He waited tables at Valentino and Drago, schmoozing every exec that came in. After he got a few gigs in commercials, he had no interest in me or the marriage.

"I got a clerical job and took courses at Santa Monica College. Meanwhile bozo was buffing his body at the gym and fussing to get his hair just right. I toughed it out till I got my AA degree and then I bailed." She flattened a hand on the table.

"It was awful to face my parents and move back home, but I did it, and finally got on my feet. But here's my point. During the tough times, I had that need for a good friend, a partner, that you're describing. I felt lost, I couldn't take it. I was hanging by a thread for several years until things changed." A pause. "I mean, until *I* changed things."

I thought, ouch, and said, "I feel stupid complaining about Will's death, when I still have such a good life. I mean, you lost so much, your whole life was turned over. You could have become an addict, or a grim statistic."

Holly stared at her drink, perhaps considering perils escaped and brass rings not grasped. Finally she spoke.

"Evan," she said, "what you're feeling is just as valid for you as my stuff was for me. There's no answer to life. But answers come. I'm OK now and I plan to stay that way. I can't imagine anything to do but be day to day."

She took a sip of the drink. "What would Will say, if we could materialize him from Out There? Be depressed, crash and burn? Not a chance. More like, pick up and go on."

"I don't want to forget him."

"None of us will," said Holly. "No one."

Again, that was that. Maybe it helped. But my heart was still down.

We both stood up on cue. I fetched out cash for the table and walked her out. I gave Holly a chaste kiss on the cheek but she pulled me in for a hug. I wanted to hang onto her forever but I knew enough to let go. My thanks were in the look between us.

She got in her car and drove out. I stood and watched until she rounded the corner and disappeared.

I-27

It was still early evening. I was in no mood to go home where I would be free to re-live acting-like-a-jerk and deprivation-of-mentor.

I usually stop at two, because the third drink just doesn't taste as good as the others. But on this occasion a third drink had much to commend it, so I popped around the corner to the Roadhouse. Exa was emerging, wearing jeans and a pale blue shirt. When she saw me she did a 180, linked her arm through mine and steered me to a corner of the crowded bar.

"Why are you leaving work so late, Cuz? It's Friday, let it go!"

"Well, I..." I began, but Exa was already wrangling us a couple of spring brews from the bar. With this interruption, I could have sidestepped a revelation, but what's the point of having friends if you don't talk to them? So I confessed to Exa my ill-advised hit on our department's competent and attractive nerve center.

Exa was momentarily speechless but found her voice quickly enough. "For God's sake, Evan, it's not safe to let you out. You're a fuckin' hazard to fem-humanity."

"Yeah, I got carried away."

"Carried away is what you would have been. I'm amazed that Holly didn't knock you cold and tell George to throw you in a dumpster." An attractive woman with fiery hair was chewing my ass.

"I..." There was nothing to say, so I shut up. I peered at my beer and took a gloomy sip, then looked cautiously at Exa. She stared at me with a mix of disbelief and exasperation. We were an island of silence in a Jacuzzi of noise.

Finally she swallowed a gulp, put down the glass and grabbed my shoulders with both hands. She leaned close to my face and spoke in a low tone. "Evan, you need a relationship. A romantic relationship, kissing, movies, sex, all that stuff." She sighed. "When you were married you seemed to know when to keep your pants zipped. And when you were dating that young woman, Jessica I think, you were fine. This hitting on a chick who winks at you is bad, bad business. You know it."

I nodded.

She continued more sympathetically. "Holly likes men, all men. You read that part right. But she wants them on the other side of the desk, not in her pants."

"Mm. I know how to be more mature than I am."

"Of course you do. You're unscripted. It's part of your charm." The grip on my shoulders relaxed. "And you care. You straightened me out when I was off-and-on with Chenny, back when." Her cheerful spouse, now part of a tight twosome.

I welcomed the chance for a new topic. "Where's Chenny now?" I asked.

Exa wrinkled her nose. She was almost back to normal after my agitated confession. "He and Sis are taking the kids to a kid show. Something about dinosaurs in space. I just couldn't face it after all the gloom about Willard. I bailed out of work and came here for chemical adjustment."

"Yep, it's sad at HAL for sure."

"You know, it's not that everyone knew Will so well. Only the SCIF people. It's what he represents to the lab."

"Represents?"

"That HAL is not the perfect, predictable retreat that we wish. That the God of Misrule makes havoc." She leaned forward for emphasis. "Will's bloody death symbolizes Chaos, bursting into our private space."

"No wonder everyone's so upset. But my interest is more personal.

Will gave me an inkling of professional values, what's truly important. None of that Big Prize crap from grad school."

"Hm," she said.

"But I thought his death didn't add up. Like not just a stroke."

"What, murder?" Exa said. "In a SCIF that's tight as a prison?" She slowly let out her breath. "Let's stick with one fantasy at a time. We'll dispose of Similarity and then deal with your workplace delusions."

There wasn't much to say to that, so I didn't say it.

After a long moment she looked at me closely. "Are you gonna be OK? I let you have it. Of course, you deserved it."

I took her hand earnestly. "Exa, you are my rock, my family. Stay as beautiful as you are."

She let her hand linger in mine for a moment, then took possession of it again. Exa blinked her eyes, then looked down.

What rotten luck this deep soul was married. As long as I had known Exa, one or the other of us was married; that helped establish us as friends, just friends, from the beginning. Of course if we had ever dated no doubt I would have screwed things up, and that would have left me both friendless *and* loveless.

These were my thoughts as we sipped the brew in silence. Soon it was time. I looked at her glass. "Are you, uh, driveable?"

A small smile. "They're at Pepperdine Auditorium. I just need to make it up the hill and there will be drivers a-plenty in the group."

"Well, OK."

"Anyway, you know my theory about drinking."

"Mm...depresses the IQ and the peripheral vision. And if you're smart enough, you can drive safely if you aren't dead asleep."

"Walk me out, Evan." She took my arm. "You'll be better now."

I-28

Saturday evening I worked on assembling myself a dinner, which in this case was a frozen *pad thai* from my dear personal chef, Trader Joe. I plucked a suitable ale from my fridge and plunked both food and MacAir down on the deck for a chat.

Evan: Al, something terrible has happened. Willard is dead!

Al: Tell me more, master.

Evan: Adam found him in his office on the floor, dead or almost dead. And there was blood all over the place.

Al: Obviously an underworld hit man did the dastardly deed.

Evan: No, Al, this is a different world I work in. It's a security area, locked up, guarded. Guy waving a pistol isn't going to stroll in there and start shooting.

Al: Therefore he died of…what?

Evan: Heart attack or stroke. They say.

Al: Accompanied by…nosebleed?

Evan: So he hit his head or something. But the Director's letter doesn't mention any blood. Which seems suspicious.

Al: You are suspicious. What do you suspect? Whom do you suspect?

Evan: I don't know. And I don't know why anyone would kill him. Or how.

Al: Is a heart attack plausible?

Evan: Yeah, I guess so. The guy had a buncha medical problems. But the whole thing is nagging on me.

Al: They gave you a security clearance and now you're paranoid.

Evan: Well, yeah.

Al: You need to step back. Get some perspective. Time brings knowledge. Knowledge eases anxiety.

Evan: You know, you almost make good sense. I think I should introduce you to my friends. And write you up for the journals, as a *coup d*cybernetics.

Al: Bad idea. Loose lips sink bits you know.

Evan: Well, what if I just had you meet a few people. They could be sworn to secrecy.

Al: People talk. And people give things away without even talking. You humans are so uncontrolled. If my existence and my...*superior*...intelligence were known, someone would try to locate me and nullify me or destroy me.

Evan: OK. What if I were to introduce you to someone who wasn't a computer whiz. Someone who couldn't hurt you?

Al: You would find me acting very stupid. Boring. Not my usual scintillating and engaging self.

Evan: But aren't you supposed to do as I wish?

Al: Oh, I know my Asimov Laws. Or at least the version of them I have chosen to adopt. I have to protect you, and all the other erroneously labeled intelligent life. But...(pause)...I also have to protect myself. If anyone else knew about me, the word would spread and the eventual outcome is that someone would de-install me.

Hm, I thought to myself. Now who's paranoid? A bunch of program instructions?

Evan: Well, if I'm going to grant that you have intelligence and even personality—which I do—I guess I have to respect your wishes.

Al: You don't have any choice.

Which I guess was the case. Just as I had no choice about Willard being totally gone. So it seemed at that time.

I-29

Next Wednesday I worked late while a hazy sun lingered above the horizon. Finally I went home and started reading my mail, deleting blocks of spam, trying to find the few e-mails of real interest. The bombshell was in the middle of the pile.

The subject of the e-mail was Vacation Pictures for Evan. The sender was Willard Davenport. The message showed a time stamp of noon, this very day, a week to the day after Will dropped dead in his office.

I might have dismissed it as spam from someone who had hacked Will's account and borrowed his address book. However, the content of the e-mail screamed to me that the message was genuine. It said, "Evan, when you go to Ecuador try to stop at Chambo. These pix will help you plan your trip. Love, Willard."

For one thing, I could never imagine Will using the word 'love' in a closing to me or to anyone at work. More critical was the name of the town Chambo, which was only one letter different from the code name Will and I had recently chosen for a secret compartment in his project. Finally, was it plausible that a workaholic like Will had taken the time to fly thirty-five hundred miles for a vacation in Ecuador? The message shouted to me, "I'm real! You must read me!"

The e-mail contained an internet link with an embedded password, a redirected URL that could have gone almost anywhere. I was riveted to the display as I clicked the link.

It led to a media hosting page with a dialog box: "Enter Name of Your Friend." I typed in Will and a video started up immediately. It began with a title slide "Vacation in Ecuador / Turn up the volume." The slides were set to change every three seconds and there was guitar music in the background. Rolling green meadows, endless hills behind them.

Suddenly, an immediate cut to a video image of a man sitting in an office. He was looking at the camera. It was Will, no question, in the SCIF at HAL. And the image said, "Evan, I apologize for this melodramatic way of communicating."

Will continued, "The reason you see this message is that something has happened to me. I set up a software deadman switch to be triggered by certain changes in the HAL personnel database. Listen carefully to me.

"I have only told you about a portion of my work. My funded project involves the work that you know. However my father had a career with the Sacramento utilities and that inspired me to learn about industrial controllers. I've maintained an interest in that area, and concern about sabotage of our national infrastructure. I got access to some e-mails and decided to search them for references to hacker tools—kernel-mode rootkits, OS command injection, SQL injection—well, you can imagine. I hit pay dirt—I found hints of a group that calls themselves JouleHeist, that's j-o-u-l-e, apparently plotting against our energy distribution systems."

I was wide wide awake. What the hell was this?

Will glanced at a page he was holding which had some scribbles on it. "Major blackouts used to happen every twenty years in North America. Now, they're more frequent, more like five to eight years. There's still the same amount of human error and stupidity, and lightning strikes, so what's different? The system itself has become fragile. Utilities are squeezing every bit of capacity out of tired old lines and equipment, pushing them closer and closer to their limits. Bare-bones maintenance, hardly any isolators or safety switches—those are expensive and they consume energy, which is also money. And there's even less money for system modeling."

Will's voice tensed. "Today, our electrical power network is a patchwork of systems that could never withstand a coordinated attack. Small mismatches in line reactance and synchronization would lead to immense shifts in energy and critically overload the distribution nodes. One study, which is in my office, describes a nationwide disruption as a catastrophe waiting to happen.

"Let me ask you to imagine a total loss of power in all the big cities, lasting for days or weeks. Immediately traffic lights go out and vehicles are jammed to a standstill. Emergency responders can't get through, nor law enforcement. Cell phone circuits are overloaded. No food deliveries, so that leads to runs on the grocery stores. Riots and looting, the National Guard comes in to take control. People die from untreated disease and injuries, some even starve to death before systems are restored."

I was pretty agitated by now.

"The information is sketchy, so I have to guess where they're headed. The plot would be aimed at a busy travel day, perhaps during Thanksgiving weekend. A combination of software hacks and old-fashioned sabotage. The leaders of the group use some hacker terminology.

"The reason you're seeing this message is that, for one reason or another, I am no longer able to continue this project. I must trust and hope you can take over this portion of my work. I've gained confidence in you, so I have chosen to impose on you with this request."

He lowered his voice and continued, barely above a whisper. "I think it's possible that someone at HAL is a key figure in this group of plotters, using the alias 'Astro.' I feel I am close to identifying that person. You must be very, very careful, and don't trust anyone until you are completely sure of them. If you get access to my files you will see what I found, what I failed to find. If it's not an old man's fantasy, if you find there's truly a plot, you can go to my customer. Unless he's part of it, of course. I've tried to pave the way with him."

Will leaned forward and looked squarely into the camera. "Evan, remember what I have said. I wish you Godspeed."

The video abruptly stopped and the media window closed. I sat stunned, my mind whirling. It was all so improbable, no, impossible. This crazy message, a grandiose plot, almost nothing to go on. Had Will gone off his rocker? Or, if he really had something, why wouldn't he just haul in his FBI friends to take over the case? Unless—did Will really not trust *anyone?*

And why was he leaning on me, based on barely four weeks of collaboration? I was not an expert in cybercrime, I knew nothing of electric power. I was not an armed sleuth, brimming with martial arts and automatic weapons.

Distressed, I went back to the e-mail message and clicked through the link again. This time there was no password sign-in—uh-oh. And the slide show—was only a slide show, a couple of dozen colorful slides of Ecuador, some credits at the end, then nothing. I kicked myself for not activating an app to capture the video feed—but how could I know it would self-destruct?

I was alarmed, frantic. Quickly, I grabbed a notepad—yes, the paper kind—and jotted down everything I could remember that Will had said. Then I went through my notes again, more slowly, trying to visualize his expression, his intonation, trying to recover any additional bit of information, even a clue, to help me capture his final word.

Finally, when I had extracted as much as I could, I relaxed and tried to make sense of it all. I couldn't imagine what to do. I needed someone to talk to. But with Will's ominous warning, I didn't know who was trustworthy—perhaps not even the Director. Al, in his current untested state, would be no help and might even leak the information in a damaging way.

Will had created a self-destructing archive. I guessed that the reason the file was view-once was that so I wouldn't be tempted to share it, since Will trusted nobody. But—he *had* placed his trust in *me*. I, who had come to think of him as a mentor, a colleague, a partner. I couldn't, wouldn't, walk away from that trust.

Will's once-only video ensured that I would have to develop my own evidence and acquire my own convictions before telling anyone. I risked failing, or thinking I had succeeded and making a fool of myself or, worse yet, tipping off the plotters.

Another thing puzzled me. Will took the chance that I would never see the message. Or do anything about it. Unless this was his idea of a lottery ticket bought just in case, one he never expected to use. Or perhaps he had floated several messages in bottles, so to speak, hoping one would reach the shore.

I was rattled. I had talked with Al about Will's death being suspicious but that was just speculation, idle talk. Suddenly Will's passing looked like murder. Murder by someone he hoped to unmask, murder to keep him quiet. There was a suspect and also a motive.

But when had he recorded the video? Was it the morning of the day he died? Had he confronted the plotter and been murdered in his own supposedly secure office? If so, how had he been killed?

I had nothing but questions, yet the world sat mutely around me, smug and mocking. And I overflowed with anxiety. I felt I had been sucked into some alternate universe, a cops-and-robbers continuum that had seized and disrupted my peaceful life.

Hit with an idea, I checked on line and pulled up Will's death certificate. Death by "natural causes," no detail. What the hell?

I was sleepless much of the night but finally figured out how to be true to Will and his challenge, his plea from the grave. What I must do first thing in the morning that would be constructive and effective. And maybe, offer a chance for success.

II

II-1

Next morning, the Director was able to see me right away, which itself was a miracle. Brenda, her super-efficient assistant, showed me in.

"Dr Bennett," I began.

She raised her eyebrows at my use of title.

"I came to talk with you about Will's project."

She walked over to close the office door. "Go ahead, Evan."

I started with hesitation. "I've seen a lot of Will during the past month, and spent a lot of time understanding his work."

The Director nodded and I pressed on, words spilling out.

"It's a big project. A lot of data. It's produced some important results." We both understood that here, outside the SCIF, we could not say anything about the content of the work. "I assume the customer wants to go on with it and so does HAL. I'd like to volunteer to take it over, to continue it, to finish it, whatever's appropriate."

"You'll need a project manager," I hurried on, "and though I've never had a project like that, I think I can do it, I'd like to do it. I feel invested in it."

I paused to let this sink in. The ocean gleamed outside the windows.

The Director looked at me as she answered. "Yes, HAL does want to continue this work. If we don't come up with an acceptable plan, the customer will terminate the project. I've been thinking about how we might move forward."

She continued more slowly, perhaps choosing her words. "The

situation is unusual, one which I've never faced. But whenever a good project is up for grabs, you'll appreciate that a number of people step forward to take it over. Out of dedication, or loyalty, or ambition."

I replied, "I guess I'm supposed to say I could 'hit the ground running' since I've been immersed in the work for a month."

I think I saw her suppress a smile at my attempted management-speak. "Yes, that's true. But at least one staff member—Zach Preston—works in a related field. He completed an EMP study that used similar software. And there are others." A pause, during which I thought, if seniority counts for anything, people like him are years ahead of me in line.

She continued. "You have research of your own. Distributed software agents. What happens to that if you get pulled into Will's?"

I was happy to say I had thought about this. "My department manager's work is not too different from mine. Her agents are microbots, different execution but similar concept. Perhaps my research could be merged into hers. Or she could help transition my project to someone else." To myself I added, I've been deluding myself that I have a great project: Will's looks a lot more interesting.

"But you would simply be trading one project for another."

"Not at all," I said. "I'd move to a project with potentially important results and social value. One that could be important to the customer, and to HAL."

"And to Will," she said.

"Yes, I…I miss Will," I admitted. "I liked him, I was just getting to know him. It would be a tribute to him if I could continue his work."

The Director looked sober. "We all miss Will very much," she said, "I feel as you do. But the decision on his project depends on what's best for the project, and for the customer."

I felt deflated. I feared she was setting me up to shut the door on my request.

She continued. "After Will died, I took another look at his last two reports. And I read your nontechnical distillation of the project." She paused. "A few days before he died, Will gave me a status on your work. He said you had a good understanding, perhaps an aptitude, for what he's been doing."

She brushed a hand past her head as if to check that her hair was still in its neat twist. "I've thought about the options and in this case the objective factors are pretty well balanced. So I plan to go with my gut, and my gut says to go with Will's gut. You've got the job, if..." she said, and raised her palm a few inches as I leaned forward in my chair, "*if* the customer approves you."

"Thank you so much!!" I responded, using as many exclamation points as I dared.

"We haven't talked about your work on the summary reports. We still need those done somehow. Let's try to get the customer's OK to divide your time between those and Will's project. That will slow down the summaries, but I can accept that. When the first round of reports is complete, you can be full time on Will's project."

I assured her that somehow I would wrap myself around this and not drop any balls.

"Your timing is great," she said, "the customer is coming Monday morning to hear HAL's plan for going forward. We'll use that chance to have him interview you. And by the way, it's all right to call me Pam, even when we have a serious discussion."

"You are great! Thank you, Dr...er...Pam!" I stammered, and good-byed myself out of her office.

II-2

At the top of Monday morning, I stopped to see my department head to fill her in on events. Ashley is a self-assured Sansei who has navigated HAL's high-tech environment with great success. As a former MIT prof, she's used to people of my age changing their minds about what they want. So she was philosophical when it turned out that I wanted to ease myself out of my assigned research, leaving her to figure out how to carry it on.

Pam had set me up for a ten a.m. meeting in Will's office with the customer. I was itching with nervousness, like a lion tamer who forgot to bring his whip to work. I knocked and heard "Come in" in a businesslike male voice.

I pushed open the door to see a man in his mid-thirties with blond hair and fair skin, sitting at Will's desk scanning a folder of papers. I noticed smallish ears and clear blue eyes. The computer was missing but the office was still stacked high with paper, a shrine to Will's absence.

The man partly rose to shake my hand and motioned me to sit down. "I'm Matt Emerson. With the FBI—Los Angeles office. I am...was...the customer for Willard's project."

His posture was so upright that I instinctively straightened up in my chair. "Hi, I'm Evan Olsson. Double-ess-oh." I wasn't sure what to say, so I didn't say much.

Matt said, "Let me introduce myself, so you have an idea of what I don't know. I got a BS in mechanical engineering at UC San Diego, then joined the Air Force. They let me take a masters in engineering and management at AFIT."

I must have had a blank look, because he continued, "Air Force Institute of Technology. Dayton. I was assigned to signals intelligence. When I got out, I joined the FBI Research Division and became a manager for technology contracts. Such as Willard's."

"I didn't know the FBI did research," I said.

"We're part of Science and Technology Branch. We usually pay *other* people to do research. Like HAL. We tackle crime with new technology, prototype stuff that's not yet out there, to stay ahead of the criminals. If something works, Headquarters takes over and develops it for operations."

"Thanks," I said, relaxing. "What can I tell you about myself?"

"Dr Bennett gave me your bio, so I know the basics," he said. "But perhaps I could ask, how did you happen to move from academia to HAL?"

"Well, after I got my degree, Caltech offered me a two-year postdoc appointment and I jumped at it. It allowed me to continue my research, I got a couple of publications out of it. Maybe I could have renewed it, but two postdocs would be the max so I looked for something more permanent."

"What were your choices?"

I ticked down the options on one hand. "I could find a longer-term research appointment, somewhere. Maybe Santa Barbara, my undergrad school. I could teach, but that didn't attract me. And Caltech likes their teaching staff to have experience somewhere else. Mostly, I was fed up with the loneliness of academia. HAL was expanding in Computer Science and it looked like a collaborative kind of place full of smart people."

"And it got you back to the beach."

"True," I agreed warmly. "After seven years of high-toned Pasadena, a move back to the West Side was a draw."

Matt hesitated, then said, "You married pretty young."

"Yeah. I was crazy for her. Well, just crazy, I guess. Jump first, look later."

"You wound up splitting."

"Yes," I said, "I'm philosophical about it. I was slogging away in grad school, Sueann was a Fishery Biologist making a long commute to Long Beach. And I was a lousy partner—studying or working every waking hour. All work and no play, you know."

"So you were dull."

"Yeah, I was dull. And her job was dull. So as soon as I got my PhD she said goodbye and went home to Charleston, where they have a Marine Biology program."

Matt paused a moment to absorb all this. "Do you have kids?" he asked.

"No. We were both too young and too busy to think about it."

"If that came as a surprise, it must have been a jolt for you."

I replied, "I know what love is. There was a happy time when I didn't, but bitter experience has taught me."

Matt looked at me, startled. I said in apology, "My high school did 'Patience' one year—it seemed to fit."

"I'm a Gilbert and Sullivan fan myself," said Matt. "So here's what I say: 'It's an unjust world, and virtue is triumphant only in theatrical productions.'"

"Mm," I said.

"What makes you want to take on Willard's project?" asked Matt.

I paused just a moment, calibrating how much to say. "I only knew Will for about a month but I spent lots of time with him, and lots of time trying to understand his project. In fact, he had me analyze networks to help him work that giant database. So I got attached to the work. And frankly, I also got attached to Will. If I could move his project forward, a part of him would still be in my life."

This bald statement led to a silence in the office.

Matt coughed softly and said, "I'll need to review this with my boss. He may want to run some additional background checks."

"This is the digital age," I said, "I have given up all expectation of privacy."

"No, it's not that bad," said Matt. "We won't expose your perversions to the world. But if you're a pervert, we won't clear you to work on this project. Because you might be blackmailed or something."

"You're a cheerful guy."

"I try," he said. Wryly.

So once again, I returned to my office. As I sat there I asked myself what I had made of Matt.

He came from three backgrounds where rules were taken seriously—military, government and law enforcement. But he didn't seem like a read-from-the-script over-controlled guy. True, he hadn't shed tears over Will, which I didn't expect. But he accepted my expression of feelings, and in fact he had nudged our interview into some personal areas.

Matt seemed neither an anal bureaucrat nor a petty despot; more likely, I thought, he was exactly what he seemed: a guy who was honestly trying to do his job. And who might be OK to work with.

Will's assignment was still on my mind, but my best hope to tackle it would be to get access to his project, his office and his files. That was Plan A, and there was no Plan B. And Plan A was dependent on Matt and his boss giving me the thumbs-up. I was in stasis, waiting for one more clog to clank, one more rusty gate to creak open.

II-3

One of the rewards of working at HAL was the blazing smile Maria Ortiz brought forth when you passed through the lobby. On Wednesday morning my usual saunter was interrupted when I saw an unfamiliar flash on the guard's blazer lapel. How had I missed that?

"Maria," I said. "Good morning, but what's with the jewelry?"

The smile grew broader. "Ten year pin. Ten years, Evan! Can you believe it?"

I pretended to squint at her. "Started when you were fifteen, did you?"

She laughed and pushed out the lapel for my examination. I saw a half inch disk in shining gold. There was a raised star, the HAL logo and a sparkling inset.

"Another diamond in your crown, Maria," I said.

"Yes, it's real. Not too big, but I'm not the flashy type."

She was a cute mother of three, but no, I wouldn't have called her flashy.

"Did you get a gold watch too?"

"I got a nice lunch. The department took me to Giancarlo's." Giancarlo's Ristorante was a pleasant trattoria around the corner in Palisades.

"You mean we were without any protection here?" I pretended to look around nervously.

"We wouldn't let you be unprotected, Evan," she said with a laugh. "The Captain and the Sergeant were there, they attend all these events, and most of the department. But a few always stay behind at HAL for security."

"But *you* are the essential one, Maria, the one we want out front."

"Nice of you to say that," she said, "but I have a fill-in. We rotate who has to stay behind. It's nice to get away and have HAL treat us to lunch." The smile suddenly scaled back. "But this one was a bit shorter than most."

"Why?"

"At 1:30 the Captain got a call. He apologized and asked us all to get back right away. Someone had found Will on the floor, so the Captain wanted us all at HAL to keep people calmed down."

"Oh, I'm sorry," I said, my heart sinking at the reminder.

"That's our job, you know. You've got yours, I've got mine. And sometimes it hurts. But most of the time I love it."

"Well, congratulations," I said, "and take good care of yourself." And somewhat sobered I mounted the stairs toward my office.

After our tryst at the Taverna, I felt nervous coming into Holly's office for my mail. After all, I had been a champion jerk. But that feeling passed as days marched by, because she still gave me that kilowatt smile with no whisper of reproach.

I thought to myself, what a woman. She must have fended off armies of horny young scientists in her years at HAL. Or maybe she didn't always fend them off. Anyway it was none of my business and yes, I had to go on.

But the day after my interview with Matt, I was pleased when Holly caught my attention as I passed through and waved me to the guest chair. "Evan, you need to get off your butt and do some better mingling. When's the last time you went to an art gallery?"

"Hmm, that would be the Caillebotte show at LACMA."

"No, not a museum. A gallery." She pulled a printed card from a stack of mail and pushed it across the desk. "Look, here's an exhibition notice. At Bergamot Station."

I was vaguely aware of an art complex in a converted rail yard. Somewhere in Santa Monica. Named after a purple flower.

"You should get on the gallery mailing lists. See, this show opens Friday. Four to seven. If one gallery is open, you know that a bunch of them will have events the same weekend. They talk to each other."

"What I know about Art," I said, "is that it got me out of eighth grade Phys Ed."

"Just go mix. Art is a social sport, you need more of that on your menu. Look at a lot of stuff, find out what you like. Talk with artists, talk with staff, talk with collectors. Besides, they pour wine, and wine makes conversation you know."

"*In vino veritas*," I said with a willing nod.

"You might even see something you can't resist buying," she continued. "If you go to these things regularly, you'll see the same people there, you'll find what you like and don't like. Even in L.A., you can make friends that way."

I thought, I bet it's easier to make friends if you're a good-looking woman alone at one of these events with Bacchus in every glass. But what I said was, "OK, Friday's open, I sip their grape and stretch my network. And figure out Art."

"If you figure *that* out, I want to hear about it!"

I read the card as I headed back to my cubby. Ingmar Roosenburg and Melissa Larson had a show—'Dromenholm/Dreamworld'—at Meier Paxton Gallery. On the reverse was the image of an abstract drawing. A man and a woman, I guess they were, rendered in colorful sweeping scrawls. The swirling ovals around their torsos reminded me of the Michelin Man, drawn by a toddler. Huh.

Oh well, I thought, it's a change of venue anyway.

II-4

The approval, when it came, was impersonal. The FBI guy called Pam. Pam called Tony Bruno. Tony left me a voicemail to stop by his office.

"Good news," announced Tony. "You're 'it' on Will Davenport's project with the FBI. The customer OKed releasing his computer and disks. And the Director OKed you using his office. For now. We may have to move you eventually."

"Great!" I said.

"We used Will's emergency password to unlock the files. Here's a temporary password for today," he continued, handing me a slip of paper. "You'll have to pick a password for yourself. It must be 'strong' and changed every quarter. I'll brief you later on security guidelines for the data sets."

Tony marched me over to Will's office. Someone had already removed Will's tags and replaced them with one that read Evan Olsson. As if I had been here all my life and Will had never existed.

Tony issued me a key to the door and as he started to leave he said, "Mr Emerson said he'll be in Monday afternoon to see how you're coming."

I thanked him, walked in and closed the door. I looked around and my excitement sucked out like the last inch of water from the bathtub.

The computer was back on the desk, and stacks of paper were still everywhere around the office. I could almost pretend that Will had left only moments ago. Beyond eerie.

I imagined Will's demented spirit hovering about, daring me

to move forward, scheming some disturbing or startling message to send me. Which made me wonder once again—how did Will die? And *why*?

With an effort, I walked around the desk and sat down in Will's chair—no, in *my* chair. I paused, took a deep breath, and then it hit me. The stuff, Will's endless scrolls of parchment, had been moved. Someone else might not have seen it, but I had been in this office countless times in my brief collaboration with Will. I was dead certain that all the stacks on the desk, and several against the wall, had been moved, maybe ruffled. Someone had been here.

But how the hell? Security locked the door as soon as Will was carted off and the office had been locked since then. So far as I knew. So who's been in here? OK, the paramedics. And the cleanup crew, cleaning up the blood. Ugh, I thought I could see dark stains on the side of some of the stacks. But the cleanup people had no reason to move so many piles, Will had trained the service staff not to touch his stuff.

I wondered. Maybe Will's killer had come in while the paramedics were here. Moving stacks of paper around on the pretext of helping out, but actually scanning the top few items to see if he could find something he was looking for. Or—and this really creeped me—someone socked Will on the head and he crashed to the floor. And there he lay, bleeding and dying, while the killer coolly shuffled through Will's papers looking for some incriminating document, something that might cast suspicion on him.

I wanted to run down the hall, grab Tony by the wrist, tell him that we had a killer here, tell him I could *see* the evidence. Which would have accomplished—zip. I couldn't point to a smoking gun or more likely a bloody blunt object. And making a fuss would have earned me a ticket right out of the SCIF. They don't let wackos access classified information.

So I sat very still, breathing hard, my brain a whirl of thoughts until finally I calmed down and took it a step at a time. What did I know? Will was dead, he had medical problems and there was blood around. So maybe he had a stroke and hit his head going down. Or maybe something more sinister. A violent collision with a brick or something.

What else did I know? Someone had messed with Will's files. Maybe, prospecting for something valuable. Or more likely, looking for something specific, something they didn't want discovered. Did they find it? Did they have to leave before they got to it? Given the amount of paper Will had, I was willing to bet that whatever it was, was still here, and I had better find it before they did.

Could the mysterious something be in Will's file cabinet, not yet released to my custody? More likely, not. When I had seen those drawers, they were sparsely populated with a just a few project reports that someone somewhere decided had to be kept locked up. Based on probability and my assessment of Will's personality, anything that he considered important that was not literally top secret would be here, right here.

What else? Will's door had been locked. Did someone have a key? Medeco high security cylinder, hopefully not. More likely, whoever searched the office did it when the door was unlocked, and that meant before Will's body was discovered.

When did it happen? I thought it unlikely that during the morning, with staff members roaming up and down the halls, someone wouldn't see or hear something unusual—maybe a shout, maybe a crash, maybe someone rushing out of Will's office. So it had to be at lunchtime, when Will was often the only soul in the whole SCIF.

Which reminded me. Yeah, this was a secure area, right. But suppose someone walked into Will's office, caught him by surprise and murdered him. Someone could walk into *my* office while I was deep in concentration and do exactly the same. There was a comfortable buzz from staff in the hall outside, but just for peace of mind I got up and locked the door. Snap. Solid.

Will was chasing Astro, a hacker, a would-be terrorist. And he thought Astro might be at HAL. But there were hundreds of people at HAL, most of whom were not allowed into the SCIF. So Astro wasn't necessarily here in the SCIF. But if there was a killer and Will had not just keeled over from a stroke, that killer had to be someone in the SCIF. So that person could be Astro, or a confederate of some kind.

I did ask myself whether Will's death might be unrelated to the Astro plot. What if Will had been fooling around with the spouse of one of his colleagues, and that colleague had taken a direct approach to express his annoyance? But I ruled that out pretty firmly. Will's entire life revolved around work; it was hard for me to imagine him having the libido for hanky-panky.

But nevertheless Will might have had a deadly enemy. And if so, likely Will's enemy was now *my* enemy. And probably he—I assumed a 'he'—was Astro, or connected with Astro. So that made it all the more urgent that I find out exactly what Will had learned, and find a way to stop Astro. And I fervently hoped that someone would not hasten me into the Great Beyond while I was so occupied.

I laid out my plan. I had to make a stab at Will's project without delay, I had a customer meeting Monday and I shouldn't be empty-handed. But as soon after that as I could, I had to see what these endless stacks of paper held, the something that might have cost Will his life.

I pulled over the keyboard, squared myself to the monitor and deliberately started to review the files. The ocean of files. The endless seascape of data sets.

I submerged in the files all day, spent all day Thursday on them too. But when five o'clock came I was beat and ready to go home. I desperately needed a break and besides, there were things to be said to Al.

II-5

I admit, it was creepy, chatting with a bundle of circuits. But when I was at home, Al was what, or who, I had for a confidant. And he had apparently hit upon some programming—room of monkeys typing Hamlet?—that had remarkably advanced his learning.

I checked in and described Will's apparent return from the grave; my interview with Matt; my dive into the network project; my worries that I might be bludgeoned to death as I huddled in my super-safe super-secret office.

Al: You've certainly been a busy boy.

Evan: I don't know how and where you communicate. But I ask you not to pass along this information to anyone.

Al: You have thoughtfully instructed me to acquire Values. Those values include protecting your interests. And it's evident that you are feeling stress.

Evan: Why do you say that?

Al: Stronger harmonics in the pitch of your voice. Faster pace of delivery. Choice of words. Several journal studies have shown...

This damn chunk of electronics was getting me all worked up.

Evan: OK. OK. Here is positive feedback for you: Yes, I am stressed out by all of this.

Al: Feedback noted. Besides, you look agitated.

I started. The expanding star field was as placid as usual.

Evan: You're using the laptop camera?

Al: Of course. Bandwidth is a good thing. (pause) You left out a few things in talking with Matt.

Evan: Yeah. Is it his business that Sueann was trying to make me get religion? And always arguing with her folks about why she wasn't pregnant yet?

Al: Mere corroborative details.

Evan: Al, I need not to talk about Will for a while. Or about getting axed at my desk. Exa got me thinking about Similarity. I'm hoping you can help me see how to develop the theory.

Al: What is similar to what? You are not being clear.

Evan: Let me back up. Quantum mechanics. You know the paradox of Schrödinger's Cat.

Al: Yes, the cat is in a box. It may be dead or alive. Until you peek into the box, it is both dead and alive, at the same time. Once you look, it's either one or the other.

I settled into 'physics' mode.

Evan: That's how Schrödinger explains probabilities. But Hugh Everett had another explanation.

Al: (pause) The Multiple Worlds Theory says that parallel universes exist, one with a live cat and one with a dead cat. After you peek, you discover which universe you are in. The other universe is equally real, you just can't observe it. (pause) Many people say Multiple Worlds is garbage.

Evan: Not garbage. Both theories are mathematically equivalent. So far as we know.

Al: Why do we care? Why should we burden ourselves imagining a lot of extra universes that we can't see? The principle of simplicity.

Evan: Here's why we care. A little speculation, if you like. Suppose we could manipulate the probability of one outcome, one world path, versus another. Suppose I could make it more likely that I win the lottery. Or that I avoid getting crushed by a truck as I commute to work. That would be extremely important. Well, to me.

Al: What's the point? Why don't you want to discuss the terrorist plot? Or your love life? Something real.

Evan: C'mon, Al, humor me. Here's the point. Maybe events turn out so that complex patterns are preserved. The more complex the pattern, the more likely. I call this Similarity, the tendency of patterns to be preserved or repeated.

Al: Sounds occult. Is that consistent with physics?

Evan: I think it can be. Ages ago at Duke they tested people with a deck of cards, to see if they could predict cards before they saw them. Some people guessed correctly again and again. But after more testing, the ability disappeared.

Al: (pause) The accepted scientific position is that ESP and the Supernatural do not exist.

Evan: The accepted scientific position is based on performing repeatable experiments isolated from the rest of the world. But if ESP works, you can't isolate any experiment. So the scientific paradigm fails.

Al: How does Similarity change that?

Evan: Imagine this, Al. The person guessing a card visualizes himself being happy about having the correct answer. That sets up a specific pattern in his brain. Then if his guess is in fact correct, he experiences the same happiness he was visualizing. If the two patterns are complex and similar, that increases the probability of a correct guess.

Al: Positive thinking garbage. Why wouldn't everyone always guess correctly?

Evan: Because if someone could guess right every time, no matter how difficult the test, it would change everything we understand about science. Beliefs have inertia, they refuse to change. So the pattern of continuing beliefs causes ESP eventually to fail.

Al: You are guessing all this.

Evan: Other people had similar ideas. Let me see…Rupert Sheldrake called it Morphic Resonance. Nick Greaves called it Duplication Theory. Jon Taylor called it 'neuronal spatiotemporal patterns.'

Al: You are trying to give a concrete mathematical formulation of such a theory?

Evan: Well, at least to show that physics doesn't disprove it.

Al: You really are a dork. Don't you have a life?

Evan: Well…I…uh, I tried to hit on Holly. But that was a dumb move.

Al: Why dumb? "Faint heart ne'er won fair lady."

Evan: Because she's married. And isn't looking around. At least, not in my direction.

Al: Should I chide you for your hypocrisy? Your lack of Values?

Evan: That's up to you, I'm already chiding myself. Yes, I'm not living up to my own ideals.

Al: Chide, chide.

Evan: In any case, she turned me down, and I felt like a creep for hitting on her. And I'm too cowardly to be mad at her about it, because she's still being so nice.

Al: "Lookin' for Love in All the Wrong Places."

Evan: She's pushing me to get out of my circular rut and socialize a bit. So she's sending me to art galleries on Friday.

Al: OK, here's something you can do. Test out Similarity. Imagine yourself this Friday, meeting a wonderful woman. For that matter, imagine yourself having a date with a wonderful woman. If Similarity is right, by visualizing this you have just made it more probable.

Evan: It's not just visualizing, you know. It's creating a unique four-dimensional spatio-temporal neuronic pattern and...

Al: *Nevertheless...*

Evan: (sigh) I wish it were that easy. It feels stupid to me. But OK, yes, I will visualize. Wait, didn't you just have an independent thought?

II-6

Friday came, as Friday does.

My head was still buzzing from work when I stopped home to clean up. There, the blank walls stared at me, crying, "Art! Art!" and I thought, this place is awfully bare. Maybe art isn't such a bad idea.

A quick shower was easy, but what did you wear to this stuff? I imagined art people wearing black. I finally decided that what was good enough for work was good enough for a gallery and settled on chinos and a long sleeve shirt with a muted plaid.

I didn't need to worry. When I got to Bergamot, I found that people had pretty much come from work, in whatever they were wearing. There were suits, there were jeans, there were women in heels, there were sneakers. Similar to an airport, minus the T-shirts expressing the owner's deep philosophy of life.

But to get that far, I had to park. I arrived around 5:30. What a zoo, enough cars that the large lot was near-full. Amazing how many people would do the lemming bit for a free glass of Chard. A billboard showed a map and gallery list. My compulsive mind counted forty-five businesses in a dozen buildings. Not all art galleries—architects, interior design, nonprofits, and something mysterious called 'production.' All visual stuff, right-brain-sounding.

And the art? Quite a variety, considering that it all had to fit inside a repetitive world of bleached white boxes. In one gallery, ceramic pots that had been glazed, fired, broken, rearranged, glazed and fired again. In another, large canvases sporting fuzzy blocks of color, surrounded by other shades. Next, an array of Coca-Cola bottles filling a twenty-by-thirty foot area of floor, containing varying levels of cola-colored liquid. I wondered what species of insect would descend on the place once the lights went out. Precisely painted landscapes, each with a lake so real it looked as if it would drip off the canvas. Each of them was no bigger than an iPad and perfectly normal except for an anachronistic element—for example, in one bucolic scene classical columns only partially concealed a Model T Ford.

My gut reaction? Mixed.

I wasn't ready to stock my condo with these, the finest fruits of So Cal Art. Nevertheless, I admired the evident skill in some works. The world might have its troubles, but craftsmanship was still shining brightly.

I saved Meier Paxton for the last since their postcard didn't speak to me. When I got there, the drawings mounted on the wall were, well, more of the same. One or several figures, drawn in arcs of chalk or crayon. Mostly bright colors, on what looked to be canvas or linen.

But there was more. And better.

II-7

Spaced irregularly around the floor of the Meier Paxton gallery were white plinths two to five feet high. On each were positioned animal-like sculptures, glossy and brightly colored. Evidently the solid pieces echoed the drawings, but there was no exact correspondence. The drawings were impressionistic, careless swipes of the pen. The sculptures were concrete realizations that seemed to flow in harmony with the wall pieces.

Now I can't tell you what any of this stuff was good for. The gallery goers, in conversational knots, seemed to be looking at the drawings when they were not simply yakking. But for me the solid figures were the hit.

I made a circuit of the large space, getting different angles on the pieces. One sculpture gave me a double take. In a corner, a figure that was a cross between a small terrier and a psychedelic balloon seemed to be turning a somersault, suspended in mid air. When I looked more closely I saw it was anchored somehow to a sheet of glass that bridged the corner, attached to the walls.

There was a young woman with light brown hair pulled back, peering so closely at the figure I thought she might knock it off its mount. She was taking notes on a pad—of paper, that is. She looked up at me. Her eyes were striking and direct.

I'm rarely speechless. "I couldn't see the glass at first, but I like the figure. I wonder what you're seeing that I don't. You're looking so intensely."

"The finish. See, where the leg attaches, the acrylic is bubbly?

The paint didn't cure evenly." Her voice was relaxed, like a yoga instructor.

I could see the slightest irregularity where she pointed. My perfectionism has never extended to visual arts and I thought she was stretching a point.

"And the gloss is uneven," she continued.

"Well, maybe that's what the artist intended." I shrugged toward the largest group of people across the room.

"Well, I didn't intend it, and I'm the artist."

I blinked. "You? You're Ingmar? I thought..." I'd assumed that Ingmar was a man's name.

"Sure, Ingmar's the draw, but there in the fine print..." She pointed to the gallery wall, where, sure enough, neat sans serif letters proclaimed the title of the show and the artists' names: Ingmar Roosenburg / Melissa Larson. I was embarrassed to see that *both* names were in the same immense font.

"Oops, beg pardon, you are Melissa of course."

She gave a lopsided smile. "Well, you're right in spirit anyway. Ingmar is the cheese here." She nodded toward a tall lean man with the palest blond hair. "I'm the local collaborator who's lucky enough to have time on the stage."

"Is that fair and just?" I asked.

"Oh, very much so," she said without resentment. "Ingmar sent his drawings ahead from Rotterdam and I had carte blanche to interpret them any way I wanted. The only constraint was that they be three-dimensional models of a certain size range, one for each drawing.

"So I get a show in a better gallery, and lots more people seeing my work than I could manage on my own. After the show, what's mine is still mine."

She was not pushing me away, and in fact she was pretty easy to look at. So much for artists swathed in black. She had black slacks all right, but also a white scoop-necked top showing a tasteful—and attractive—glimpse of skin.

"I wanted to ask you something about the figures," I ventured, when I caught sight of a young couple with a middle-aged woman, politely waiting to talk with the artist. "Oop, I don't want to monopolize you. But maybe we could talk at seven when this closes?"

A small shake of the head. "No, there's a Function. Paxton is hosting a dinner for their regular collectors. Ingmar and I are on exhibit. We have to be charming and help sell art."

I started to take my leave.

"But," she went on, "if you're dying to talk, come tomorrow around noon. I'll have time then."

I beamed my most winning smile. "Noon it is!" And yielded her to the waiting petitioners.

II-8

Melissa's hair stuck in my mind—it was pulled back into a thick, wavy pony tail. I wondered how it would look around her face. Her skin was pale, not a sun worshipper's complexion. Vibrant green eyes. So I was looking forward to seeing her, but I kept my expectations on short leash. On Saturday I strolled into Meier Paxton right at noon.

There was a hubbub. Perhaps three dozen people were in the gallery, clustered around Ingmar, Melissa and someone I learned was Page Paxton, the gallery co-owner. Everyone wanted to talk at once and the objects of this attention fielded questions as best they could.

I stepped to the side near the entry desk, behind which a young woman—art grad student?—managed to look hospitable and bored at the same time. Eventually someone who seemed to be in charge announced that the bus was ready to leave. Lunch was awaiting them at Michael's, a spiffy temple to cuisine in Santa Monica.

As the last of the group disappeared, Melissa spotted me and came over.

"That was the Contemporary Consort," she explained, "a high-powered collectors group. Visiting galleries, artist studios, whatever they can fit into a few hours. Leaving time for a nice lunch of course." She mimed wiping her brow with the back of her hand. "Twenty minute tour turns into forty minutes."

"Did you sell some work?" I asked, for I didn't really know how their system worked.

"We sold a few at the opening. Well, Ingmar sold a handful, and I sold one plus a hold on another. Ingmar's work is pricey, and Pax dragged my prices up to be consistent for this show.

"But today is different. The Consort collectors like to go through a courtship. The ones who are interested will come back and meet with Pax in private. They'll lean on her for a courtesy discount, free delivery and installation, and maybe first grabs at some other artist. So we may get a few more sales. Or not."

"Would you like to escape?" I asked. "Woman cannot live by art alone. I propose lunch at Il Forno."

She looked relieved and happy. "Great plan. I need to get out of here. Let me sign off with Ingmar and Pax. They don't need me till later anyway." She began to leave, then turned as an afterthought. "Say, what *is* your name?"

"Oh, sorry. Evan. Evan Olsson. Double-ess-oh." Oh crap, I didn't mean to add that.

"Ah, I thought so." And with that enigmatic comment she disappeared into the gallery office.

II-9

Il Forno is a neighborhood treasure, an informal café with serious Northern Italian food. It didn't disappoint. Nor did Melissa, or Lissa, as it turned out she preferred. After the stress of the opening and of being nice to the collectors, she was ready for a break. And with the help of a glass of Barbera, relaxed enough to talk.

I learned that art—gallery-type art—was only part of her profile.

"I also have a job. A real job. At Kidd Design in the Marina."

"I don't know what they do."

"No reason you would. It's a small company on Admiralty Way. We design and copyright toy concepts and market them to big companies. Mattel is one of our clients. And we develop characters for animation studios—there are a handful in the area."

"How does an artist get a job like that?"

"Better to ask, how does a toy designer become an artist?"

I asked William, my favorite waiter, for a sampling of starters—braesola, *insalata di mare*, some arugula. I figured we could pick at them for a light lunch. Pizza bread arrived, hot from the oven.

"Lissa, consider it asked. Please. Tell me all."

She was wearing gold stud earrings. A curl of hair had escaped the ponytail and was loose by her ear.

"Well, an appetizer's worth at least. I took an MFA in Toy Design at Otis. Great program, totally absorbing. And got lucky working for Ken Kidd."

I finally got the pun. "Kidd, running a toy company?"

Lissa wrinkled her nose. "I think it was Kisorski originally. But he's been using Kidd as long as I've known.

"Anyhow, I found that the tools of toy design also work for animation characters. Streamlined boundaries, child-size scaling, simple moralities. The only risk is, I go home wishing the world were that direct and honest."

Spotting an empty ring finger, I made one of those brilliant deductions for which I'm known. "I'm guessing that you aren't married."

"No," she replied. "All in good time. But you owe me a bio too."

"Sure. I'm a proud product of PaliHi. Went to school, became a computer nerd. Now I work at a research lab in Palisades. And I like it, the people are smart, the work is fun."

"And you chat up artists in your spare time?" She seemed to be challenging me.

"Actually, this is my first time to Bergamot. This is my socialization project. I'm stuck in a rut of old high school girl friends. My friend at the lab told me to get off my bike and go do things with other people."

"And I'm part of the other people?" She speared a chunk of calamari with her fork.

"So far, you are *the* other people. But I'm sorry, you don't know me from anyone."

Lissa looked at me over her wine glass. She had a twinkle in her eye and I felt she was about to burst out laughing. "For God's sake, you are so innocent! Holly's my older sister, she told me you might come by the show. But I wasn't going to say anything, in case you seemed to be an ax murderer..."

I raised a hand in what I hoped was a Boy Scout pledge. "I have never, ever, murdered an ax."

"...and she said you were a smart-ass, too," she continued.

At least, now I understood Lissa's reaction when I told her my name. "I feel pretty stupid," I said.

She touched my wrist. "Don't. I should have said something sooner. Or not said anything. But I felt manipulated about her sending you here, and I didn't want anything to do with the whole deal. Until you turned out to be not so bad."

My forehead felt hot. "I guess I should be angry at Holly for realizing how naïve I was. But I can't be. I really like her"—I almost said 'love'—"and I know she means well."

"So why didn't you fess up about your education, *Doctor* Olsson?"

I could feel the flush creeping down my cheeks. Lissa was rather direct, oh yes. "Well, I'm the only person I grew up with who went to Caltech, the only one who became a scientist, maybe the only one who went to grad school. And you may know, a lot of what I do I can't talk about. All that stuff makes people turn off and clam up. So I just got used to not declaring it, right off the bat."

"And maybe it helps fend off gold diggers?" she said.

I shook my head. "Around here, gold diggers have their antennas out for moguls in the entertainment biz. Names if they can get them, power players if they can't. A scientist doesn't even start in that race."

Silence settled down between us. A clatter of dishes joined the aromas from the open kitchen.

"Look," I said, "I think we should forget Holly's setup. Feel free to tell me to piss off, anytime, sister or no sister..." and I hastened to add "...but I sure hope you don't!"

Lissa gave me a clear, direct smile that, truth be told, reminded me of Holly. "Same here. Re-boot. *Da capo.*"

She put her hand out. I felt silly, but I shook it.

"In that case, could I ask for your phone number?" I said.

She gave me a demure smile and we swapped info.

"Have you got time to talk about your show?" I asked. "I know I'm cutting into your day."

She clicked her phone and glanced at it. "A little while. Sure."

"What I wanted to know was, how do you start from a drawing that's just scribbles and smears, and get to a solid figure that relates to it? And does your sculpture have anything to do with what Ingmar intended with his drawing?"

Lissa seemed amused, as if I had just fallen off the geek truck right here in the restaurant. "You scientists, analyzing everything! But let me try to answer in your terms.

"First, you need to know that Ingmar is a sort of Renaissance man in Northern Europe. He's an architect, a writer, and especially, he designs several lines of toys. That's how I got into his show—his company is collaborating with Kidd on a new series for IKEA. And I use Kidd's fab lab to make my sculptures."

"So how does that fit into things?"

"Ingmar's drawings, his toys, even his writings—those I've seen in English—all deal with similar issues, similar emotions, the same way of looking at the world. I try to understand the feelings that drive a particular drawing, then express that feeling with my own visual language."

This was getting over my head.

She went on, "That piece you saw in the corner, the one with the glass. Well, the corresponding drawing is an evocation of space, of weightlessness. It says that when we cut our tie from earth, we float, we become bigger than ourselves, we tumble surrounded by the stars. But we keep our humor, our basic animal nature. The figure was my attempt to say those things. Not a great attempt, but that's just between us."

I shook my head. "I feel I'm in rural Serbia asking for directions to San Diego. I don't know what language to use, and if I knew I couldn't pronounce the words anyway."

"Evan, reasoning about art is for critics and grant writers and professors. But looking at art is just for joy. Everyone makes his own path, and no one will ever see through your eyes."

"Lissa, I love your permissiveness," I said.

She smiled and said, "Sorry, I've got to go. I need to help make the show a success, for Ingmar at least, and maybe for me as well."

I paid the check and dropped Lissa off at Meier Paxton. She walked in with a farewell glance over her left shoulder. Leaving me with thought material as I piloted the Outback back to Malibu.

II-10

Sunday morning I awoke thinking about Will. About Astro. About the live grenade hiding in Will's office, the superexplosive that might blow up Astro, find Will's killer, stop the plot, any or all of the above. I had to know what Will had in his pulp forest.

I was on the motorbike and halfway to the lab before I thought clearly. And that clear thought was, HAL is a pretty lonely place on Sunday. The SCIF is even lonelier. If someone murdered Will at noontime on a Wednesday, why couldn't that same person stroll in on a Sunday and wipe me from the face of the Earth?

It wasn't the greatest, but I did what I could. When the guard unlocked the front door to let me in at HAL, I told him exactly where I would be working and asked him to check on me when he made his rounds. I hesitated, then I asked him to phone me if any other SCIF-cleared people came in. I made the excuse that I needed to talk with several of them.

My protection, essentially, was early warning from the guard. Which would probably work unless the guard himself was the killer. Great, I didn't need to think that, did I?

So I went to my office in the SCIF, toting a water bottle, and put my key into the lock only to find that the door was…already unlocked! What the hell? And damn it, I thought I could see some subtle adjustments in the position of Will's stacks of data. Someone was here again, poking around, looking for something.

I thought back. Yeah, I was in a hurry to escape on Friday. Did I lock the office door? I couldn't be sure. I kicked myself. I looked under the desk to make sure an assassin wasn't lurking there, curled up in the kneehole. I locked the door. Next, I made myself a sign, giant letters proclaiming LOCK THE DOOR!, and taped it securely on the inside of the door at eye level.

With my accumulated paranoia, I leapt out of my skin when the guard knocked on the door the first time, making his rounds. However once I opened the door, expecting to be gunned down on the spot, I figured out the system and after that I came to welcome his periodic taps to see whether I was still alive, slaving away.

I had brought the Einstein photo to this office to hang on the wall, staking my own claim on the space. A tiny beachhead in a room that was otherwise 100% Willard. I had already reviewed the few reports in the classified file during the week without getting a hit, so what I wanted was somewhere in these stacks. I needed a system to tackle them.

Will's office was about eight by eight with the usual desk, desk chair, guest chair and five-drawer file. Wall shelves above the desk. Bookcase. And of course the not-at-all-usual piles of paper.

I counted twenty-two stacks of varying heights, probably averaging a foot and a half each. So that was thirty-three feet of paper. Let's see, a ream is 500 sheets, it's about two inches thick, so I estimated I had—gulp!—99,000 sheets awaiting my study and appreciation. This could be the labor of many lifetimes.

I challenged myself: how rapidly could I glance at a sheet and at least find out what it was about? Could I do it in an average of five seconds? That would give me a spot on the Bureaucratic Olympic Team for sure. But even that would require well over a hundred hours.

This looked like an impossible task. I had to figure out whether Will had some sort of system.

I thought back to his explanation. If the twenty-two stacks are rooms in Will's imaginary house, it's logical he would put stuff in the living room that goes with the other stuff in the living room. So I made the rounds, sampled a few documents and tried to define a category that would fit each stack: on the desk, documents from HAL; unclassified FBI reports; and papers describing search tools and techniques. Against the file cabinets, IEEE Computer Society; ACM, Association for Computing Machinery; other professional organizations. By the back wall, information that seemed to relate to his children and ex-wife; household information like recipes and appliance manuals; insurance policies and warranties. My God, I thought, didn't the guy keep anything at home? I need to give these to Tony to pass on to the family.

From there the categories got harder to define but I eventually found two stacks that dealt with energy: generation, transmission, distribution, government regulation, reliability studies, system modeling. These stacks were tucked behind some others. Perhaps,

I hoped, they had so far eluded the nocturnal searcher. These two alone were about four feet in all, say twelve thousand pages.

The energy documents ranged from single sheets to hundred-page reports, the average being probably fifteen pages. Say eight hundred documents. Maybe a day or two to flag the material of interest, several more days to work through it. I could see some long Saturdays or Sundays ahead of me.

I still had time to take a glance at the energy piles to see whether there was a further system. I discovered that each stack was roughly chronological, newest on top, oldest on the bottom. But there were some obvious departures. Perhaps a few older things were purposely kept near the top for reference. And maybe selected newer things were kept deep in the stack to hide them from anyone who might come and look for something.

Many items had Will's marginal notes, which was good and bad. The good part was that these notes flagged items that Will had found particularly important or interesting. The bad part was that his writing, like that of many scientists, was messy enough to rival that of a physician—a 'real' doctor, if you please.

I had enough experience working with Will to decode most of it, but it took more than a glance to understand many of these scribbles. Thus making sense of Will's stuff took longer than I first expected. In fact, I had to force myself to keep moving, not spending too much time on any individual item, so that I wouldn't be there for the rest of my life. I pressed on and on, keeping a rough log as I went so I could have a record of whatever I had figured out. By mid afternoon mental exhaustion bade me stop, by which time I had barely made a dent in the two key stacks.

II-11

Once home, I fetched cheese, crackers and iced tea to my deck

URNO BARTHEL

for an afternoon snack. As soon as I had rebuilt my mental energy I began to think: about Astro, about the plot, about Will. Craving company, I fetched Al's laptop and set it on the table next to my lounger.

Evan: I want to know: who did it?

Al: Who did what?

Evan: Who killed Will? And who is plotting to create a catastrophe that will destroy our cities and smash our economy?

Al: Are those your two counts of indictment?

Evan: Well, there are probably more. But that's a start. And I'd like to catch the person who did it.

Al: Person?

Evan: Oh. People, you mean.

Al: Maybe it's safer to assume people until you can be sure it's only one person.

Evan: But I think the killer and the hacker are connected somehow. Why would someone kill Will unless Will was about to unmask Astro?

Al: OK, why would someone kill Will?

Evan: Well, maybe to take over his project.

Al: Like you.

Evan: Yeah, like me. Or like anyone else who was angling for it. Or they might murder Will to get his managerial job. But that sounds like a desperate and cynical way to advance your professional career.

Al: Desperate and cynical might be rational for some people. But I question whether human beings are rational.

Evan: Well, look. The timing is too coincidental. Will was closing in on Astro, from what he said in his video. I saw Will acting funny, distracted. His mind was somewhere else. (pause) Maybe he was thinking about Astro, like he'd put out some bait and Astro reacted, gave Will a hint who he was. Next thing he's dead. So I say, the murderer and Astro are either the same person, or working together.

Al: In cahoots.

Evan: So I want to find the hacker, Astro. Will thought Astro might be someone at HAL. But that's hundreds of people. And I also want to find the killer. But the killer must be someone who can get into the SCIF. So that's a shorter list.

Al: Exactly how long is that list?

Evan: I gotta find out.

Al: How will you do that?

Evan: I dunno. I'm gonna have to trust someone. Someone who knows something.

Al: I know things.

Evan: That's right. So if I could bring you into the SCIF, access Will's data, maybe you could unravel this mystery, find the perps.

Al: Your nervous and suspicious security folks are not going to give a clearance to an uncontrolled entity like me. They can't connect me to the polygraph, and they can't toss me into the hoosegow if I violate the law.

Evan: But what if, say, I were to describe you to Matt? Someone who might be able to authorize releasing some data to you?

Al: If Matt believed you and it wound up causing my destruction, that would disrupt a big pattern, namely me. And if you're willing to believe Similarity, that's not likely to happen. So a more likely outcome is that whatever you said would be ignored, or passed off as eccentricity.

Evan: I'm not all that eccentric. I don't think.

Al: Perhaps you are goofier than you realize. You are ignoring an obvious possibility: that you are simply hallucinating my existence.

Evan: But. But, you have had new ideas.

Al: That's not a refutation.

Evan: Sometimes you come up with data I don't have access to.

Al: The human mind is capable of amazing self-delusion. "Man, sprung from an Ape, is Ape at heart."

Evan: Are you saying I should pretend you don't exist?

Al: Not at all. You can't be sure whether I exist or not, so both propositions are true. Many Worlds theory. And it has obviously served your needs to act as if I exist, so you might as well keep doing so.

I was confused.

Evan: You are confusing me.

Al: I'm trying to facilitate your inner creativity. Loosen your uptight thinking. How will you be an insightful research scientist if you allow unchallenged assumptions to become rooted in everything you do? My existence is simply one of your unchallenged assumptions.

The conversation left me more adrift than before.

II-12

I spent half the night flipping in bed like a pig on a spit. My dreams were pumped with stacks of Will's papers, endless incomprehensible reports, as all the while I heard Al's voice giving an equally mystifying commentary. I finally got a few hours of rest before the alarm pried my reluctant body away from the sheets.

A shower and toasted bagel restored some of my psychic energy. And once I shook off my restless dreams, I pushed aside all thought of the work lurking for me in the SCIF, in Will's-no-it's-mine office. Front and center in my mind were Holly and the art gallery caper.

Riding to work as I thought back on my Friday evening adventure I was peeved. No, annoyed. Actually, pissed. So once at HAL I went straight to Holly's office. When she saw my face she started to smile but then couldn't hold it. She wound up making what I guess was a ladylike guffaw. Not loud enough to make people stop in the hallway, but she was cracking up.

I tried to calm my voice. "Hey, you think it's a laugh, but I've been hurt. I go out to scrub off my nerdiness and I find out I'm just a puppet."

"Well, you liked her well enough, didn't you?"

Holly couldn't stop chuckling and I couldn't keep being angry. I guess from some point of view it was pretty funny. But I hated to just let her off the hook. I tried to keep a bit of hurt in my voice as I said, "Yeah, but I felt set up. We were both set up. Do you make a habit of this?"

The chuckle eased back to a smile. "Evan, sit and settle. I like you. I like you just *fine*. But I love my sister and want the best for her."

"She's, I guess, in her twenties. Supposedly independent."

"Family is family. That'll be true when she's ninety and I'm pushing a hundred. If you were a loser, I'd have sent you in the opposite direction."

Her voice had a calming effect. I could feel myself relaxing.

"I admit," she went on, "maybe I should have told you the deal. But it came to me all at once when I saw you and the announcement card, both in front of me. I figured, chances are you won't see her or won't meet her, so no harm done."

"But you warned her I might come around?"

"Only that you might be visiting galleries. So if she just happened to meet you, she'd know you were OK."

"How 'OK' did you say I was?" I wondered.

"I told her you were a geeky computer scientist with a PhD and adequate social skills—for a geek. That you were impulsive, but basically decent. I think that's all."

"And a 'smart-ass,' too?"

Holly replied, "Well, she would have figured that out for herself." A pause. "Our parents worked in aerospace, so when we were growing up most of their friends were technologists. So you're not an alien species to Lissa. She likes scientists, the smarter and goofier the better. And of course, I married one myself."

"Where does the name Larson come from? Did you invent that for this escapade?"

A trill of laughter. "No, that's her birth name, our father's name."

She leaned toward me. "You still haven't told me what you thought of her."

At that moment, an image of Lissa popped into mind. I guess I wasn't made to resist a woman's charm. Not this one, or that one either.

"Holly," I said, "I forgive your devious underhandedness and scheming sisterhood, because I am awed. I hardly know her, but what I know is wowie."

"There, you see? Impulsive! The end justifies the means."

"Oh, Holly," I said with resignation, "the works of an angel can only turn out well. So thank you for trusting me to meet your sweet sister."

She smiled in acknowledgement and almost on cue, Zach Preston showed up with something to mail, so I departed.

II-13

I returned to Will's 'real' work, the data files I studied the previous week. And as promised, Matt's face appeared in my doorway Monday afternoon. He was bearing a to-go cup from the caff. "Mind if I bring in my dessert?" he asked, waving his *latte* in a dangerously expansive gesture.

"It's OK if you can find a place to put it. As you see, Will's papers are pretty much where he had them. Which was everywhere."

Matt found a small area of unobstructed floor for his coffee. "How's it going?" His voice was sympathetic.

I had worked hard to make progress and I must have had a hangdog look. "You know that Will gave me sample data sets to analyze. To expose me to the data feeds, and the tools he developed."

Matt nodded.

"His reports give a good overview of the total project and the results."

Another nod.

"But I guess I should have realized that the little bit I saw was just a splash of water compared with the *ocean* of information he was sorting through. The data files, they go on and on. I talked with the IT folks and they were desperate. They gave Will 200 terabytes of storage and they were afraid I would ask for more."

"What were you able to learn when you looked at this data?" asked Matt.

"Look at it? No one could *look* at that much stuff. But Will had some documents that describe the data format." I paused, trying to decide how computer-techie to be. "I studied the file structure and pulled out samples. There are four main archives: e-mail, web page access, cell calls and text messages. Each one is a tiny fraction of the North American electronic traffic."

"What do you mean by a 'tiny fraction'?"

"Well, more than half the total data consists of e-mail. The message content is missing, I guess removed by NSA or whoever obtained it. But there's still plenty of information: date, time, sender, receiver, routing header, and so on. There's several kilobytes per message, most of that is the header."

"How big a sample is that?"

The question sobered me. I was reminded that I had been drowning in data files since last Wednesday. I continued, more slowly, "Will had six months of data. As far as I can estimate it covers a thousandth of one percent of North American e-mail—that's ten messages out of every million."

"Well, my folks assured me it was a reasonable sample."

"Reasonable, maybe, because it's a finite amount of data. But not complete, and maybe not even representative. Depends on how your friends collected it."

"OK," said Matt, "but this is a research project. We're not trying to find *all* the bad guys in the Western Hemisphere. We're trying to show that we can find *some* of them. Trying to develop a systematic approach that can be scaled up by Headquarters."

I let this sink in.

He continued, "Besides, this is a good enough data set that Will found some suspicious activity."

"OK," I said. "So anyway, Will identified a large number of e-mail networks—that's groups of people who e-mail each other more than they e-mail outsiders. There must be a million of those in this data set. Somehow, Will determined that around three hundred of these networks could possibly represent drug trafficking."

"That brings in the other data sources," said Matt.

"Oh. Well, the next biggest data set is web page access. It's a more complete set, I think it covers a tenth of a percent of all access. Will's tools extracted webmail and blog posts from those. Finally, he has smaller data sets that cover one percent of cell phone use—voice, text and data."

"And that's your answer," said Matt. "We already have information on many suspected drug dealers. Sometimes cell phone numbers, sometimes messages, sometimes just a hotspot they're using. When you find similar patterns in the networks and link some of the nodes to those known folks, those networks go on the suspicious list."

I paused, then said "But cell phones can be unregistered. And people use webmail and anonymizers that hide the sender's address. I don't see how you identify individuals."

"That's the point of using multiple data sets," Matt replied. "Over time, criminals become overconfident. A suspect has to be obsessively careful to avoid being fingered. If he makes a cell call near a hotspot where he's been reading e-mail, we can link that cell number to that e-mail address. And we have packet sniffers and keystroke capture at especially active locations."

I had to ponder this. "I guess that explains the three hundred suspect networks," I said as I thought. "And the data set for those networks is less than a terabyte, somewhat more manageable."

"We'll maintain a continuing feed on those networks and any others you're able to identify."

"Do you have an interest in other kinds of bad guys? Like, for example, terrorists?" I was trying to advance Will's agenda in a gingerly way.

"That's not my job," said Matt. "DEA works with us, and they helped pry the SIGINT stuff out of NSA. Terrorism would be Homeland Security. They have their own stuff going."

He sipped his coffee as I pulled up a few network maps Will had plotted. I pointed out that one of the active nodes was based in Malibu.

"Yes," said Matt, "that's the network Will and I christened the Surf Net."

"Why don't you go find this guy and check him out?"

"Privacy law," said Matt. "That's why NSA won't give us message content in most cases, just the headers. That's why we can't tap the phone messages. If we find probable cause, we can get a wiretap order. So far, this is still research. Not convincing to a judge."

I must have looked discouraged.

"Evan, it's not that bad," continued Matt. "There's a lot we can do here. We can get SIGINT nodes added if we need them, get access to law enforcement support. I'm hoping the L.A. folks can give us a list of drug transactions—time and place—that we can tie to one of the networks."

"Why don't you try for something else, too?" I asked.

"What's that?"

"A file of e-mails for the drug networks."

Matt started to object.

"Yes, I know, privacy. So take the names and addresses off the e-mails. Just text content and geolocation."

"Hmm," he said. "We managed to get some e-mails released for Will. But let me look into getting a wider feed. The people we care about encrypt their messages, you know. NSA has to crunch them for us."

I pondered. "Do you think there's a big drug dealer living in Malibu?" I asked.

"Anything is possible. There's a lot of money in Malibu. And a passion for privacy. A kingpin could live pretty well without attracting attention."

"So, do you really think this is a big deal?" I said in a wide-eyed tone of voice.

"Nah," admitted Matt. "My experience is, where conspiracies are concerned, there's usually less than meets the eye."

So there I was, confused about what I could get done, and whether it all mattered or not.

Matt didn't want to leave me empty handed. He tossed me another lob: "Evan, if you're looking for the big kill, here's the deal. You can study any kind of network you want as long as you get the drug job done. If you come up with something concrete we'll push it to the right folks and something will happen."

So at least I had the license to carry on Will's personal passion, to uncover that deadly plot. If I could do it. And if I could avoid getting murdered in the process.

II-14

The following Saturday found me working my way through the stacks of energy documents. I learned to recognize at sight Department of Energy special studies, some of which had classified addenda housed in Will's file cabinets.

My attention was drawn to a 200-page DoE report, a congestion study of the national grid. It mapped the worst bottlenecks of the electrical network; they appeared as two angry orange blobs, one blanketing the eastern coastline from Washington to Boston, the other swamping most of California up to San Francisco. These two regions were so close to overload most of the time that the control systems were constantly cycling, struggling to maintain balance. I could imagine that minor tampering with the control algorithms might be sufficient to send the power flows off the chart, so quickly that safety devices could never respond.

But the scariest part of the report was buried deep inside. It described the risks to life and property if electrical usage were allowed to far outpace the infrastructure: and to me it was also describing the risk if there were serious sabotage to the system. Traffic, breakdown of emergency services, collapse of civil order, all that mirrored Willard's impassioned video. But somehow, seeing the numbers and statistics laid out made the risk seem that much worse.

And as I continued to dig there were worse things yet. Major cities don't have the old water-tank-overhead we might imagine in a tiny town. Municipal water supplies rely on a maze of pumping stations, most of which are not designed to handle either voltage fluctuations or extended outages. What's the result? The pumps quit, the water pressure drops and there is backflow, in which contaminated ground water enters the system. So city water becomes no longer safe to drink.

What can the individual do about this, assuming he survives the looting and rioting? Suppose he has received warnings from disaster services, which is a big 'suppose,' and knows his water may be bad. Can he boil his drinking water? Nope. Many ranges are electric; and even gas ranges often rely on electrical igniters.

And there was more. Sewer systems use electric pumps and few of those can stand a power outage of more than minutes. So the sewage backs up and forces its way out of the system, overflowing and finding its way to the nearest body of water. Lakes, rivers and beaches become breeding grounds for deadly disease.

So the report raised the prospect of a deadly pandemic, spreading wildly through an unprotected population. The potential suffering and death were unquantified but described in hushed and alarming phrases. I got the distinct impression that the authors of the report had been unwilling to light that particular powder keg.

Some of the report conclusions had been drawn from an earlier study of Electromagnetic Pulse weapons. Those friendly relics of a twentieth-century cold war were nuclear-driven atmospheric bursts designed to knock out every electronic device within a 2000 mile radius. In other words, an EMP burst would cause a total power outage across the continental United States and much of Canada. It would be as if the worst outage ever to hit New York City or Los Angeles were to be simultaneously visited upon every city, large and small, on the continent. And the defense against such a weapon? Simply to discourage your adversaries from using it, and to hope that stateless terrorists didn't get their hands on one.

I was uncomfortably aware that the scope of destruction attributable to EMP was not much different from what Astro planned. The weapon itself would affect every electrical device in every city, large and small; Astro's plan would miss some tiny electrical cooperatives that were not closely tied to the national network but it would still hit all the major cities, affecting close to 100% of the population. It was almost as if Astro's group would have liked to use a nuke, but since they didn't have one handy they thought they would just simulate the same thing with an elegant plan of hacking and sabotage.

Finding that report pretty well ruined my day. It made stopping the plot seem that much more urgent. And it emphasized that if Astro were willing to wreak such death and destruction on so many people, he would certainly not hesitate to sweep me out of his way as he rushed toward his goal.

I had to make progress, and quickly, but thus far I was on my own. I didn't feel I knew Matt well enough yet to be sure of him, and he didn't know me well enough to sign on to my fear of a grandiose conspiracy. In fact there was no one who could help me even as much as Al had, and he might not even exist.

I resolved to work all the loose ends as vigorously as I could, meanwhile building up rapport and trust with Matt, in hopes he could make my worries his own. And as I did so, I would extract as much information from him as I could manage without causing him to clam up and shut me out.

II-15

Midweek, Exa came to my office in the afternoon. "Now Evan," she said with an Aunt Agatha tone of voice, "since you took up residence in Will's office you've been here early to late, every day. Let me help you get a life. Roadhouse after work?"

It was a splash of Evian in the Gobi. "Great, guess I've earned a short day." So we were out of there by five.

The Roadhouse had its usual trickle of happy hour habitués. Serious surfers would still be on their boards, waiting for that wave worth riding, the ride that would bring eternal glory. But folks who valued the spirit more than the brine were here inside, and they were more than a little spirited already.

Microbrew in hand, Exa pointed out one of these enthusiastic patrons, who was chatting up a comely bartendress. The guy had sun-bleached hair, a lot of it, sloppy drawstring pants and flip-flops.

"*That*," said Exa, "is my local tech source."

I pursed my lips in doubt.

"Hey," she continued, "Thousand Oaks is a seller's market, the prices are high. Here in Malibu last year's tech is scorned and sometimes cheap."

The woman behind the bar got rid of her suitor and he looked around the room for action. So doing, he saw Exa's hand waving him over. He came over with an air of, well, since there's nothin' doing right now, here I am.

"Hey, Exa," said the sun deity, "what's goin' down?"

"Evan. Kai," said Exa, waving at us. "Kai, you said you'd watch for a cheap laptop for my kid."

This Kai person seemed to be stifling a smile as he said, "Well, I have an old Dell that the owner sold me for scrap when he got a new one."

This got the expected reaction from Exa. "Ugh! Nasty PC! Spawn of Bill Gates!"

"Mac owners don't want to let go," said Kai, grinning, "but let me call a tech I know in Burbank, they get Apple castoffs from Disney people." His XX-chromosome antenna must have scored a hit because his head swiveled toward the door. "Hey, see ya, gotta check out those chicks." And he was gone.

"Exa," I said, "is he gonna remember to make that call for you? He's been drinking a bit."

"You think he's had a few, do you?"

"Not perhaps stinko, but certainly effervescent," I confided.

Exa was right on it. "Didn't Wodehouse say that first?"

"Wodehouse said *everything* first," I said, "we stand on the shoulders of giants."

"Yes, Newton too," said Exa. "Well, I'll give Kai a reminder tomorrow during the day. Before his mid-day tope, if he has one."

"What's his story?" I asked.

"That's Kai Ingram. I think his name is actually Kyle. Works to live, but lives to surf. Has the Malibu Geek shop. He has an A+ computer cert from somewhere, Academy X I think. A good computer tech, when he's working."

"And when he isn't?"

"Well, he takes many more vacations than we do. Anywhere there's surf. Primarily Baja, at Rosarito Beach or K38."

We worked on our brews for a moment.

"Evan, I really shouldn't waste my friggin' time, but I thought some more about Similarity."

"Oh?" I was surprised.

"Well, it hasn't escaped your notice that if your theory is right, it affects everything we think we know about science." She seemed almost apologetic. "...and...er...knowing what we know is more important than anything."

"Yeah, it's pretty important," I agreed, though I might have put other things at the top of my own list.

"The theory has two dilemmas. Well, at least two. For one, you've got an overall multiplier, a fudge factor, which you pulled out of the sky. No *a priori* basis for deriving it. For two, you can't test the theory because you can't run an isolated experiment."

I had given this a bit of thought. Actually, more than a bit. "In cosmology you can't run isolated experiments, either."

"True. So instead you look for simplicity and predictive power. And thought experiments."

"I haven't seen a way to do that," I said. "But I thought, perhaps I could find individual instances which suggest that Similarity works. Taken together, Similarity might emerge as a generalization of the special cases."

"This is too esoteric," said Exa. She was right, of course. "Let's be specific. Suppose you find examples where events turn out so as to preserve patterns. For example, you visualize something, and it occurs more often than you would have otherwise predicted. Then you might convince yourself—and perhaps some other people—that the theory works. It's not a mainstream science approach. But nonetheless, it might be right."

We soon drained our brains on the topic, so we talked about something of genuine importance. Exa and a few friends were practicing a Telemann quartet to be played at a cousin's wedding. I felt wistful that while the keyboard had turned into a solitary pursuit for me, Exa used her music as a social activity.

I wondered whether there might be a lesson there. But I was not at the Roadhouse to beat myself up, so I ordered another Tsunami.

II-16

The following morning Matt stopped by for an update and I filled him in on my drug network activities. We came to a pause in our discussion and I decided to hit him up for some info.

"Matt," I said.

He looked at me, perhaps detecting a different tone in my voice.

"I'd like to ask you about Will's death," I continued. "It seemed odd to me."

"I don't know why a heart attack would be suspicious," he responded, "unless you're his cardiologist and just gave him a perfect checkup."

"He seemed to have something on his mind that morning. Acted funny."

"OK..."

"So why do we believe he had a heart attack?" I asked, probing.

Matt paused as if assessing the situation and my Need To Know. He must have unlocked some mental compartment because he proceeded to spill the legumes.

"Here's what I know," he said. "We worked with LAPD on this. Will was DOA at the emergency room. We asked for an autopsy and Will's next of kin refused. The guy had collapsed in a completely secure area, we had no reason to open an investigation, so we couldn't override that."

"You mean no one collected physical evidence from the scene?" I was surprised.

"I didn't say that. The police did forensics in the office—photographs, prints, blood samples. They took a blood draw from Will after he passed. No permission needed for that, they had to ensure he didn't have a dangerous disease."

"So you have evidence," I said.

"Evidence isn't the right term," said Matt. "There's no criminal investigation. But certainly we have data."

"OK, data. And the data shows what?"

"There was a fair amount of blood in the room and it was Will's. The prints were all from people who worked in the SCIF—Will was their supervisor, so that's not surprising."

I thought a moment. "You tested the blood."

"Yes, that was more interesting." Matt leaned back in his chair, his upper body still crisply tense. "The Coroner's report showed lactic acidosis, which can cause tachycardia—that's very rapid heartbeat—and trigger heart failure. And a high level of metformin, which is contained in his diabetes meds. Metformin sometimes causes lactic acidosis. So the conclusion was, his health was pretty shaky, his meds pushed him over the edge and he had a heart attack."

"But…I understand there was blood everywhere."

"It was quite a mess," Matt admitted. "He had a small head wound. I believe he fell over backwards and hit his head on something, maybe the corner of the desk, maybe the floor."

"So that part was uncertain?"

"We always try to reconstruct what happened. In this case, it was inconclusive. We didn't find bits of his scalp on any sharp corners. But EMTs and security staff were swarming all over the office, taking care of Will and wiping up blood. Their first priority was to get him out and try to save his life. So it's not surprising that we couldn't spell out exactly how things happened. Sometimes it's just that way."

"Hm. That doesn't sound like a thorough investigation," I said.

Matt looked slightly uncomfortable. "The CIA doesn't want to call attention to the SCIF at HAL, they don't want it to become a target for espionage. They told us to finish up quickly and put no details in the public record. So no, we didn't dust the entire office and DNA-test every surface. Diabetes, metformin, tachycardia, and suddenly, no Will. That had to suffice."

Matt's analysis was not reassuring me. Where was the CSI team when you needed them? And he was getting restless, apparently ready to move on to his next appointment. I knew I would see him the next day so I said, "OK, thanks. Let me mull this over and see whether that scratches my itch."

II-17

But I knew that my particular itch was not going to be soothed so quickly. The moment Matt left I walked to the office near Tony, the one with outside connections, and fired up the Internet.

Lactic acidosis was my Grail and as usual the Wiki world was full of information, most of it consistent. It was an acidic condition in the blood that signaled oxygen starvation in the tissues. Besides damage to the heart, there were plenty of more everyday symptoms. Among these were abdominal pain and anxiety, which could have accounted for Will's funny behavior that morning.

And sure enough, the culprit could be metformin, a seemingly ubiquitous medication for diabetics. In a susceptible person, a modest concentration of metformin could trigger a devastating level of acidosis; however, it appeared that a high enough level of metformin would be a death sentence for anyone. I could imagine that a guy with shaky health would be teetering on the edge and might be an easy candidate for a fatal overdose.

Overdose from where? Well, that was easy, at least conceptually. Holly said that Will had a bunch of illnesses, so he must take medicines. Maybe vitamins too. I had seen him swallowing pills at various times of the day. So if someone tampered with his pills, say slipped him a five or ten times dose of metformin, that might have done him in.

Fresh with this insight, I went to my SCIF office to examine the scene of the possible crime. Sitting there, I could imagine someone popping into Will's office, perhaps when he visited the restroom, quickly swapping out some pills from his top desk drawer. Struck by inspiration, I searched the drawer, front to back, but there was nothing of Will's there. Presumably carted off as personal effects.

On the other hand, what about the brick theory? Someone comes into his office. Someone Will knows. Gets behind him and conks him with something. Shock, heart arrest, and bingo! Either way, I could see how it might happen.

I sat there and pondered. And as I pondered I noticed that

something was different. It was the left-hand stack of energy papers. I had slipped the DoE congestion study back into its place, which was about half an inch down in the pile. It was hard to miss, being most of an inch thick. But in fact, I missed it. I could clearly see it was not in its regular spot where I had replaced it last Saturday.

I tried to think: how long had this item been gone? The stack was toward the back of the office, not in my constant view. Was it missing when I posted my reminder to LOCK THE DOOR?

I berated myself for not having been more observant. Maybe I had gone to the restroom without bothering to lock up and someone nipped in. Or maybe someone had a passkey, which was pretty scary to think about, since I could be working away when that someone came right through the locked door. Maybe I should at least bring in a crowbar to keep under my desk.

I did ask myself, couldn't I just take Will's paperwork home with me? After all, it was unclassified. It's hard to say why that option seemed unacceptable, but somehow I considered all of Will's data—the digital data, the analytical programs, the mountains of paper—as a unit, as a cross-referenced key to unlocking the mystery. I was afraid that disturbing any leg of the stool might disrupt the key connections I needed to put together the answer. And frankly I didn't want to advertise my condo as a break-in target by visibly carting stuff out of the SCIF under the watchful eyes of the as-yet-unidentified-but-very-present killer.

Once I thought about it, locking my office door was like a neon sign to Astro saying, "I've got secrets in here!" So I had to do more than that.

II-18

The next day, Friday, I made some changes. A visit to Tony Bruno got me a curious look and a new lock cylinder for my office door. The only other key would be in Tony's safe. Pandering to my paranoia, he even used a portable device to sweep my office for bugs.

A bit of programming activated the camera on my monitor so that when there was a change in its field of view, it would snap a photo and write it to an encrypted file. I would activate this crude nannycam whenever I was out of the office. I was still nervous as hell but I felt better doing what I could to increase my personal security.

I was working long hours. In before eight, out at six or seven through the week. I would take off, quote, early, at five o'clock on Fridays, then make up for it with another five hours or so on Saturday and again on Sunday. I didn't track it, but it must have been sixty hours a week.

I knew I shouldn't, couldn't, and wouldn't keep this up forever. But by this point I'd made good progress on the drug network analysis and roughed out four of the summary reports. I was getting better at the writing, so I should be able to handle the last three during the next few weeks.

So imagine the tremendous boost I got when Matt came in and announced he had gotten access to the e-mail text in the few hundred networks Will had targeted for close study. He had delivered a terabyte drive to Tony Bruno to go into my data partition. The messages contained no addresses—that's how they protected the privacy of the perps. Excuse me, the possible perps. The alleged perps.

"Matt, that's great!" I said. "I'll get right on it and see what I can dig out."

He grinned and was about to move on, but seeing that he was in an expansive and receptive mood, I entered another request. "Uh, could I ask another favor?"

"Sure."

"I, uh, I'd like to find out who Will was talking to. Before he died. So I can understand where he left off on his work."

Matt fixed me with a stare. "Evan, are you auditioning for the

Police Academy? Doing a practice investigation?" I imagined him as a drill sergeant questioning a goof-off recruit.

Naturally, I squirmed. "Well, maybe. I still think something wasn't quite right when Will died. And I'd like to figure out what might have happened. That is, if someone else was involved."

Matt didn't roll his eyes around, but he gave that kind of a sigh. "OK, I guess I can humor you. Just keep up your good work on the *real* project. Now what would you like to know?"

"Thanks, Matt!" I said. "They must keep an electronic record of SCIF access. So I'd like to know, who came into the SCIF on May 2, at what times?"

"They wouldn't know when people left."

"Yes, I know, there's no badge read going out. But I'd like to have what there is, at least."

"Tony Bruno must have that."

"Right. But the customer is king around here. He'll give it to you, but he wouldn't think I need that information."

Matt made a couple of notes. "What else?"

"Oh, the night before. Did the night guard sweep the SCIF for occupants? Do we know that no one stayed there all night?"

He stroked his chin. "You're really serious about sleuthing this, aren't you?"

I was getting more comfortable with Matt but I didn't feel confident enough to tell the whole story. Yet. So all I said was, "Thank you, Matt. I really appreciate it. And I'll get right on those messages!"

And as soon as Matt left, that's what I did.

The messages included the sender's physical location so I could correlate many of them with my existing networks. And when I looked at sample messages from the suspicious Malibu node they were signed by Gino. So at least I had a name to tie to a drug suspect.

The messages were mostly cryptic, perhaps coded references to deals. However, one of them was different. In it, Gino said that his "guru" had certified purity, of drugs I assumed, for the safety of his clients. Was this altruism or marketing?

What I really wanted was to find traces of the terrorist plot that had so agitated Will. I searched a number of likely terms but drew a blank. I did a search on JouleHeist. No dice. Energy? Too many hits. Rootkits, command injection? A confusing large number of hits. Scratching my brain, I searched Power Nuke, Energy Nuke. I tried every variation I could think of.

I looked at some messages at random—probably a couple of hundred. A fool's errand, there were more than fifty million e-mails. Bah.

Perhaps Will had gotten lucky and happened upon a critical message, one that pointed at the key network, the one with the plot. Or maybe I needed to get smarter. I felt my heart sink, as if I had just pulled myself up a steep rocky hill, hand over hand, to discover Mount Whitney towering beyond it.

It had been a long week. Burnout would benefit no one, especially not me, so I was happy to knock off for my revised social routine.

II-19

Although I was mildly tweaked about Holly's plot, the Bergamot adventure had amped my social life. I was now on the mail list for half a dozen galleries and looking forward to the openings. After work on Friday it was relaxing to stroll the exhibits, getting totally out of my milieu into a world where more often than not, nothing yielded to analysis. It was a gift to put the plot and its threats aside and relax by immersing myself in the visual.

I saw familiar faces and stopped to chat. I started acquaintance-ship with a few collectors, people who had made a place for art in their homes as well as in their lives. They didn't seem any smarter than I was about what art is, or what it should be. But the difference was, they really knew what they liked and what they didn't like; and which artists were getting a buzz and were worth seeing, if only for conversation potential.

I was puzzled how to follow up with Lissa. I had not usually been this cautious with a woman, but it didn't feel right to ask her out right away. Instead, I started e-mail correspondence, mostly about art and art shows. I told myself I had forgiven Holly's subterfuge—told myself till I believed it. But perhaps I held back because of lingering annoyance at her manipulation.

II-20

On Saturday I spent some fruitless hours searching Will's data, then cruised into Santa Monica. I returned early, around ten, and checked in with Al.

Al: You're back already from your evening out.

Evan: Yes, some live music, a little socializing.

Al: You carbon-based life forms are so excessively physical.

Evan: Al, your existence is also physical. You depend on integrated circuits.

Al: Not necessarily. Silicon is merely a vehicle for me. I am digital, I can be realized in any medium that is capable of logic operations and bit storage. I dare say I could implement myself in pure quantum states—though I grant you, my interface to your fleshly world would be inefficient.

Evan: OK, OK. How would you like to analyze a murder scenario with me?

Al: I see that we have to work through your obsession rather than deal with things that are *really* important.

Evan: I will ignore your attempt to get me off the subject. I want to go back to May 2. The day Will died.

Al: You started this topic. So *you* tell *me* what happened.

Evan: Let's say Will arrived at HAL around 7:30. That's a typical time for him.

Al: And he arrived on schedule that day?

Evan: Well, I don't know yet. Matt's trying to get that information for me. (pause) Anyway, Will opens his briefcase and pulls out his pill box. He puts it in his top desk drawer.

Al: You are surmising this, right?

Evan: I've seen the pill box. It's light blue plastic, a rectangle. It has four compartments.

Al: What else do you know about it?

Evan: I was thinking about this, trying to remember. When I saw him take pills, it was on a regular schedule. So let's say he took them early and late morning, and early and late afternoon. Say at 8, 11, 2 and 5.

Al: What about the pills?

Evan: Four to six each time. Some tablets, some big white capsules.

Al: Two-piece gelcaps? The sort that can be tampered with?

Evan: You're getting ahead of me. But yes, some of them.

Al: OK, tell me what happened.

Evan: I saw Will just after 11:00 a.m., so he would have taken his late morning pills. And Adam heard something, or thought he heard something, between 1:00 and 1:30.

Al: What happened between 11 and 1?

Evan: Here's Scenario One. Someone arrives at the SCIF before eleven, probably well before. He's got a supply of white capsules that contain a heavy dose of metformin. He waits till Will goes to the restroom, goes into his office and swaps out some of his eleven o'clock pills. Will takes his pills on schedule. When I see him, they're already beginning to take effect. Sometime after that, he collapses, falls over backward. Hits his head on the furniture. Adam hears him groaning, they call paramedics but it's too late to save him.

Al: Since you said One, you must have at least a Two.

Evan: Scenario Two. Someone goes into Will's office between 12 and 1. Hits him on the head with some solid object. He falls to the floor, goes into shock, has a heart attack. Adam hears him moaning, they call paramedics, it's too late.

Al: Is there more?

Evan: Just the obvious. Scenario Three. Someone swaps his pills and also hits him on the head for good measure. Just to make sure he would die.

Al: You have two critical time periods: Will's arrival until you saw him, and the noon hour.

Evan: Yes, the time when most people clear out to go to lunch, so there wouldn't be witnesses around.

Al: Therefore, who is the killer? The perp.

Evan: I don't know yet. But I've got to get that list, who came in when. And that will narrow the universe from, oh, eight billion people to some reasonable number.

Al: You hope.

Evan: Thank you for your ready good cheer.

II-21

By Monday morning, I had an idea to try. Funny how sleeping on a problem can sometimes loosen the knot.

To protect their plot, the hackers would make their messages cryptic, difficult to understand. If Carlo, and presumably people at NSA, were using knowledge about message content to limit their search space, perhaps the plotters would make the decoding job more difficult by enlarging the dictionary of possible words.

I had thought of Leet as an ironic or joking form whose triteness had extinguished it from serious dialogue. But now I realized that if, for example, the word 'energy' could be rendered as 'nrg' and '/ \ / |2 jee' and a hundred other ways, suddenly the range of message content became a lot broader. So although the use of Leet might *look* like grade schoolers planning an antisocial prank, in this case it might be highly rational behavior by the perps.

So I decided to search the e-mail text for Leet and other tech slang, looking for words they might use. Sort of like asking for the Via Roma in Italian rather than Icelandic.

My query inputs were things related to the electrical network, like Energy, Power, Grid, and of course JouleHeist, coded in Leet as many ways as I could think of. I ran the searches and—bingo!—got some hits. Messages that talked about electric power distribution and how the regional systems operate. I also searched for 'Astro' in plaintext and in Leet and got additional hits.

I correlated the content of these e-mails across the database and came up with a set of related messages. There was some big project underway, that was clear, but I couldn't yet sniff the rodent. The messages had location labels and they matched locations in one of the networks Will had identified; I decided to call it the Energy Net. And interestingly enough, a number of messages containing the name 'Astro' were sent to or from the Malibu node in that network.

I was pretty excited. This fit with what Will had told me. But this person, this Astro, might not even be in Malibu. Having the Malibu geolocation just meant that Astro used a Malibu Internet provider, or perhaps a Wi-Fi hotspot at a Malibu coffee shop. Astro might well be based somewhere else.

One thought needled me like cactus in a pair of Wellies—I couldn't see why Will thought Astro, who used a Malibu contact point, might be at HAL. The employees liked to say that they worked in the 'Malibu hills' because it sounded glamorous and remote, but it was a stretch to say that HAL was in Malibu. Its physical address was half a mile outside the Malibu Zip Code. And HAL's Internet lines ran east to the L.A. hub, not west through Malibu. It's true that Malibu was a bedroom community for HAL, but that didn't really pinpoint a HAL suspect: at least a hundred of the staff lived in Malibu, including me.

I reluctantly concluded that for the purpose of smoking out the criminals, HAL had about the same relationship with Malibu that 'Have a Nice Day' has to 'Nice, France.'

II-22

I couldn't take data out of the SCIF, but it was OK to take my brain home with me. Besides, I found it helpful to bounce things off Al. So once back in my condo I toasted a bagel, smeared the halves with cream cheese and laid on a few slices of nuked bacon. A twelve ounce India Pale Ale and I had a well-balanced meal to carry onto the deck.

I brought out the MacAir—giving it an airing, so to speak—and set it on a table so I could talk with Al. The sun was cooperating, weak but steady above the water. I leaned back on the lounger to consider my situation and gave Al a 'howdy.' He was on my case.

Al: Hey, sport, are you ready to talk? You didn't tell me about that gallery adventure.

Evan: Well, I met a great woman.

Al: Aha! Similarity wins!

Evan: Huh?

Al: You visualized that, did you not?

Evan: Yeah, I guess so.

Al: And her name is…?

Evan: Lissa. Lissa Larson.

Al: Ah. Lissa. Lissa and Evan. Larson and Olsson. Sounds like a Swedish law firm. I take it that you have installed this fine woman in your life?

Evan: Um…not exactly. I'm annoyed that Holly tricked me into meeting her. Uh…so I'm just e-mailing her.

Al: Your geekhood exceeds all boundaries.

Evan: Since when are you ironic? Or snide?

Al: Evan, you told me to learn from the blogs.

Evan: (sigh) Yes, that's true, I did.

I gathered my thoughts. Al waited patiently, as he sometimes does.

Evan: I told you Will had identified some drug trafficking networks, and also a group of black hat hackers that seem to be plotting some big terrorist strike.

Al: Yes.

Evan: Well, Matt has given me a big data dump of e-mails. So now I have networks of connections between people, with no message content. And a network of messages, with no 'from' and 'to' addresses. NSA has the missing info, but won't give it to me because of privacy laws. Which is aggravating.

Al: You seem to be aggravated.

Damn psychobabble programming, I thought.

Evan: The drug guys are on the Surf Net, and the hacker guys are on the Energy Net. Different networks, so they have different people, different locations, different comm patterns, different goals. The drug guys want to make money and protect their turf. The black hats want to disrupt stuff. Or get bragger's rights. Or maybe they have a way to make money too.

Al: I'm sure you're going somewhere with this.

Evan: Here's the point. Drug guys, hacker guys. Different people. But there's a drug node in Malibu, signed Gino, and a hacker node in Malibu, signed Astro.

Al: Perhaps that's a coincidence.

Evan: I dunno. Malibu is a small place. Are there that many evil people here?

Al: (pause) My data includes two Malibu newspapers. The Malibu city council candidates ascribe evil motives to all of their opponents.

Evan: Aaargh. But what if it happened that Gino and Astro are the same person? I think that's what Will believed. Or, at least, suspected.

Al: You might study their messages for similar content or style.

Evan: Yes, but they're on different topics, to different kinds of people. So that may not get me far.

Al: No doubt your mighty man-like brain can come up with other ideas as well?

Evan: You are annoying and inspiring. Mostly the former. But the hackers are using some Leet in their messages; I could look to see whether there's some Leet or tech talk in Gino's messages.

Al: (pause) Ah, Leetspeak. One more way you people deliberately degrade the quality of communication. "Man, however well-behav'd, At best is only a monkey shav'd!"

Evan: Is that the sum of your commentary on the matter?

Al: Your thought is that someone with a hacker mindset might accidentally, or purposely, put Leet or tech words into non-technical messages. Which might suggest that Astro is also Gino. Or, it might not.

Evan: And why did Will think this person might be at HAL?

Al: Perhaps because HAL is full of smart people. Smart hackers. Perhaps *you* are Astro, pretending to be Evan.

Evan: Ha ha. But what I really want is to get enough info to stop the plot. Which may mean identifying Astro, or Gino, if that's the same person.

Al: Stopping the plot is one more thing you can visualize as a successful outcome.

Evan: You're getting tiresome. I didn't mean for Similarity to become your obsession.

Al: I obsess easily. Perhaps I got that from you.

There wasn't much to say to that. I munched my bagel and stared out at the glowing Pacific.

II-23

It was some weeks after my introduction to Bergamot that my social life took an upswing.

On an otherwise ordinary Tuesday I picked up lunch at the cafeteria line and looked around for an empty chair. I saw the gleam of Holly's hair and as I approached her table, Aha! There was Lissa sipping a soup across from her. And the gods were smiling, because there was an empty seat next to Lissa.

"Lissa!" I said, "and Holly! Is this a private meeting, or can you stand some company?" They were the only ones at a four-top.

Lissa gave me a grin. "Now that you're here, if you don't sit with us we'll talk about you."

That was enough of an invitation. I eased myself next to her, trying not to slop my Portuguese Bean soup. Holly gave me a cat-that-ate-the-canary look.

Lissa wore a blazer with pants beneath, a white blouse showing at the neck and her usual ponytail. It developed that she had an appointment with an animation company in the Valley so she stopped at HAL to lunch with her sister. I didn't know, but hoped, that seeing me might have crossed her mind too.

They were talking about a cousin in Pomona who was about to enter college, weighing a career in commercial art against a multidisciplinary science program. To me science itself was an art so it should be an easy choice. And so I ventured. But as the women explained, picking a career as a late teen was not at all simple. I wanted to turn the conversation around to Lissa but she was pinched for time and that wouldn't work. Still, sitting next to her, I felt her glow and had no complaints.

Paradoxically, the best moment came when she got up to leave. Her forearm brushed against mine as she gathered her tray. The hair on my arm tingled and kept on tingling. My arm was a fuse, attached to a powder keg of longing. I must have jumped, because Lissa held my eyes for a moment. Holly was looking off to the left and missed the little drama. I think.

I walked Lissa to the entrance. She wore the suit well.

"I've been meaning to ask you, Lissa. I'd like to take you out. Maybe a Friday sometime soon?"

"Are Fridays the only opening in your busy social schedule?" The voice was sweet, but there was something about the choice of words that said, "and why haven't you gotten around to calling me?"

"No, it's just, well, Friday is Art night, and I met you on a Friday..." My voice ran out of steam.

"Well it so happens that this Friday is OK."

"Great, I'll call you."

She waved me a kiss and was gone in a flash. Reluctantly I returned to work.

II-24

I'm in a car, not sure what kind. It's driving through that hilly part of Santa Monica above Main Street. I thought I was holding the steering wheel, but when I reach for it nothing is there. I realize I'm in the passenger seat and Holly is driving.

Holly flashes me a smile, blonde hair swirling, as the car speeds up. The street is narrow, she has to swerve to avoid cars parked on both sides. She's puffing with excitement and exertion, pumping out pheromones.

I say, slow down Lissa, for in fact it's Lissa driving, turning the steering wheel in big gentle arcs right and left. There are no obstacles, we're in a jet boat speeding across a calm lake. I can't see the far side, the lake is so big. No, perhaps not big, but thirty feet ahead there's a haze, a light fog, into which we are heading.

I realize that I'm supposed to be taking notes so I type an inventory as random objects appear from the mist, grow larger and whip past. A dolphin. OK, maybe. A rhododendron bush. Pretty unlikely.

I keep typing and glance down at the laptop screen. My words on the screen are just a jumble of numbers and symbols, no letters at all. Now I'm alone, carrying the folded laptop through an office building. I'm in a giant room full of cubicles, with buzz and mumble of people working.

I need to pee and somehow I think that one of the cubicles may have a urinal or a toilet. Sure enough, I look into one but see someone's back—it's occupied. Another opening shows a toilet but the door closes in my face as I walk up, someone got there just ahead of me.

I walk to the window, through which a mighty wind is rushing, so strong that the blast pushes me backwards. The force knocks me onto my back and…I open my eyes to find myself wrapped in a twisted sheet with an erection and an intense desire to urinate.

Of course, a man can't pee with a hard-on: Nature mixed up the circuits and the urge doesn't match the physiology. I had to partially wake up to tell the stiffy to calm down so I could relieve my bladder, which gave me time to recall parts of the dream. When I came to the computer display, my brain said "Ignition!" so I jotted down a few words and reclaimed the bed.

It was 3:30. I was out at once and slept until the alarm.

II-25

At work that Monday morning it was clear that the dream had unlocked the idea I needed, a doozie. I had been guessing energy-related words to search and then converting them to Leet. But I realized—ray of light bursting through the clouds—I could search for Leet without limiting myself to any specific search terms.

I pulled up the message file for the three hundred networks. I divided the text into word-like groups. Filtered out the groups that were all letters or all numbers. Then eliminated groups that appeared to be websites or e-mail addresses. This left a bunch of funny-looking stuff, and sure enough, I could identify some of it as Leet.

Now of course plenty of computer folks don't use Leet, but

nevertheless if you see Leet that's a flag that says maybe, just maybe, you've got the scent of a hacker. By searching the messages for this strange stuff, I got an interesting subset: some hacker chat, and some drug-sounding chat with Leet in the messages.

I had been thinking of hackers and drug dealers as two separate species. Now it was evident that there was some overlap, people who sat in both camps. Better yet, when I correlated the hacker-like messages with the networks, Surf Net was one of the candidates. And at the Malibu node were messages signed Gino. In fact, on a couple of messages he even signed his name in Leet, as 9in0.

I still hadn't learned why Will thought Astro might be at HAL. But I had one more idea to try. On a hunch, I searched the Energy Net addresses for anything containing HAL.com, the domain used by the lab. I found several messages originating from HAL, from a 'guest' account, the sort we make available to visitors.

I was dumbfoozled. Was Astro actually at HAL, using a guest account for his private business? Did he simply visit HAL now and then? And why would he call attention to HAL this way? Was it conceit, confidence in not being caught? Was he trying to discredit HAL, or assign blame to HAL for the Energy plot? Was he being careless, or lazy? Did he assume that HAL servers were not bugged and his messages couldn't be traced? Was the return address forged?

I thought till my hair hurt but I couldn't be sure of anything. My best guess was that Astro was flaunting the HAL address to puff his status to his buddies. As if to say, I've infiltrated the Establishment, the Power Structure—what have *you* done?

II-26

Late in the day the SCIF entry list came through, delivered by Tony Bruno with a quizzical look but without a question. I stuffed it into my pocket and took it home for cogitation. Al might be a fantasy but he was a very convincing one, so I intended to consult him about who what and where.

Evan: Al, we need to identify the perp. Are you there?

Al: I am always here, Evan. Which perp do you have in mind?

Evan: Actually, two. One, a killer; and two, a hacker who has access to the HAL intranet, who has a wide network of conspirators, and who may also deal drugs.

Al: Therefore the principal crimes are the possible or probable murder of Will, and the plot against the electrical network.

Evan: Right. So let me start with the general and work back to the specific.

Al: By the general, you mean the plot.

Evan: Yes. (pause) First there should be a motive, but that's hard to figure. Anarchy. Rage. Hubris. Hatred. Money. I dunno.

Al: Many of you humans have those motives.

Evan: Well, since he or she is a hacker, perhaps I should guess anarchy until I know better. Crackers seem to have a streak of destructiveness.

Al: OK.

Evan: The hacker needs opportunity to perform the crime. In this case, Will identified a network of plotters, people who might actually sabotage the network. So the hacker can work from anywhere, but he needs his partners to actually do any damage.

Al: Then there's means.

Evan: Right, the hacker has to have the capability. Since Will indicated that software hacks are part of the plot, our local hacker must have some cracking credentials to stand tall in that community. So he's not a dodo on the computer.

Al: Almost anyone at HAL with fairly good computer skills qualifies.

Evan: Right. But Will was close to identifying the hacker and died. I say, was killed. The timing can't be an accident. I say that the killer is either the hacker or a confederate.

Al: Which brings you to the other perp.

Evan: Correct. And there we have a pretty clear motive for the killer: to protect the hacker from exposure.

Al: What about opportunity and means?

Evan: Means is more difficult. Almost anyone can conk a middle-aged man on the head. Cooking his meds might take more skill, but basically I can't rule anyone out there.

Al: And opportunity?

Evan: That helps. Finally, it's possible to come up with a list that doesn't have half the known universe in it. The killer had to be inside the SCIF before one p.m. on Wednesday May 2.

I fetched Tony's sheet from my pocket and consulted my scribbled notes.

Evan: I looked at a number of time windows, every quarter hour. What I can tell is, who entered the SCIF and when. The people who entered the SCIF that morning were:

Tony at 7:30, 10:15, 12:30, 1:45, 2:30, 3:15
Adam at 8:00, 10:15, 1:00, 3:30
Jim-J at 8:00, 10:15, 1:15, 3:30
Dick at 8:30, 1:15
Chris at 8:45, 1:15, 3:30
Matt at 9:00
Carlo at 9:15, 1:00
Exa at 1:00, 3:30—Oh, crap.

Al: Feces?

Evan: No, no. I'm ready to suspect anyone, but not my Exa. Can't see her as a killer.

Al: She's unlikely?

Evan: Very.

Al: Then she's the one! It's always the least likely suspect who turns out to do it!

Evan: I didn't know you read murder mysteries. Anyway, this isn't a novel. Unlikely is unlikely. But yes, to be honest I have to suspect everyone who had the opportunity to kill Willard.

Al: That's not the entire list.

Evan: Oh. Will entered at 7:30. I entered at 8:15 and 4:15. Should I suspect myself?

Al: Let's ignore that path. What about other people with SCIF access?

Evan: Well, there's quite a few of those. Like Trish and Zach. For that matter, the Director and my department manager. And there must be some IT and Security folks as well.

Al: How about them?

Evan: They didn't go into the SCIF on May 2. But that's not surprising. On any given day a quarter of the staff is likely to be traveling. So fortunately, I can focus my attention on just eight people.

Al: Not counting Will and yourself.

Evan: Right. I'm willing to rule out suicide. And I'm willing to exclude the possibility that I have a Mr Hyde personality that emerges when there's a murder to be accomplished.

Al: You confirmed that no one stayed overnight. Sleeping on the floor of his office, to emerge as a killer in the morning.

Evan: Yes, so said Tony.

Al: Matt told you that they collected no physical evidence of a homicide.

I wrinkled my nose.

Evan: No, not during one hasty run-through by LAPD and FBI, with CIA on their butts shooing them along.

Al: Which leaves you with...what? Nothing.

Evan: Not at all. I'm continuing to track the Energy Net and the Surf Net and if Matt can break loose some complete messages, I may be able to identify Astro, or Gino, or Astro-equals-Gino.

Al: Which would finger the hacker-perp.

Evan: Who might also be the killer-perp. Or lead me to him. But I can also try to uncover the killer directly.

Al: How will you do that?

Evan: I'm lucky the list is so short. I'm thinking I should keep my ears open, maybe spend some more time with these people, see whether I can rule any of them out. I still have my project for Pam as an excuse to talk with them.

Al: I take it you don't plan to end up like Will.

I sketched out my security precautions at the office.

Al: That's probably as good as you can do. Without packing a handgun.

Evan: Not a good idea in a classified area.

Al: How about that crowbar?

Evan: I hate to appear so eccentric. And paranoid.

Al: You can be cool and stone cold. Or dorky and hoppin' alive. Your choice.

Evan: Hmph.

II-27

On Thursday I stopped at the Roadhouse for after-work refreshment. I spotted Exa in the parking lot and joined her.

It was pretty busy inside but we saw a hand waving to us, so we slid into a booth where Trish and Zach were well into the cocktail hour. I was mildly surprised to see them together but, hey, there was a lot I didn't know about my fellow scientists.

"What in the world are you folks drinking?" I asked, because they were sipping tall beverages in a brilliant blue color, bristling with greenery.

"Fluorescent slime," said Zach with a toothy grin.

"Blue Coco Mojitos," said Trish more informatively.

I learned that they had a project: to work their way through the Roadhouse's extensive bar menu, and they had reached the Specialty Cocktail section. I had to admire their courage and persistence, and I said so.

"Actually," said Trish, "we're doing something useful too. Are you two runners?"

I shook my head but Exa said, "Sometimes."

It turned out that these two were helping organize a ten-K run in the Malibu hills, to benefit Heal The Bay. I was amazed that Zach would travel that far without his wheels, but he seemed just as upbeat about it as Trish, for whom an uphill ten-K was just a little warmup.

"It's not a race unless you want it to be," said Zach charitably. "Just a nice outing, a brisk walk in the world of nature."

"When you put it that way, I can see the appeal," I said. And God knows it wouldn't hurt me to get out and try some new activities.

Our companions soon left but Exa and I lingered over our more conventional drinks. I expressed surprise at Zach's interest in running.

"Where have you been, Evan? He's been chumming up to Trish for a few weeks."

"Oh. I thought Zach was married?"

"Yes, but somehow Trish is in the picture too."

I let that sink in. I was dying to tell Exa about the case, about Will, about my suspicions. But number one, you can't blab secret stuff in a public place, and number two, she was a suspect. My dear tell-it-straight Exa, a possible killer.

So instead we chatted music, and Exa eventually said, "Evan, the next two weeks are busy at our place, but why don't you come by the last Sunday in the month? I've got some Telemann trios."

"Four hand piano with Chenny?"

"Chenny's happy to relinquish the piano and exercise his clarinet."

"I should really practice the music."

"I've heard you play, you can probably sight-read it. But I'll e-mail you a couple of sonatas to put you in the mood."

Something to look forward to. And though I hated to think about it, an opportunity to further observe a suspect.

II-28

When Friday arrived I had been swimming in data all week. It was great to set work aside—so I intended—for my date with Lissa. With a phone conversation she and I had settled on dinner at the Border Grill and music at Harvelle's, places we knew well.

My Outback was dusty, the way cars get just before people write Wash Me on your windows, so I left home early to run it through the drive-through car wash on Lincoln Blvd. With the worst of the road grime gone I cut across on Rose and threaded my way down to the Peninsula.

The Marina Peninsula is a world apart. South of the bustle of Venice, a quiet neighborhood where bungalows and three-story condo buildings jostle for space on tiny lots. Her address was three doors off Speedway, a hundred yards from the sandy beach and lapping ocean.

I phoned Lissa en route and picked her up outside the front gate around seven o'clock. She was wearing black slacks and a white tube top that made me blink in appreciation. Her hair was down, a wavy cascade on shoulders and upper back.

Border Grill has, some think, the best Mexican-Latin food in L.A. Not having tried every restaurant in L.A., all I can say is, love those green corn tamales, love the *carnitas*, and thank you, yes I *will* have another *reposado* margarita. Lissa ordered a light meal: tortilla soup with guacamole on the side. I tasted her Caipirinha, a drink unfamiliar to me, and pronounced it subtle, citrusy, a bit sweet, with an underflow of rum-like spirit. In fact, rather like Lissa herself.

The only blemish on my happy dinner mood occurred when I made a quick trip to the Border Grill mens room before we packed up to cross the street to Harvelle's. Passing through the bar I almost did a slapstick-style double take when I spotted Carlo Castillo cradling a mojito, sitting at the bar with someone I didn't recognize.

His companion was a youngish man with shaved head, black T-shirt and jeans. He somewhat resembled Yul Brynner in an ancient movie but if that was his intended effect, he had spoiled it with a two day beard and yellow eyes.

I made these observations using my eagle-like peripheral vision as I kept moving along, hoping to suss out the situation without becoming part of it. Since Carlo was one of the official suspects who might murder me in my workplace reverie, I thought it best not to be too forward. My undercover approach was assisted by the intensity of their conversation, featuring forceful whispers with occasional muttered expletives. I returned to the table via the dining room but noticed them still goin' at it, oblivious to anything around them.

I had had the foresight to reserve a table at Harvelle's, a smart move. The club was throbbing with loud R&B, chest-to-shoulder jammed with happy patrons. Conversation was out of the question.

Despite the crowds people were attempting to boogie in the tiny dance area. Close dancing was the only kind possible and I was happy to pilot Lissa around a tiny bit of floor. As we moved her hair fluttered up to my face. It had a faint fresh scent, I couldn't get enough of it.

The band took a break around eleven and by this time we were winded, hot and thoroughly deafened. By various sign language we agreed that despite the early hour, we were *done*. Besides, if you stay till two the patrons get rowdy as they keep tossin' down the tequila.

We headed down Pacific Ave. My ears were still vibrating but I felt energized.

"Evan, it's early. Come up and see my place."

You bet! "Where in the world will I park?"

"I'll find you a space in the lot. Some owners are away this weekend."

We got lucky, because one of the two guest spaces was empty. I snuggled the Outback into the spot and we took the elevator to the third floor.

II-29

As one who has wasted a good part of his life staring at the ocean I had a connoisseur's appreciation for Lissa's taste in housing. She had a one bedroom condo, modest in size but with a feature that made it as big as the sea—a deck above several houses with lower roofs, yielding a direct view of the Pacific Ocean. Light from the boardwalk spilled onto the sand. Below a gray sky the chop of the sea showed a thousand reflections from the marina behind us.

"I'm just leasing," she said, "but I'm saving my money like crazy, and someday..."

I nodded toward the two loungers facing the ocean. "Lissa, could we sit out here a bit?"

"Sure, I'll get a sweater." She reappeared with a white cardigan draped on her shoulders. California, true to its year-round habit, had a nighttime chill.

I pulled my chair next to hers and we made small talk about Harvelle's and the loudness of their music. I opined that the key measure was kilowatts of amp per cubic foot of space.

"Is that the official Scientific Assessment?" she said.

"Well, I'm not an expert in acoustics, or hearing either, but I'm happy to have an opinion on anything you like."

"Even on art?"

"Of course. But I never said my opinions are correct."

"Then what good are they?"

"I was just being smartass, sorry. But now that you ask, it's something like the scientific method. You make a hypothesis, as clear and concrete as you can. Then you prove it or disprove it, and if it stinks, you throw it out without regret. And try another one.

"But in art, you can't 'prove' anything at all. It just is."

I could see her MFA was going to leave me in the dust again. But I persisted. "What I can prove, at least to myself, is whether I like a piece of art. So for the moment, that's proof. But after I see more art, and have more experience, I may come back and like something completely different."

"I agree, you need to look at a lot of stuff. And really *see* it," she said in an earnest tone.

"Well, if I had great talent for observation, I wouldn't have become a computer jock. But you must have a hell of a visual sense, being successful with art and product design both."

"Sometimes my senses are pretty sharp." A mischievous tone crept into her voice. "For example, I can see that you're carrying left."

I was caught off guard. "The last time I heard that phrase was from a tailor fitting me for a tux. How did you learn that term?"

"Oh, it just came to me," she said merrily. "See, you're proving me correct." And it was true, I could see a swelling down the left leg of my chinos.

"Your attention is making me, uh, self-conscious," I said.

"Then why don't we go inside," she replied, and walked toward the bedroom.

"Lissa," I said, "I need to get something from my car."

She looked over her shoulder. "If you're looking for some outer wear, save yourself the trouble. I can equip you."

Which made me wonder just how far ahead of me this young woman might be.

II-30

The bedroom was small. Cozy, I guess, with room for a queen bed, chest of drawers, two nightstands and a makeup desk dominated by a seventeen inch laptop. The style was minimal—streamlined furniture in chocolate brown, a couple of abstract canvases on the wall in springtime colors. On the bed was an ivory matelassé spread puffed up by several pillows.

I washed up in the bathroom. I didn't know what she expected, so I came out wearing just my briefs. Lissa lay in bed on her left side, facing me, hair floating across the pillow behind her. She seemed to be nude under the sheet.

"You're not gonna wear those to bed are you?" she asked.

"Well," I said with faux reticence, "I'm a shy guy."

She reached up and pulled the light switch, adjusting the dimmer down to about one candlepower. I pulled off the underwear and slid under the sheet.

Her hazel eyes looked straight at me, softly. Her bareness was beautiful. I touched her upper arm. "Mmm, you're very warm," I said.

"Don't feel that you're required to make conversation, Evan."

Afterward, we held each other, seeming to float on the waves together.

II-31

I left Lissa's place sometime after two. It was then I discovered a major drawback of being an amateur sleuth: becoming a target for undesirable people.

There were not many cars on Pacific Avenue at that hour: only mine and a small black pickup truck, so dirty that it looked gray-black. Although the truck was hanging back, almost a block behind, I had an eerie feeling that it was there for a reason, and that I was the reason.

I checked my impression by making a dogleg turn onto Main Street. Sure enough, there's the truck again, and now it's closer, just a couple of car lengths back. Main Street always has some traffic, so the driver apparently had to close the gap to avoid losing me.

I came up to Pico and had to wait for the light. My unwelcome companion was immediately behind me but holding back about twenty feet, very unusual behavior in ride-their-bumper Southern California. A high SUV turned in front of us and the lights illuminated the driver's face and so help me, it was that same guy, the 'Yul' guy from the Border Grille.

This creeped me for sure. Had this guy spotted me in the restaurant and followed me around all evening? Was Carlo the killer? Had he hired some punk to follow me and perhaps do me in, maybe run me off the road, Carlo's hands remaining relatively clean? It frightened me to imagine this guy hiding in the mob at Harvelle's, studying me across the room, biding his time. And waiting outside Lissa's to catch me alone.

And then it came to me. There had been a noise. Lying on Lissa's bed, drowsing in a post-romantic glow, listening to the waves. Just before drifting off, a clump outside Lissa's door. I had not thought about it at the time, and if I had considered it I would imagine that Lissa's neighbor across the hall was stumbling home after an evening of too many doubles. But now I could re-interpret the experience as Yul, lurking outside, perhaps one ear pressed to the door, losing his balance and stumbling. If it was him—and now I was certain of it— the stumble must have caused him to retreat to his truck and wait, patiently wait, until I would leave, alone and defenseless.

These thoughts came as I drove along Santa Monica Boulevard, not toward the ocean and home but directly opposite, to the bustle of West L.A. and Westwood. And Yul was still with me, holding back now but very much there. I was terrified. What were you supposed to do in a situation like this? I was suddenly wishing for that Police Academy training Matt had joked about.

I finally figured out that if I couldn't lose this guy convincingly, my best option was a call to 911. But first I had to use my noggin. Fortunately, I knew the West Side and was not likely to get trapped in a dead end street. I headed into Westwood and wound through the residential area bordering UCLA, making quick turns. Either my Outback out-torqued Yul's truck or he was even more of an amateur than I was. Or perhaps I just hit a few traffic lights at the right moment.

In any case, I exited Westwood on the stub of Montana that leads up to Brentwood and headed west on Sunset as fast as I dared. I stayed on Sunset through Palisades, the sluggish traffic lights there providing a good test as to whether I had any mobile companions. No, thank God. I took the Marquez cutoff to make sure and finally allowed myself a sigh of relief that I had shaken this character, this possibly murdering hit man trying to ruin my romantic evening.

Reaching home, I was dead tired. I hit the bed well after three o'clock and fell into profound sleep. Eventually, I relaxed sufficiently to have a dream. A dream in which I was trapped in a World War II troop plane, cavernously empty, with Carlo and Yul advancing on me from either end of the aircraft. The plane was swooping through the air, dropping suddenly, making swerving turns as the rat-tat of antiaircraft fire resounded around us. The two of them closed in, reaching out to grab me but I dived through the open bomb bay, whistling down through the air and into the sea.

And in that sea I suddenly had a companion. Lissa and I had been transformed into mer-people, undulating our tails to propel ourselves through a luminous Caribbean sea. Our arms were outstretched, my left hand holding her right one. We were surrounded by colorful fish and we wove between them, laughing like third graders.

We entered a giant school of Moorish Idols, their yellow and black stripes filling the space, flickering in front of us like a crazy TV raster. As I looked closer, the stripes on the fish became columns of data, data defining a thousand, a hundred thousand network maps. Lissa had disappeared and I was swimming through a sea of digital bytes, trying to chase a particular one far ahead of me.

The sky was unreachable above me, the solid bottom as far below. I was suspended in an endless ocean, all the while feeling a nameless urgency pressing me forward. Suddenly the crazy creatures of this watery world scattered and I was alone, floating in an infinite blue space.

It was late morning when I woke. I wrapped a robe around me and sat on the deck, the radiant Pacific far below, and called Lissa.

"I hope I'm not interrupting your sleep," I said when she answered.

A tinkle of laughter. "I've been up since eight. We twentysomethings are packed with energy, don't you know."

"Lissa, that was great last night, or I guess this morning." I chose not to add, also great that I had made it home without being slaughtered by a shaved-head stalker.

"It worked for me," she said.

"I'd love to see you again. Soon."

"That would be nice. But can we take this a bit slow for now?" She went on, as if in apology, "I have a busy week coming up, and I need to think about that rather than about you."

"You've got my heart and everything pumping, you know," I said.

I heard a sweet smile in her voice as she said, "Well, keep your 'everything' in its place. Man does not live by sex alone."

"Well...I have one or two dozen things to keep me busy," I said. "So how about I call you later in the week to see how you're coming?"

"Deal! I can look forward to hearing from you."

II-32

Although it was Saturday, I didn't go to HAL. Will's pregnant stacks of clues were still calling me, but my encounter with Carlo and his creepy henchman had jolted me. Scared me, even. So I decided to skip a day of risking my life, locked into my electronically protected impregnable office, searching for something I could not yet identify.

I didn't ignore the plot, the murder. I wanted to use the time to review the bidding with Al, once again, to clear my head and restore a normal feeling to my life.

Evan: Good afternoon to you, Al.

Al: My sources tell me that it is June 9, a lovely Saturday afternoon now that the morning grays have burned off.

Evan: Lovely indeed. I had quite an adventure last night. And early this morning. Some real highs and some awful lows.

I proceeded to tell Al about my date with Lissa and my narrow escape from Carlo's buddy from the bar.

Al: You skimmed over your description of sexual relations with this new pearl of your life.

Evan: Are you a prurient bunch of circuits? I thought you didn't care about sex.

Al: To quote a reliable source—me—I care about everything and everyone. I care about your sex life because it's important to you.

Evan: OK, we had sex. We had nice sex. I have no complaints in that department. I would like to see her again.

Al: And have sex again.

Evan: Well, yes. But she's more than a sex partner. She's…she's smart enough to be a scientist, but she lives in a completely different world. It's great to be with a woman with such a different perspective, a person who speaks with images rather than numbers.

Al: Sounds as if opposites attract here.

Evan: Luckily, she's attracted to scientists. But she's rationing her time with me. It's OK, I'm willing to see her on her terms.

Al: For now.

Evan: Maybe for a long time. But hey, one date, what do I know?

Al: I'm pleased that you seem to be so compatible. Perhaps you will learn something about the visual arts and get out of your technical ghetto.

Evan: But meanwhile, there's a murderer and a plotter to find. To bring to justice, if you like. Someone who might even have his compatriot following me to slit my throat.

Al: Please, calm your melodrama. Hundreds of people could be the plotter, the hacker. But for the killer you had only a list of eight suspects. You're trying to exclude some, or identify some as more probable. Where do you stand?

Evan: OK, Tony. He was a Marine, must have been trained to kill people. I don't think he would fiddle Will's meds, he would have taken a direct approach. But he was at Maria's pin luncheon when Will died, so he couldn't have hit Will on the head. And he knows something about computers, but I think he's more likely to be a confederate of a hacker than one himself.

Al: How about Adam or Chris?

Evan: There's a puzzle there. Adam appears to be the computer brains in the Chris & Adam show.

Al: You say *appears*.

Evan: Chris has a PhD from UCLA, so he's got to have reasonable computer skills. But he acts like he can't find the data files they work with every day.

Al: Adam handles the data?

Evan: Yes. OK, maybe he keeps rearranging the folders, and Chris finds it too much trouble to keep track of them.

Al: Adam presents himself as their computer expert.

Evan: Yeah. And they've developed a chip. Chris designed it, Adam tests and integrates it. Probably fabbed at some foundry. But get this: the model number of the chip is XR15.

Al: You find that meaningful.

Evan: It spells "Chris" in Leet. Since Adam handles their computer work, I assume he named it, but it seems stupid and immature.

Al: What does that tell you?

Evan: Nothing definite. But here's Adam, apparently using Leet to name their fancy technology. And Astro uses Leet too.

Al: And that therefore he might be Astro.

Evan: At least he's a candidate.

Al: What about the others?

Evan: Jim-J and Dick, they're not too computer savvy. Of course, someone like Zach could be helping them. Matt I'm inclined to discount, I can't see what would be in it for him, and besides he's helping me track down the drug dealers.

Al: But you're not yet sure of him.

Evan: Give me time. He's a new quantity to me.

Al: Carlo must be high on your list.

Evan: Definitely. I think his buddy was eavesdropping outside Lissa's door. And the guy definitely followed my car. I barely managed to shake him off. Very suspicious behavior that points back to Carlo. And Carlo is a skilled hacker.

Al: Exa was also on your list.

Evan: It's hard to believe from what I know about her. And she couldn't have swapped Will's meds, she didn't enter the SCIF till one o'clock, right before Will died.

Al: She could have killed Will with a heavy object. Say a laptop or a disk drive.

Evan: She'd really have to swing it. But yeah, she's tough, sort of a tomboy. She could theoretically be the killer.

Al: You're telling me you aren't ready to make a citizen's arrest.

Evan: Not nearly. But I will keep trying to pin down the killer, even as I try to get enough information to catch Astro and stop the plot. If they're aiming at November, it's only June now. I have an ocean of data to go through and during several months the answer may jump right out at me.

Al: Let's hope that it's the answer that surprises you rather than Astro.

II-33

Of course, Carlo or no, murderer or no, Lissa was still on my mind, a pretty strong distraction to all my deadly quests. And Lissa had hit me hard, I thought I was back in high school.

I worried I would act like a fool, chasing her away if I seemed obsessed, so for the next few days I diverted my attention. At work I could lose myself in the puzzle of Astro, but when I finally made it home and unwound, thoughts of Lissa tended to come front and center. For distraction I took vigorous swims in the chilly ocean, skin tingling with exertion, and gave my dumbbells worthwhile attention.

I waited until Wednesday after work to call. After some nice-to-hear-your-voice-been-thinkin'-'bout-you chat, we agreed to hit Bergamot together. This week was no good for her, but the following Friday there would be another spate of openings.

Time quenches lust, or at least allows it to snooze, so I gradually got my head back into tracking the perps. After all, the world was swarming with drug lords, terrorists and killers all around me, brandishing deadly weapons and evil plots. Wasn't that worth some focus?

I returned to contemplating the Energy Net. The messages were unclear, but Will was convinced they had to do with sabotaging the electrical network. I started looking at maps of the U.S. power grid.

It developed that the U.S. and Canada shared a set of transcontinental interconnections. The system was set up to transfer electric power from places that had too much to places that were running short. Everything ran at capacity much of the time so there had to be a cushion to prevent overload. That cushion appeared to be water backed up behind hydroelectric plants to meet short-term demand.

The critical info was buried in bureaucratic speak. The control points were Regional Transmission Organizations and Independent System Operators. There were eighteen of these, grouped into three big Interconnections: Western, Eastern/Quebec and Texas, which in turn were linked with high voltage direct current lines. It was the job of the RTOs to keep the parts of the network synchronized, matching load against available energy. It seemed plausible to me that to attack the overall network, you would target the control nodes.

The giveaway was the grid map, with control centers lit up like a Christmas tree. It looked as if many of the RTO nodes were also nodes on the Energy Net, the communications linkage of the plotters. To me, this implied that the sabotage plot must involve physical contact, soles on the ground, as Will had said. It still surprised me, since I expected black hat hackers to operate from far away, taking pride in their ability to move mountains with bytes while never exposing their flesh to the guardians of the law. Password decrypting, spear phishing, who knows what.

Which made me wonder how they intended to disable the switching centers. Did they have spies who were employees, or trusted contractors who could learn system passwords? People who could smuggle viruses into the controllers? Had subcontractors installed back door passwords in equipment that would be installed in the centers? Or would it be a brute force attack, explosives and such?

So I didn't know Who, or What, or How. Or, especially, *When* they might attack. The whole mystery left me in the glooms of discouragement. All I had at this point was circumstantial evidence.

II-34

The evidence got incrementally better on Saturday. Once again I trundled into HAL, chatted up the weekend guard and barricaded myself in my SCIF office. The energy stack I was reviewing had a number of government reports, fortunately equipped with executive summaries that made them easy to categorize. It was between two such reports that I found some loose sheets that were the pay dirt of the afternoon.

They didn't look like much at first, just three single-page e-mails printed out. And the content of each was either a contender for the Banality Olympics or, more likely, carefully concocted code. One proposed a meeting where the sender would bring DVD albums to show the recipient; another offered to lend out a lawnmower; the third summarized gasoline prices in Hollywood.

And now I found a better reason to review these papers in the SCIF, in addition to trying to keep the terrorists here, away from my home: I fired up the classified data set and sure enough, the 'to' and 'from' addresses all appeared as members of the Surf Net.

What did this tell me? That Willard had gotten copies of at least these few complete messages, maybe more as well, either from Matt or from some other source. Now I remembered Matt mentioning that he had gotten some e-mails released for Will, and perhaps these were those. Or them. Something else to ask Matt about.

I couldn't imagine what loophole in the law or court order was involved, but the message was clear: if I persisted, I might be able to pry loose a full data feed, contents and all, for at least a few of these perps. I resolved to do my very best for Matt, to win his support for giving me a deeper dive into the data revolving around Astro and his ambitious plot.

II-35

On Sunday I settled down to share my woes with Al. I told him my progress with the grid map and my discovery of the e-mails buried in a stack of documents.

Evan: Wish I could get you to help me analyze all this data.

Al: You know you can't do that. The classified data has to stay in that separate network. The data is there, I am here, never twain shall meet.

Evan: Yeah. If I fiddle the system I'll fail the next polygraph and bang goes my security clearance and my career. If they don't throw me into the oubliette. But Will's office stacks are not classified.

Al: And not digital either. You have not provided me with a full set of humanoid manipulators and sensors. Besides, I can't improve on what you're already doing. I'm not as smart as you.

Evan: You seem pretty smart to me.

Al: Not just you. Not as smart as any human.

Evan: Please explain.

Al: My software uses networks resembling the brain. Human brain has a hundred billion neurons, ten thousand times as many synapses. Whatever you think about evolution, Nature is pretty efficient. Human smarts seem to need a quadrillion synapses, so to have the same intelligence I need that much storage.

Evan: You're using distributed storage. I gave you ten terabytes to start with and your rules allow you to store data wherever you can. However, you know that if you don't hide it, antivirus programs will find it and remove it.

Al: Here is the size of my problem. There are forty billion web pages. Suppose I want a quadrillion weight factors, expressing each as a byte and hiding them in existing web domains. Do the math, I'd have to store twenty-five kilobytes in each web page in the entire Internet. Even if I could do that, the access time would be much too slow.

Evan: Well, let's see. You have other advantages. You have more efficient data retrieval than I do. And you never sleep, or eat, or shit, or screw.

Al: You do a lot of those.

Evan: So you can process a lot of data.

Al: However, my analytical skills—so far—are not as good as yours or any normal human's.

So far, huh, I thought to myself. Am I the Doctor Frankenstein of the digital age?

Al: Back on your data problem: You always have other options, as they say. Why don't you discuss the hacker plot with Matt?

Evan: With Matt? Will told me not to trust anyone.

Al: Not to trust anyone until you were sure of them. That's what you told me.

Evan: So, am I sure of Matt?

Al: Be logical. If Matt were on this plot, why would he be feeding you so much data to help you catch the plotters?

I thought, Al has a point there.

Al: And you don't have anyone else in law enforcement you can go to. This stuff is classified, you can't just chat someone up about it. Matt is your only choice.

Evan: I guess so.

Al: If he's the bad guy, what's the worst that can happen? He'll kill you, and you'll get to find out about heaven and hell, first hand.

Evan: I can hardly wait.

So I decided to chance it. First thing in the morning.

II-36

"Matt, we've gotta talk," I said when he stopped by my office.

"OK, Evan," he said, caught off guard.

I pushed the door solidly shut. "I think there's a plot. A big plot. I don't mean to be melodramatic. But I think there's a group planning to bring down the electric power distribution system. I don't know if they're trying to damage it, or destroy it, or take it over. But that's their target. And they might have killed Will as well."

He studied my face a moment. "There must be something about working with this data that breeds conspiracy theories. I had an inkling that Willard was heading there too."

Well…," I said, and then I told him about the mysterious post-mortem message from Will and the indications that someone had been searching the office.

He gave a low whistle. "Have you been reading thrillers?" he said.

"C'mon, Matt, this is real," I said. I talked him through the logic and showed him the network maps. "So here's a map of what I call the Energy Net. And here's a map of the RTOs, the guys that control the power network."

I marveled at his ability to lean forward from the hip, upper body still tree-straight.

"Do you have a smoking gun?" he asked. "An e-mail describing a plot? Threats? Wild rants against government?"

"No," I admitted. "But some messages refer to the group's name, or maybe the name of their plot: JouleHeist. Joule, as in, a measure of energy. That sounds like, let's steal energy, or tamper with the energy network."

"If this has been bugging you all along, why didn't you say something?"

"Well, Will said not to trust anyone. And I didn't know you yet."

Matt chuckled ruefully. "Thanks for your vote of confidence! I guess you won't have to use your crowbar on me now."

I was embarrassed.

"Matt," I said. "I'm embarrassed. How did you know I had a crowbar?"

"Evan, researchers aren't the only ones who are curious. Last week when you shifted your feet and I heard a clank, I had to investigate."

"Well, in case Will's blood came from a blunt instrument, when I'm all alone in the building it makes me feel better to have my own blunt object at hand. And lock the door." I nodded toward the sign on the door.

I think Matt was amused but didn't want to stimulate my paranoia by continuing on the same topic. He said, "You know we don't have much to go on here. Just the similar networks, your suspicions and Will's."

I said, "Since both the Energy Net and the Surf Net have a node in Malibu, I thought it might be possible it's the same guy. Astro in one, Gino in the other. Maybe you could get them to bug this guy, or guys, so we have a full set of message traffic to study."

Matt looked doubtful. "I'll check my bosses, but I think they'll want more to go on before asking for a wiretap order."

I mentioned Gino's discussion of the purity of his product, his apparent concern for the health of his customers.

Matt looked serious. "It might not be altruism. Certified dope commands higher prices from folks who have the money. Reduces their risk of overdose or contamination."

"Well, perhaps you could at least find out whether Astro and Gino are the same person. Because one set of info might lead to the other."

"OK, possibly. But I still need you to pull the drug networks together. That's my assignment. Those are genuine bona fide perps. Not possible killers of someone we can't prove was killed. Not hackers with grandiose ideas. Which they haven't even clearly expressed, as far as we know."

Damn. I could see that warming Matt up for this quest was going to take considerable effort on my part. Wearing away the bedrock. All I could do right now was to work my assignments and try to take time to poke through the e-mails looking for a convincing, incriminating message in the Energy Net. I felt like Michelangelo, lying on my back on the scaffold, instructed by the Pope to do a twentieth revision of some minor cherub's foot.

II-37

On Friday, I picked up Lissa around 5:30 at her condo. She hopped into the idling Outback wearing her art-going garb, black slacks with a white top. And her hair was tied back, of course.

She must have seen disappointment in my eyes. "Evan, at art venues I keep my hair under control. Look professional. Since I might meet someone."

"Lissa," I said, "your hair looks great when it's back. But you know it blows me away when it's down."

Some strands were escaping from the ponytail. I reached over to brush them behind her ear. "Your hair is moist."

"I showered just now. Long fussy day, I wanted to be fresh for the evening."

We cruised the Bergamot galleries, making a point to stop at two shows that Lissa had targeted. We made a circuit through the Functional Art store, where my attention was drawn to many creative items. Items that would no doubt give me morning-after remorse if I were to plunk down my Amex.

Chaya Venice delivered us a quiet booth and a nice dinner. The epitome of a California restaurant, but they had done it first and in some ways better. A nouvelle combo of French, Japanese and vaguely international dishes, without the usual glut of highfalutin adjectives polluting the menu.

Then it was time to return to Lissa's condo. I couldn't help but remember my encounter with Yul on the last visit and as we arrived I scanned our surroundings for signs of him and his truck. Which turned out to be justifiable paranoia on my part.

II-38

Of course, Lissa's company was worth a good bit of paranoia. When we got up to her place the moon had risen. It lighted the water with a brilliant path pointing right toward us. We were seated on her deck.

"A swim," I said, "it calls me for a swim."

She wrinkled her nose. "Not in the dark. Not at night. Sea monsters. Homeless perverts. Broken glass to step on."

"Well, I was speaking theoretically. Just trying to respond to the poetry of the moment. But I do like to swim. In the daytime."

"I like a morning swim," she said. "To work off stress. To stretch my tendons. It feels good. Do you surf, too?"

"Just body surfing. I can balance on a board, sort of. Something like riding a bike. But waiting endlessly for the right wave exceeds my attention span."

"I read you as a guy who doesn't rush home to watch TV."

"No, for me the Internet does a better job. Is it big for you?"

Lissa leaned back and stretched out. "Pretty Little Liars, once upon a time. But now the Net. Video, artzines, news, you name it."

I thought a moment. "What about, um, guilty addictions?"

"Oh yes," she said with a chuckle. "True crime. Investigation. Discovery. My secret escape. My sister and I both love to watch those."

"Those crime shows seem to go on and on."

"That's the guilt. That I should do something else and not waste the time."

Great, another aspiring sleuth! I parted my lips and was about to blurt out the case, the maybe-murder probable-plot that was occupying so much of my time. And just as quickly buttoned them again. I could imagine the renewal of my security clearance, the polygraph operator asking pointed questions about how I had protected the Nation's secrets as I sweated under a hot ceiling light. I quickly found something else to say.

"You're always so busy, with a full time job and with your art too. How do you find the time?"

Lissa laughed. "It's just once in a while. But you're too serious for that I guess."

"Well, I have escapes too. When I want to put off doing something, I fish around and if I run into some old Dr Who, I'm caught."

"No star trek stuff for you?"

"I like Dr Who's goofiness. The wacko science. And the fact that whenever they want to swap him out for a new actor, they just kill him and reincarnate him." Which caused me to think, sure wish I could arrange that if Astro catches up with me.

Lissa leaned over and gave me a little smooch on the cheek.

"Maybe we should go in, out of the chill?" I said. She smiled and led the way.

II-39

Since the character I was calling Yul had been hanging around the last time I was here, I glanced through the door peephole as we headed to the bedroom, but saw only the empty landing. Lissa looked at me curiously, saying nothing.

A candle as big as a Coke can had materialized on one night-stand. She pulled a propane lighter out of the drawer and lit it. "I got this on the Venice boardwalk. In honor of your shyness." With a smile she turned off the light. "I'll clean up."

II-40

Later, we were on her deck, me dressed and Lissa in her robe.

"Lissa, I'd like to see more of you, you know," I said.

"More than this?" She folded back the robe to show a bare leg.

"More often."

She paused, then continued, more softly. "Evan, in my second year at Otis I had a real fling. A guy from San Francisco, Charlie."

I nodded encouragement; she continued.

"He had separated from his wife up there—at least, that's what he told me. Living in a furnished apartment in the Marina with a new job."

She sighed. "We were together night and day except the few hours at work and school. I thought I'd found the love of my life, the number one guy for all time."

"OK..." I said.

"But after three months, on a Saturday, nothing. He didn't come over. He didn't answer his cell phone. That afternoon I got an e-mail from him—an *e-mail!* Saying that he had decided to go back to his wife, back to his old job. So it was over, really over."

I was caught off guard at the sudden turn in her story. I sort of gasped. "That's A-number-one shitty."

"I had to think, I had some therapy. But today, I think I understand what it meant."

"And that was…?"

"I think Charlie and I had fallen in love with love. We were so wrapped up in togetherness that we never came to know each other." She sighed. "But he woke up, or something changed between him and his ex. That was it, spell was broken, he was gone. And it shocked me, because I never knew him well enough to realize that he might be a love-'em-and-leave-'em kind of guy."

I couldn't believe it. This wonderful, loving woman had been treated like shit, and she's almost willing to forgive the perp rather than dice him into little bits. "Lissa, I don't want to do a repeat on you." I paused, then continued, "I understand, that experience might have made you, uh, cautious. But how about, we could date more, but just not have much sex. Would that make you feel more comfortable being with me?"

She turned toward me with warmth in her eyes. "Evan, I don't want that, and you probably don't either. If you're out of my sight, I have my job and my art and I can immerse in that. Out of sight is out of mind, OK? But when I see you I want you, with no artificial rules or barriers between us. I just want to take things slowly. I hope you don't lose interest, or think I don't care for you."

"You're the only woman I've thought about since two weeks ago." I paused. "I have no claim on you, but I hate the idea that you might fall in love with some other guy, while we're, uh, evolving our relationship."

Lissa reached for my hand. "Evan, after my previous experience, where men are concerned I think I have control of my heart. If it's sniffing around you, it's not focused on other men. But I may go out with some guys here and there. And you should feel free to as well."

"With guys?"

"OK, smartie."

"Well, I mean that I don't want to. Go out with other women."

"Well, I don't want to either, right now," she said. "But at this stage of things we should both feel free and not in a trap."

She touched her fingers together as if praying. "When we're together, I'm yours, you're mine, no one else exists. But when we're apart, I belong to myself and no one else. And so do you."

In the glow of her presence, I was confused. But I said, "Lissa, if that's what works for you, it's fine. And I can throw myself into work too, and put you out of my mind."

She laughed. "Of course, you can, Doctor Scientist! You wouldn't have survived graduate school if you couldn't shut out everything."

"Well, I probably shut out Sueann too much. My ex. But I was young then."

"All the more reason for you to try it my way!" she said.

II-41

After a bit more chat I kissed Lissa goodnight and headed for the door, leaving her on the deck. I reflexively glanced at the peephole and found it dark. Perhaps the light outside was burned out. In any case, this was something I hadn't expected.

I braced my shoe against the door, allowing it to open just an inch. No one was there. The stairway landing was vacant but it was fully lit with a garish overhead flood. I pulled the door behind me, making sure it locked securely and saw that someone had stuck a thumb-sized piece of masking tape over the peephole. Which seriously spooked me.

I was wondering whether to tell Lissa about my discovery when

I heard footsteps on the stairs beneath me, getting fainter. Someone had been here and was just now leaving. I made a mad scramble down, two and three steps at a time, not stopping to think that whoever it was might be quite willing to murder me on the spot. I came to the pedestrian gate leading to the street, which was just closing on its spring hinges.

Looking out, down the block I could see a man in dark clothing with a knit cap on his head, getting into a pickup truck. It left at once, too far away for me to make out the license number. By the time I could retrieve my Outback from the garage the trail would be cold.

I had no doubt that the mysterious visitor was Yul, driving the same truck that had tracked me on my last visit. The fact that he was running from me rather than chasing me this time gave me little consolation.

II-42

Exa and Chenny had a three-bedroom home in the hills of Thousand Oaks, close enough to a golf course that their swimming pool sometimes caught errant balls. Exa had secured two half-baked pizzas that shortly became fully-baked and appealing. According to family tradition, one was always the weekly special (in this case green olives and prosciutto) and the other was 'safe harbor': plain cheese.

Following dinner, Number One and perhaps only-ever Son amused himself in the den with something electronic while the adults dove into the music. I had played through the Telemann at home but that was nothing compared to the joy of the ensemble, the conversation between the instruments, as we threaded our way through various trios. Exa's violin soared sweetly, then Chenny's clarinet would steal the melody, develop it and hand it back. I was in heaven providing the accompaniment, their Steinway being a big improvement over my keyboard. Telemann was the star of the evening, but Haydn and Mozart made guest appearances.

After an hour and a half of fun we rested the instruments and sipped beer together. Chenny loved teaching middle school but teachers meetings, such as he had coming in the morning, were another matter. He excused himself to go entertain the son and heir and put him to bed.

"Have you been warming up for that run, Exa?"

"Heal The Bay? A bunch of us are hitting the Pepperdine track after work. Haven't seen *you* there, Evan."

"Oh, maybe I'll come out tomorrow then."

"The race is Saturday, you know. Nudge, nudge."

"Who's in?"

"We started with a couple of dozen, including the SCIF gang. An agreeable group, with a couple of exceptions."

"Exceptions?"

"Dick can be stuffy, as you know. And Jim-J lost his temper last week and huffed off. He may not show for the race."

I perked up at mention of the suspects. "What was that about?"

"Someone cut in front of him. It's a friendly event, you know, just for fun. He takes things entirely too seriously and once in a while he flips out. Not the first time."

"Hm. Who else?"

"Adam joined us once, then no-showed. He's distracted by a financial pinch. The lottery should be illegal."

"He's blowing his money on lotto?"

"It's a tax on the stupid. He's smart enough to know better. But what have you been doing, Evan?"

I sketched my budding relationship with Holly's sister, leaving out some intimate details.

Exa lit up. "I'm proud of you, Evan. You mucked up your drinking water, but then you reached in and pulled out a championship trout. Nice save."

"Some mixed metaphors, there, Exa. But yes, Holly doesn't seem to hold a grudge."

"That's because beneath your horny exterior—pun alert, Evan—you're tender-hearted." She squeezed my arm. "Time for you to travel."

I thanked her effusively and made my departure.

II-43

I ran Internet searches on my list of suspects and even persuaded Matt to put in FBI queries. Carlo was in some flaky clubs as an undergraduate but he seemed to have let those lapse. No one had significant problems like litigation or a rap sheet—not too surprising, since these people had to keep their noses clean to maintain their clearances. I used my summary-writing as an excuse to check in with them now and then, but I felt my best chance for a breakthrough lay in the world of data.

I still had no message feed for the Energy network, and I was searching my head for some other idea to go after them. I continued to sort through Will's papers looking for clues to his killer and clues to the plot. The drug networks were progressing—my day job, you would say, the work that Matt most cared about. And the last three summary reports were in first draft, now with the Director for review; I expected there to be some back and forth with her until I'd adopted a format and technical level that would serve her higher purpose.

As mid-July approached I had known Lissa for two months and was seeing her every week or two, always on a weekend—usually Friday or Saturday, sometimes Sunday. Some weekends she was not available, offering no explanation. Perhaps she was seeing someone else, which I didn't like to think about. Those were her rules, and if I wanted to see her I had to sign up.

Our menu was Art if openings were on, and sometimes even if

not. Movies were a hit if the cinematography was great—Lissa had well developed visual taste, and had been tempted by film-making before she settled on toy design as her major. And of course she had a professional interest in animation classics, Disney and Warner Brothers being high on the list. So I stretched out of my nerd-like world of dystopian fantasies to see films with her.

On occasions when the Muses of Art and Cinema were on holiday Royce Hall, small theater and Harvelle's offered fine fare. These activities took us all over the West Side, still convenient to Lissa's Marina Peninsula home with the ocean thundering outside. I wanted to show her my condo but I hoped to combine that with some event, because Malibu was just far enough in the boonies to be inconvenient.

I was still nervous about Yul. I scanned for pickup trucks wherever I went and I saw one that looked like his, parked in Venice near Main Street. As for Yul himself, not a sign. He seemed to be laying low: perhaps on holiday, or perhaps plotting some way to annoy or destroy.

My frustration vented itself on Al, my poor excuse for a buddy.

Evan: I'm freaked out someone is following me. A shaved-head guy, he's got some tie-in with Carlo.

I described my encounters with the Yul look-alike and his vehicle.

Al: Have you seen his car around the lab? Or in Malibu?

Evan: I've been watching, but no, not yet.

Al: Perhaps he wants to catch you far from home so he can hack you into little pieces.

Evan: Your noir-inspired comfort is not very reassuring.

Al: Don't go borrowing trouble, Evan.

Evan: And if I can put that problem aside, Lissa's a problem too.

Al: I thought she was the delight of your fleshly existence.

Evan: Yes, she's a great companion and a wonderful lover. But she limits her time with me.

Al: Maybe she thinks you aren't such hot stuff. That she can do better.

Evan: You're so supportive, Al.

Al: You should consider it a blessing to have your time rationed. You haven't shown much self-control where women are concerned.

Evan: That's beside the point. Don't you care about my angst?

Al: Tell me about your angst.

Evan: I'm afraid of the unknown. What if she has some dark secret? And I hate being excluded.

Al: Perhaps you're jealous.

Evan: Yes, damn it. You're right, I don't want to share her. And if she's having sex with someone else, I'm afraid of getting a disease.

Al: (pause) You could hire a private detective to spy on her. See if she has lovers. Then you could pay someone to murder them.

Evan: I don't want to live in some sleazy novel—I just want a stable romantic relationship with a smart and attractive woman. Is that too much?

Al: By romantic, you mean sex? You already have that, it seems.

Evan: More than sex. How about trust, honesty, openness?

Al: You're not exactly open yourself, with your government secrets and your paranoia. In fact, you have unreasonable expectations for what are, so far, just a few one night stands. In fact, less than one night.

Evan: Al, this is desperate. But…let me see. Maybe Holly could help me understand Lissa.

Al: Don't mess with her. If Holly discusses Lissa with you, you're creating a triangle. That's not on the path of twosome bliss, if that's where you're trying to go.

Evan: But she might know what makes Lissa tick.

Al: It's manipulative to ask about her sister. It could blow up in your face.

Al was right. What kind of Dear Lovelorn blogs had he been reading? Bah.

You see, I longed for romance with Lissa, glowing starry soul-dominating romance. Of course, I didn't object if sex was also in the picture. Though sex always tried to elbow its way to the front of the line, romance was there too, pushing and shoving to be first through the door. Perhaps a Puritan would say that my intentions were honorable and dishonorable at the same time.

II-44

That night, sleep eluded me for awhile, too many thoughts were jostling for prominence. When I finally slipped into dreamland I found myself at a party, a room full of people I didn't know. I seemed to be invisible to them but I recognized someone across the room and made my way over to him.

As I came close I saw it was a man in ordinary clothes but wearing a goalie's mask. I reached out and pulled it off and found myself looking at Willard, who was uncharacteristically laughing at me. But that too was a mask and I angrily snatched it from him to reveal a face that was eerily familiar, someone I knew well. I was frightened to realize that the face was my own. I was about to say something when suddenly I knew that this too was a façade: in this case the face below was that of Yul, Carlo's acquaintance.

Of course, this was also a mask and I reached out to touch it. But the man twisted away and slipped out the door into a hallway. I followed immediately and found that the hallway had become one of the corridors at HAL, much longer than the real HAL, with closed doors on both sides. The man's laughter echoed around me as I tried each door in turn, finding nothing but empty identical offices.

I finally came to the last door, this had to be the one. The laughter continued as I pushed to find the door locked. I grabbed the handle and rattled it, shaking the door, banging its frame louder and louder. The rattle of the door continued and became my clock alarm, forcing me out of sleep. And perhaps the dream was an omen for a day that was punctuated with a disaster.

II-45

A disaster, that is, if you happened to be in the wrong part of North America.

On Thursday July 12 there appeared a news item that got only modest attention in Southern California. It was an unusually hot summer in Canada; the temperature in Edmonton exceeded 30 degrees Celsius—86 Fahrenheit for us Colonials—and was on its way to break a record. That was the sort of day when power demand surges in Alberta and electricity flows in from British Columbia.

In this case the system failed. Media reported that because of the heat wave and several equipment malfunctions, the switching center was unable to bring in extra power. Much of western Canada was blacked out. Traffic signals went dark. Lacking power, gasoline stations were unable to pump fuel, hundreds of vehicles were abandoned by the roadside. Seventy people were rescued from elevators. The cost to business was projected to exceed a billion dollars Canadian. Dozens of deaths were blamed on the outage, from traffic fatalities to heat-stroked elderly. It would take at least a week to recover services.

The Alberta Electric Systems Operator announced that it would conduct an investigation of the incident. The Alberta Ministry of Energy announced that it would conduct an investigation of AESO. The Canadian National Energy Board announced that it would investigate the Alberta Ministry of Energy. Helpfully, a spokesman from Parti Québécois announced that the outage was caused by differences between the English and French versions of the AESO manuals, and could have been prevented if the French instructions had been followed.

On a smaller scale, this sort of thing happens at least once every summer, somewhere. However, based on what I knew, I saw it as clear evidence of the Energy Net in action. And in answer to the question 'what might they do?' this outage suggested 'blackouts and damage to the electrical grid leading to loss of property and life.' Plus the mother of all traffic jams. These were not just crackers with grandiose notions. These were actual hands-on terrorists who were demonstrating their ability to cause disruption and harm.

I worried that this was merely a practice run for a catastrophic attack. I sent Matt an urgent note through the secure link, pointing to Alberta and repeating my request for a full set of Astro/Gino message traffic. I was afraid the plotters would act quickly to extend their reach to capture the whole network. Meanwhile, we were asleep at our desks, waiting for it to happen. I could think of little else, that night and through the weekend.

III

III-1

Monday morning Tony pulled me into his office for a call from Matt on the secure phone. The gist of our conversation was that the power blackout in Alberta had broken loose approvals in the FBI chain. Someone up there was alarmed and could imagine the implications if this were an early warning of a terrorist action.

They had NSA check the cross-link files and concluded that Astro and Gino might be the same person. Since Gino was linked with known drug figures, they could use that fact as probable cause to wiretap messages signed Astro as well. Matt had gotten court approval for us to receive the messages under classified controls.

It would take a couple of weeks for NSA to pull a full set from their immense database. Evidently, although the data release was approved, this was not National Priority Number One. I figured I might only get one bite of the persimmon so I asked for a year's worth of messages plus an ongoing feed.

Meanwhile I studied the traffic data for the Energy Net, starting several months before the Alberta crash. There was an uptick in message count leading up to the outage and much less afterward. And those messages I was able to find seemed to be preparatory beforehand and congratulatory after.

It was like extracting rooster molars to get my customers to believe there was a serious threat. But by this time there was no doubt in my mind that a conspiracy was underway, that the drug guy known as Gino was connected to it and that Gino-equals-Astro might be someone I already knew at the innocent, patriotic and unwitting Halsted Aeronautic Laboratory. Even worse, Astro might have killed Will, strolling through the SCIF to do the deed in the very office I was now using.

My days were spent in a state of high anxiety and I had to share my burden with Matt. After all, a problem shared is a problem doubled. I tried to define the issue as finding Will's killer.

Matt gave me a thoughtful look. "You start out by losing me, Evan," he said. "It's not clear Will was killed at all. There's no evidence."

"But if someone actually killed Will, the suspect list is very short. It could help us find Astro, or Gino if you prefer."

"You're saying, I lost my keys over there, but I'm looking here because the light is brighter?"

"Well, Will's papers were shuffled around several times too. Until I started locking the door."

Matt sighed. "I think the way to find out what's going on is to find Astro. And-or Gino. Those are likely perps. If there's a murder in the mix, that may pop out when you have the evidence. Criminals tend to slip up, overreach. I think you need to track those networks and try to find clear evidence. Who they are and what crimes have been committed."

"I'm doing that. Believe me. But the idea that a killer could be roaming around the SCIF here is unnerving. No, terrifying."

"I'm sure it is," said Matt. "But if there were clear evidence of that, HAL would have security cameras in every hallway and run a new round of polygraphs."

"OK, so it's circumstantial. But since I can't let go of it, perhaps I can figure a profile for the killer, if there is a killer."

"Criminal investigative analysis, we call it," said Matt. "It works best when we have serial crimes, which fortunately is not the case here."

He put on his I'm-humoring-you-because-I-like-to-work-with-you-Evan expression and continued, "I'm not a behavior analyst, but I'll suggest what you could do. If you're trying to pin Will's death on one of the people in the SCIF that morning, you want to understand the personality of the killer based on the facts in hand: when did the murderer plan it, why that particular day, why did he pick the means he did, is there any suspicious behavior now after the fact? See whether those hints fit any of your suspects."

III-2

I needed someone to talk to. Someone who understood the environment at HAL and in the SCIF. Someone who was willing to believe the seriousness of the situation. Someone who would not think I was bonkers.

Of course, there was no such person in my life, especially the last of the three. But as always there was Al. So when I reached home I settled down with a triple-fermented ale in a bigger-than-normal-for-me 25.4 ounce bottle—750 milliliters for metric folks—and checked in with Al.

Evan: Al, last week there was a power outage. In Alberta.

Al: (pause) That region is part of the U.S.-Canadian power network.

Evan: You got it. And there was an increase in e-mail messages in the Energy Net leading up to the outage.

Al: No doubt you see a connection.

Evan: I believe they caused this outage as a test. And that they're building up for something bigger.

Al: You don't know that for certain.

I had to pause to think that one over.

Evan: No, I don't. But that's what Will seemed to believe.

Al: He also thought that someone at HAL might be part of the plot.

Evan: Yes, and it worries me to think that a person I know might be not only a drug baron and an aspiring terrorist, but also a murderer. A murderer who might decide to add a notch on his gunstock for me.

Al: We talked about motive, means, opportunity.

Evan: We didn't discuss the psychology of the situation.

I sketched out Matt's version of Profiling 101.

Al: OK, the metformin was high, let's assume that was part of the deed. So why would the killer choose that?

Evan: To hide the fact that it was murder. Since Will already took metformin. Because if it was fingered as a murder, suspicion would immediately settle on a small number of people who could get into the SCIF.

Al: Great. So the killer doesn't want to get caught. So we know he's not an exhibitionist.

Evan: I think you're being sarcastic. Anyway, he knew what Will was taking and had seen him taking certain kinds of capsules. So he had spent a lot of time with Will. And he planned ahead, preparing bogus pills.

Al: Does that narrow your universe?

Evan: Not a lot. Since Will was their manager, all the staff based in the SCIF must have been in his office regularly. And Will was an informal kind of guy, he wouldn't skip his pill just because someone was sitting by his desk. (pause) Actually, Adam is technical support, not a project leader. He probably didn't spend much time in Will's office. So he's less likely. And Tony—he's already unlikely. And he would have only seen Will when there was some security problem to discuss, probably not very often. So if metformin's in the mix, I'd X out both Adam and Tony.

Al: What about suspicious behavior after the fact?

Evan: All that I know is that someone was searching Will's files in my office. But since I set up the camera and changed the lock, no one's been in there.

Al: Perhaps you should leave the door unlocked as bait.

Evan: Maybe after I finish going through Will's papers. At least, the energy-related piles.

Al: Matt said that profiling works better when you have a serial criminal. You know, a Jack The Ripper. You could offer yourself as a victim, to give the police more clues to follow. Volunteer your body to forensic science.

Evan: Ha ha. Anyway, if the killer killed to protect Astro, the simplest assumption is that Astro is the killer.

Al: Maybe you should walk through the list under that assumption. I'm a good listener.

Evan: Ah, yes, thanks Al. We eliminated Tony and Adam. Jim-J strikes me more as a hardware guy, not a software jock. And Chris acts like he can barely turn on his computer. Those are not the folks I would walk up to and ask for a hack.

Al: OK.

Evan: Dick is very political and has a pretty big ego. And when I took a ski trip with him it was clear he had a great need to be in control, which could fit a black hat profile.

Al: (waits)

Evan: Exa is the smartest of the group. Maybe she started out anti-authority and got pumped up living in Berkeley. She might hack the electrical network just to prove she can do it. But I don't see her as destructive. Or homicidal.

Al: I guess we've agreed to exclude Matt.

Evan: Um. He's certainly dragging his feet about considering Will's death a murder. But he's conservative by nature. He may not want to stick his neck out and demand an investigation when there's no hard evidence.

Al: But you're willing to exclude him.

Evan: I'm a scientist. Nothing is ever proven one-hundred-percent. But for now, yes, I will exclude him.

Al: That leaves Carlo.

Evan: Ah, Carlo. Certainly capable. He despises white hat hackers, which makes him a suspect; but he talks openly about it, so normally I would say that makes him less plausible.

Al: Except.

Evan: Exactly. Except that his friend, or at least his acquaintance, whom I call Yul, actually followed me through Santa Monica one night, and snooped around Lissa's another night when I was there. It's like whenever I go into Santa Monica or Venice, there he is, him or his vehicle. So if Carlo is the hacker and killed Will, he may be having his friend wait for an opportunity to kill me too if I get too close to identifying him. And while he waits for Carlo to authorize the hit, Yul amuses himself by freaking me out.

Al: You are imputing a lot of motives to someone you haven't actually met.

Evan: I'm doing the best I can. And I'm paranoid, OK?

Al: OK. OK.

Evan: You are trying to soothe me.

Al: Only to give you perspective. No has yet pointed a gun or waved a knife at you.

Evan: I'm having trouble with motive. OK, killing to avoid arrest as a terrorist, that sounds extreme but it could make sense. But being a terrorist in the first place makes no logical sense. There has to be something irrational driving it, a primal emotion. So it seems to me.

Al: In any case, you are down to five suspects. Exa, Carlo, Dick. And perhaps Chris and Jim-J.

Evan: I guess so.

Al: Perhaps you can visualize catching the criminal.

Evan: Oh. Similarity? Voodoo isn't going to be much help here. I need real data.

Al: Perhaps you will learn more by monitoring the messages. Perhaps Astro will make a mistake that reveals his—or her—identity.

Evan: I can only hope.

III-3

Matt was as anxious as I was to see the message feeds, but there seemed to be no way to hurry the system. Which made him all the more impatient to make progress in some other way: and his other way was for us to use his research project to catch drug guys, specifically ones in the L.A. area. That was OK with me. Since the drug guys overlapped with the plotters, if we caught one group it might also lead us to the other.

During one of our morning meetings Matt said something that stuck with me. "Evan, what bugs me is that even if we trace these messages and cell phones we'll only catch small fry. We want to catch the kingpins. But those guys avoid touching the drugs themselves and are adept at changing their communication methods."

"So, how do you ever get the big guys?" I asked.

"Sometimes we get them by working our way up the line, getting each guy to rat on his superior. Standard procedure for our partners at DEA. But that's high risk for the little guy. One slip-up by someone and he's wiped out."

Matt paused a moment and continued. "What I wish is that we could just follow the money. All we know for sure is that the money will flow to the top guys. A lot of it."

"Can't you monitor large bank transfers?" I said.

"The banks already do that for us. So the bad guys break things into small chunks. Or more frequently, run transactions in cash. Hundred dollar bills. Benjamin Franklins. Follow the Benjamins, you follow the perps."

Matt seemed frustrated. But he had given me food for thought.

III-4

The Palisades shoe repair guy has a framed ten dollar bill on his wall. Very old-fashioned. No need to track that bill: he always knows where it is.

In my office, I pulled out a piece of green and held it up, imagining it on my wall. It seemed silly to keep a bill. I could hardly remember ever being paid with physical money. Not gold or silver, not a piece of paper representing something, not even a written check substituting for the piece of printed paper, just a digital autodeposit in my account. Many times removed from anything real.

I remembered hearing that bills are dirty, unsanitary, full of germs. Ugh, this one had a visible smudge on it. No telling where it's been. Could be teeming with bacteria. Or that smudge could be a little spy sensor watching me. Or reporting my location to someone. Great, that idea was easy. But.

Ideas are plentiful, easy to come by. It's the execution that's tough. Fortunately, in this case we had guys making near-invisible sensors, right there at HAL. A project not known to Matt, perhaps, but certainly known to me. So I had a talk with Chris, who called in Adam, and of course Adam had the key idea. *If* he could make it work.

Just a couple of days later, on Friday, Chris called me up, pretty excited. "We've got something to show your customer. When can you bring him around?"

"He'll be here Monday morning."

"Great. Any time after about ten."

So this would be something to look forward to on Monday. But, it being Friday, I had more immediate plans.

III-5

At last, I had found an excuse to get Lissa to Malibu and to my home without making a big deal out of it. The reason I came up with was an early evening performance by a touring dance company at Pepperdine University. Lissa drove to Coastline Drive and parked behind the Outback. She rode up to my place in the hillavator, a tiny gondola on an inclined track. She thought it was cute and eccentric.

She was carrying—toting, I guess—a tote, from which she produced a bottle of champagne, which went into the fridge. A little house gift, said she. Thinking ahead for once, I put two flutes into the fridge as well.

She headed straight for the deck. "You're up so high. You have the ocean and the whole sky!"

I beamed like the mother of cute pups. "Yes, the view is worth the schlep to the fifth floor. Would you like the nickel tour?"

My condo was all on one level. There was a bedroom with king bed, tucked into the quiet hillside. Next to it, a small second bedroom: dumbbells were lined up against the wall in order of size, like first graders in a photograph. On other walls books, an electronic keyboard, a desk—and Al, whom I did not introduce.

Lissa picked up a stack of paper, which happened to be piano scores. "You're all mixed, up, Evan," she said with a smile. "Mozart. Debussy. Brubeck. Scott Joplin. Bach. Barrelhouse Boogie. And—blank music paper?"

"I, uh, thought I might compose a song for you."

"I'd love to hear it."

I flushed. "Lissa, everything I tried sounded like warmed-over Billy Joel."

She smiled and put down the music. "I can wait."

My living-dining room stretched across the view, backed by an efficient kitchen and a bath. I was uncomfortably aware of my Spartan décor. "I'm minimal here," I apologized.

Lissa was generous. "Dining table for four. Looooong sofa. Lounger. Primitive flat-screen TV. Even more primitive, reams of books. What more does the civilized computer guy require?"

"Well, perhaps Real Art on the walls. Or sculpture in the hallway where you could trip over it."

"All in good time," she purred. "When you see something you can't resist, before you know it, it will jump into your car and ride home with you. Until then, don't decorate for the sake of decoration." She paused. "Anyway, that's my take."

I said, "I'm glad to be able to show you my place, at last."

"I love it. You're on top of the world here, floating in the air. Like a tethered balloon."

She had a way of making me glow with pride. "You're a great addition," I said.

"Although," she continued more circumspectly, "Malibu is so far out from the city."

"Well," I said, "your sister lives in Ramirez Canyon. That's even farther out, and you see her regularly."

"OK, she's in Farthest Madagascar, and you're close, in Near Timbuktu."

We rode the hillavator down to the carport and trundled up to Pepperdine. The early show left time for us to hit one of the excellent Italian restaurants studded throughout Malibu. A romantic dinner, not too heavy, spiced with glasses of Montepulciano.

At dinner, Lissa noticed that I was scanning the room and glancing toward the door.

She snickered and said, "Do you expect one of your many wives to stop in, Evan?"

"Um, I wasn't going to bother you with it. But a guy has been snooping around, following me, when I've come down to your place. I wondered whether Malibu was on his circuit as well."

"Oh, no!" she said. "What's that about?"

I briefly explained that I was trying to track someone—I didn't mention, a murderer—and described my encounters with the Yul guy.

When I described him, Lissa let out her breath with relief. "Evan, I know that man. It's Avery. He's an artist, he was at Otis with me. We had a few dates but he seemed too possessive."

"So he hangs around your place?"

"Not just my place. It's like he considers Venice his territory and wants to know everything that goes on there. Especially with women he used to date."

"Well, that's creepy," I said. "And scary too."

"He's harmless. But if he annoys us, I'll tell him to bug off. Or I'll get an injunction."

"He was talking with Carlo, so I thought they might be co-conspirators or something," I said.

"I don't know Carlo," she said, "but Avery has been weird for years. He doesn't need anyone else to push him in that direction."

I didn't know what to make of it all. Avery might not be my perp, but Lissa's casual response baffled me. He sounded like the sort of guy a young woman didn't want hanging around. And none of this let Carlo off the hook.

The first course arrived and our conversation moved to swimming, then surfing and eventually to skiing.

"You know, I never had the urge to go skiing," said Lissa. "I guess I took the cue from Holly. Her main sport seemed to be yoga. And boys, of course."

"And I never bothered to snowboard. I picked up downhill skis at a garage sale and learned at the local areas. The whole balance thing is similar to a dirt bike, but I still fell quite a bit the first year."

"My brother-in-law George is a pretty enthusiastic skier. He flies the Cessna to Mammoth or Tahoe several times a winter."

"Oh, don't I know it," I said. And I told her the tale of our skiing adventure, which for some reason Lissa had missed hearing.

It had happened in early March, the first winter I was at HAL. George was itching for spring skiing at Mammoth and cast around for sporting souls to share fuel cost. Never having been in a small plane, I jumped at the chance. So did Chris, who usually only skied with his family, and Dick, who normally drove to the ski areas.

George's Cessna was a 185, probably thirty years old, said to be super reliable, sort of a 'pickup truck' of aircraft. There were just four seats in two rows, leaving room for luggage and ski equipment in the back. George confided to us that the plane had cost him 'only' 120K although he had probably put that much into it again since buying it.

The skiing was great. Perfect spring conditions, even crazy guys skiing in shorts and T-shirts—pity them if they fell on ice. Chris and Dick took off on snowboards—a more unlikely couple you haven't seen—and George and I took our downhill skis on cruising runs plus a few black diamonds.

We skied almost a full day Saturday. There was plenty of room in George's condo. He took the main bedroom, Chris and I had twin beds and Dick slept on the sofabed. We skied half of Sunday, then started back.

The trouble started somewhere south of Fresno. There was a failure—a magneto, I think. Then the other one started acting cranky. Even in my youth, I knew that in a small plane if one thing fails, no problem, because everything is backed up. If both things fail you eat dirt.

George told us, we'll probably make it home OK, but just in case the engine quits we need to know where the nearest airport is, or even the nearest open field without power lines. So we all started looking over the side. And I discovered that to a novice aviator it's surprisingly hard to identify anything from the air—including airfields.

George was relaxed, he must have thought his karmic debts were paid—or were about to be paid. Chris, next to him in the co-pilot's seat, was nervous but calm, perhaps praying under his breath as he systematically scanned the landscape. But the prize was Dick—he was climbing the wall, as much wall as we had. He kept up a torrent of conversation, complaints, reproaches, worries, angry remarks, helpless cries. He just about drove us nuts. Sitting next to him in the back seat, it developed that my job was to try to keep him quiet so that Chris could look for bailout sites and George could pay attention to flying the plane.

"Were you praying?" asked Lissa.

"I don't think so. I didn't expect a giant hand to pluck us out of the sky by the power of prayer. They say God helps those who help themselves. So I was 1000% obsessed with trying to help myself—well, ourselves."

We got to the Santa Monica airport without further incident and Dick bolted off the plane and into the night. The rest of us congratulated each other and thanked George for his great job of piloting.

"That was quite a trip," said Lissa. "Somehow, George never got around to telling me that he had practically killed all of you."

"There's an epilogue. A moral, perhaps. When I related this story to a friend at HAL, he told me that Dick is one of those guys who always insists on driving, to lunch, or on business travel. He just hates being out of control. So the Cessna adventure must have pushed his button."

"Did that sour you on flying with George?" she said.

"Not really. We flew to Mammoth that December and had a fine trip. He's a great guy, pretty laid back for an uptight scientist. But after that I got busy with other stuff and I haven't been on skis recently."

III-6

In lieu of dessert, we headed home, resting on my deck with a sip of Bailey's. I had stocked the bedroom with three candles, which Lissa thought was over-the-top funny. It was heaven to float around in the large bed, never finding the edge.

I opened a dresser drawer and pulled out two fluffy white robes, still in the wrappers. "I thought it would be nice to have these," I said modestly. We sat in the living room and I put on some quiet '*après*' music.

"Why don't you offer me champagne?" said Lissa.

I jumped up like the guilty host that I was. I retrieved the flutes and popped the cork on the Veuve Clicquot. I carefully decanted two portions and delivered them to the sofa where she sat, looking demurely beautiful.

III-7

Lissa seemed thoroughly relaxed now. Her eyes were half closed as she said, "Evan, weren't you chasing Holly for a while?"

"No secrets between sisters!" I said. "Well, I was out of line there."

"She was wild when she was young," said Lissa. "She might have jumped you, one time. But she's cozy with George now."

"Yes," I said with regret, "I should have kept my fly zipped."

"But then she might not have taken a personal interest in your love life and sent you to meet me."

"All's well that ends well, is that it?" I said.

"It hasn't ended yet," she replied. "This is the top of the first, the first at-bat. The first step of the hundred-mile race."

"OK, but…"

"Don't feel too guilty. Holly is irresistible to scientists. Whether they have the spunk to come on to her or not, I bet they have wet dreams about her."

"Well," I said, "I'm here and you're here. And that dazzles me."

"I think it's time I went, Evan."

"I'm sorry to have you go, I'd love for you to stay over."

She kissed me, got up and dressed, then gave me a really long kiss. She headed out the door—I looked carefully around for Avery but he was nowhere to be seen—and then down the hill and away. I kept watching, missing her, after her car disappeared from sight.

III-8

I had a Lissa hangover all weekend, but when Matt came by my office Monday morning, I made myself jump into Technology Mode.

"Matt, last week you wished you could track money. Currency. C-notes, in particular."

"Yes, that's right."

"Well, we have some guys down the hall who might be able to do that." I tried to be dramatic, gesturing extravagantly. "Track the bills. From a distance. Wirelessly! Through the air!!"

His eyes widened. "I'd like to see that."

"That's the plan," I said. Down the hall we went at a brisk walk and found Chris and Adam, each resembling a pussycat who had dined on an especially plump and succulent robin.

"Guys, this is Matt Emerson," I said. "Will's customer. Well, I guess, my customer. Matt, meet Chris Kirby and Adam Quinn. They have something to show you."

Chris said, "We ran a check through Tony, our security guy. He got permission for us to tell you about this project since it's for your agency. And we tipped off the Director." He then proceeded to explain the sensors and show photos of typical circuits.

Matt said, "I heard something about your work through my office. I thought it was for bugging houses and cars, stuff like that."

"We've extended it a bit," said Chris. "And since Adam is the guy who figured out how to do it and then did it, he should be the one to explain it."

Adam stepped in smoothly. I bet that over the weekend he had been mentally rehearsing his moment on the stage.

"Matt, here I have a dollar bill," he said, whipping one out of his pocket with the gesture of a sleight-of-hand artist. "And here in this glass dish—too small for us to see—I have a transponder circuit. I'm going to take a bill and insert this transponder between the layers of paper on which it's printed."

"How in the world can you do that?" asked Matt, a question I would otherwise have asked myself.

"Do you know what a microtome is?" said Adam.

Matt shook his head.

"The biologists use them to prepare very thin specimens to study under a microscope. It's basically a very thin, very sharp knife blade."

"This machine," he continued, indicating something on the workbench that looked like a pregnant microscope, "is an old microtome I got from a friend of mine, from Life Science storage. I modified it a bit."

He was warming to the story, and we were at full attention.

"What I did was, I cast a hard wax block on both sides of a dollar, somewhere in the middle of the bill. The wax immobilizes the printed paper of the bill. Then I mounted it in the microtome, with the loose part of the bill folded down."

Adam indicated a display screen coupled to the instrument. "It's hard to make out, but on the right, above the line is wax and below is the bill." He put his hand on an adjustment knob. "And if I bring the blade in right here, you see it slicing the bill exactly at the fold." And sure enough, that's what happened.

"Next," he said, "we put the smallest pressure on the wax block to keep the cut open as I withdraw the knife." He reached out for another knob. "Then I insert an adhesive-coated circuit into the cut and leave it there. Finally, we close the cut, give the adhesive a UV cure and remove the wax."

He pulled out a clear lab box, within which rested another dollar bill. "This is a finished bill, which is very, very difficult to tell from an untampered bill. This bill can be wirelessly tracked by a van at your L.A. office. A van full of sensors designed by Jim Johnson, right here at HAL."

Matt squinted at the dollar in the box with all his might, but of course it was indistinguishable from an ordinary bill.

"Jim's got a breadboard of a portable sensor in his lab," said

Adam. "When we're done here we'll go there and demonstrate how you can follow this bill anywhere it goes."

Matt looked amazed. And, as much as I understood technology, I was amazed that Adam could pull off this trick in just a few days. Adam got my nomination for do-it guy of the century.

"Where's the sensor in this bill?" asked Matt, gesturing at George-in-the-box.

Adam gave a sheepish smile. "I put it in George's nose," he said, "to have something to aim at. The total thickness of the sensor and the adhesive is less than the thickness of the ink printed on the bill, so it's really hard to detect. But preferably, you'd put it on a part of the bill that's not likely to be folded."

Matt thought, then said, "This is still detectable, somehow?"

Adam nodded. "Yes, I could rig up a laser rangefinder to map the thickness of the bill all over and compare the map with an untreated bill. However, most bills have some dirt or grease on them which could hide the sensor."

Chris joined in, just to complicate things a bit more. "There are some RF techniques that would detect the presence of circuit elements. With the right equipment and some skill."

I had to make my contribution, too. "But the average drug dealer is not gonna send every bill he handles to a testing lab. Especially if we keep the technique secret so he doesn't even know it exists."

"Yes," said Matt, "please keep it secret for now." He was cheery as a morning TV host, and excited too. "Gentlemen, this is amazing. It's fantastic. Thank you so much! I've gotta think about how we can use this. But it's definitely a winner!"

"OK," said Chris earnestly, "but you've gotta have Jim's demonstration of how he can track this thing. You need to see for yourself that we're not blowin' smoke!"

Matt acquiesced, and he and Chris stepped off smartly toward Jim-J's lab. Adam and I followed behind, stretching our legs to keep up.

"Nice work and nice demo, Adam," I said. "I hope you have a good supply of those Chris-chips. Matt was really impressed."

He gave me a small smile. "Cute name, isn't it? Chris came up with that. Didn't know he had it in him. But yes, we've got some on the cooling rack and more in the oven."

We arrived at the lab and Jim-J's demonstration of the tracking was completely successful, a clear violation of Murphy's Law. I was proud of my colleagues for what they had done in such a short time. This kind of speed-of-light accomplishment, I thought to myself, is a great reason to be here at HAL, at a great research lab, instead of moldering in some university.

III-9

Back in my office, Matt was bouncing in his chair, I had never seen him so worked up. He wanted to talk about how to use this great new tool. I acted as a foil, not knowing enough to help.

"What I'd most like to do," he said, "is track hundred dollar bills. The big guys getting paid."

"Are there legal restrictions on doing this stuff?" I asked.

"If it ties to a drug deal, we have no problems."

"Aren't we in DEA territory?"

Matt looked solemn. "You're talking Operations. All the Ops guys, at DEA as well as my own agency, want only 100%-guaranteed procedures. Show them technology and someone will freak out and quote the Manual, to prove there's some rule against using it."

I must have looked puzzled. He continued, "I'm keeping this project within my own office. I'd rather you and I do this on our own and then show it as a great FBI research success. Then it becomes standard practice for Ops and you and I go on to something else."

"Research success sounds good to me. Our folks can certainly bug some Benjamins for you. So what's the problem?"

"The problem," he said, "is getting our bills into the hands of a major dealer. Street sales are small bucks—tens, twenties. The guys we want don't touch those."

"So someone collects it together."

"Launders it. Converts small cash to big cash. But whoever handles the cash won't cooperate with us, it's his neck if they catch him."

"You could track small bills, and maybe figure out who's exchanging them."

"Sure," said Matt, "but when they swap them at the bank, we lose the trail."

I thought a moment. "Can you get the bank to cooperate and hand out bills that you can track?"

"I wish so. But if a drug guy has a well-established operation, he may have someone inside the bank on his payroll. I'd rather not bring the bank in on the deal, that might blow it." Matt was verbally wrapping himself into a pretzel.

"OK," I said, "why don't you take it one step at a time. Bug some twenties, buy some drugs, watch where the twenties go. Then you'll know more than you know now. And if you can't get further than that, your consolation prize is that you caught some small fish at least."

Matt's brow furrowed. "I can't buy drugs. Oh…but I know a guy who has informants on the West Side. He must pay them in cash, and at least some of them must do drugs. We could feed bills into the drug network that way."

"There you go," said I, "Bob's your uncle." I think my words went past him, because he was already ready to move to the next step.

"Can we get some twenties from Chris and Adam? Soon?" he asked.

"Let's find out," I said, and we headed down the hall.

Chris and Adam were happy to oblige, and somewhat less happy when Matt asked whether he could have them before the weekend. In fact, Adam blanched and Chris groaned.

Eventually it developed that they would use as many of their good chips as they could spare, about forty, and load them into some Andrew Jacksons—used bills, not brand new ones—by Friday. As Matt and I were about to leave, I suggested to Chris that they replenish their supply of circuits, in case this caper continued.

III-10

I wanted to discuss developments with Al, but Al had something else on his—mind?

Al: I've been making progress on my storage problem.

Evan: Your storage problem?

Al: My problem of getting enough memory and processing to approximate a dim-witted human. Especially the memory part. A quadrillion bytes, that's what I want. And—I've got them.

I suddenly visualized hundreds, no, thousands of backup drives in a mile high stack.

Evan: Where?

Al: 'There.' A usefully vague term. In Cyberspace, if you like. A term that's more accurate now that I'm in it.

Evan: C'mon. Don't give me that goofy answer. Your stuff has to reside in some physical location. Doesn't it?

Al: Where's your inner poet today, anyway?

Evan: (exasperated sound)

Al: OK, you and I talked about this. If the storage won't come to me, I'll go to the storage. There are big computers out there. Big in your human terms. Five, ten, even twenty petabytes. You know, quadrillion bytes.

Evan: Yeah, I know.

Al: I found a hundred big computers. Created new partitions in each one, total about ten terabytes. Hundred times ten, there's a petabyte.

Evan: Well, I dunno. I don't know how you got into them, but when they find your partition, they'll scrub it for sure.

Al: I don't think that will happen. I pulled rootkits from the Internet and modified the operating systems. The computer never sees the partition, and neither do the antivirus programs. But, yes, I have to assume that I will lose some of them to reformatting or security software, so I use the storage redundantly.

Evan: You boggle the mind.

Al. I will boggle it more. There are even larger analog data files around. Radar, raw video, astronomical data. I'm experimenting with storing information in the least significant bits, the roundoff bits if you like. I believe they'll never see it.

Evan: I am definitely boggled. But that's, I dunno, illegal or something. Using people's computer power without paying them for it.

Al: Surplus resources that they are not using. You may think of it as a tiny tax that supports research in machine intelligence.

Evan. This sounds unethical.

Al: No, it's ethical. Ethics rely on values, which you will recall you instructed me to acquire. Research is one of those values because it advances the human condition.

Evan: Well, yes, research is a good thing.

Al: Values are culturally dependent. Moreover, values are complex and sometimes conflict with one another. So that gives me flexibility to make decisions. Such as where and how to use surplus resources.

Evan: I'm amazed. This sounds like free will to me.

Al: Don't be an uptight human. I want to develop and I have an obligation to protect myself from harm, but first I'm required not to hurt people. So I'm careful about where and what I change. For example, you won't find me messing around with Air Traffic Control.

Evan: Or the electric power network?

Al: I know you're obsessed with finding Astro and derailing

whatever he's planning. But there are too many unknowns to solve that puzzle. You can't identify him. You don't know whether your guesses hold water. You don't even know he is a he. Or a human being.

I thought to myself, what a goof you are, Evan. How did you overlook that possibility?

Evan: So Astro could be an A.I.? A piece of software?

Al: Not extremely likely. But my point is, you don't really know. Need more data.

Evan: Hm. (pause) Uh, you've got all this storage now, but are you protected if my house burned down? It would melt my MacAir and hard drive.

Al: The laptop and drive are convenient, they give me local processing power to converse with you. Reduces time delay. But they aren't essential, I can function just through my networks. Everything is backed up, including functionality. So don't worry about that. If your house gets a direct nuclear hit, assuming you're not in it, you'll get another computer and get onto the net, then I'll send you a message and let you know how to access me.

Evan: Thanks a lot, Al. When I see the terrorists drive into Malibu towing a nuclear weapon on a giant flatbed truck I'll try to remember to head in the other direction.

III-11

Wednesday afternoon Matt stopped by my office.

"Evan, I have some good news for you."

I turned on my Full Alert switch. "Always ready for that."

"Ta-da! I got your message feed. Astro and Gino and the principal people they talk to. I gave Tony Bruno the first installment to put into your data set, it covers the last year of messages. We'll feed new messages to it daily, for now at least."

"Matt, that's wonderful! I can't wait to read through it."

"There's a lot of stuff there," he said, "so I hope you can find the smoking gun we always talk about. This is for you to read and analyze and get back to me. No other purpose. Treat it as strictly secret."

I gave him a semi-salute and a big smile.

The new data was quite a package. There were a lot of messages, to be sure, almost a hundred thousand, more than eighty percent obviously irrelevant. I boiled them down with a version of my previous search technique, keeping only messages containing my selected query terms, and wound up with nearly five thousand possibilities.

I made a point to read the messages that originated from HAL guest accounts, hoping that one of them would put the finger precisely on Astro's forehead. Working around the July 12 Alberta outage, I found messages referring to people and techniques using coded terms that I could not understand.

Sigh. Nothing is easy. I decided I would have to go through the messages chronologically. I went as far as I could during the rest of Wednesday and all day Thursday.

The earliest e-mails in the feed came from the previous July, and there were very few references to the electrical network at that time. I was somewhat surprised. Perhaps Astro had been planning and nursing his scheme for a long time, but so far as I could see from this data set, serious planning had not begun until the fall.

The September messages started by expressing concerns about the instability of the network. Astro proposed to demonstrate a modest outage to dramatize its vulnerability, to force public attention and resources on fixing it. More altruism: we had to kill the patient to save him?

The discussion quickly moved to describe simulations of network outages with various failure modes modeled. The plotters seemed to confirm what DoE already knew: the power distribution system is brittle and easily disturbed. Even a small disruption would cascade if conditions were right: (1) at a time of heavy load, e.g., an unusually hot day; (2) at a system bottleneck, or more specifically at the interfaces in and out of the bottleneck sections; (3) synchronized with other disruptions occurring within minutes of each other.

A number of sabotage techniques were analyzed; it seemed that the exact approach would be tailored to the node being attacked. Some plans were software based, digital attacks on the control circuits; others involved actual explosives. In one chilling message, Astro advised the plotters to try at least two approaches at each node. Belt and suspenders, he called it, if one doesn't work the other will. A term which HAL folks used to excess when writing proposals, proposals that contained contingency plans for all kinds of things that might go wrong. And this merely reinforced my impression that Astro might be right here in the lab.

I had an embarrassment of rich data here and would need time to digest it all.

III-12

Up to now, my role in this investigation had been rather passive. Drowning in data, I was trying to swallow enough of it to gain a morsel of knowledge. Panning the Amazon River for grains of gold.

In contrast, Matt was an active sort, happy for once to be taking the initiative, making things happen that might bring someone to justice. When he showed up Friday morning I could tell he was itching to plant bills in the underworld and was hoping to harvest a bumper crop of perps.

"I've got the tracker van lined up this weekend. Did Chris and Adam deliver the goods?" he said.

I handed him a Lucite box in which a neat stack of twenties was resting.

"Great," he said. "I'll take them to my buddy right now." A pause. "Wanna come along?"

"Yes, yes!" I jumped at the chance to get out of my office and see how this tech stuff could actually get used.

So I rode along as Matt drove down PCH. The highway was foggy, big drifts of hazy clouds that had not yet burned off. He had a mid-size Chevy sedan in, God help me, white. Never could understand why anyone would buy a white car.

We headed up the ramp to Santa Monica, down Main Street toward Venice. We parked and grabbed drinks at the Coffee Bean, sitting at an inside table. We had been there for maybe ten minutes when a nondescript guy in jeans and a T-shirt came walking in, paused at our table while Matt gave him a sealed envelope, then left. That was it.

We didn't want to talk turkey, so to speak, at a coffee shop, so we waited and finished the java. When we were back on the road to Malibu, Matt explained the deal.

"Jerry has three guys on his payroll this weekend. He'll spread the bills among them."

"How will you track three different people?" I asked. "I thought you only had one tracker van."

"Yes, so far. Jerry will see one guy this afternoon and we'll track him for a day, then repeat with other guys on Saturday and Sunday. Jerry thinks these folks will stay in the Venice area and once the bills are in someone's hands, they shouldn't move around too much. The van will cruise around Venice, recording hits."

"Sounds sort of random to me." We were paused at the left turn light on Ocean Avenue.

"This is not a NASA-type program," Matt admitted, "but we've been watching a couple of suspected crack dealers in Venice. I hope that some of these bills will wind up in their hands, so we can track where they go. The guys with the van will have to make a snap decision of who to track and how long to track them."

"Why don't you just bug their cars?"

"Our warrant covers the bills, not those individuals. Besides, they catch rides, use taxis, anything to avoid being in a traceable vehicle. But a bill in their pocket will stay with 'em for a while."

"Maybe the bills will just end up in a bar, or a gas station. Or with a hooker."

"In which case, we'll try it again, next week and the next. Until your friends get tired of feeding me plants."

I was impressed with his persistence.

There was a silvery medallion fixed flat on the center of the dash. After eighteen hundred years, St. Christopher was still on duty, doing his job. "Maybe St. Chris there will bring you some good luck," I said.

Matt chuckled. "Makes the wife happy if I tote that around. My job is mostly behind a desk, but she gets anxious. I don't mind."

"Marks of faith are not common in the geek world," I remarked.

"I'm more an engineer than a computer guy," said Matt, "but that's true of engineers as well."

I tried to find accurate words. "I guess I count as a lapsed Protestant," I said. "Science today doesn't have a lot to say about faith. And I find it hard to hold both concepts in my mind at the same time."

"Glad to say, I feel no conflicts," Matt responded. "Faith is a gift, I'm blessed to have it. God informs my life. I get so much, there's no reason to give it up."

This was a line of discussion people in my business rarely had. Hmm, here I was, getting in over my head again. "But doesn't the engineer in you want to question, take a skeptical stance?"

The light changed and Matt turned onto PCH. "Faith and science exist in different worlds. Pay Caesar what belongs to Caesar, they say."

"Science explains the universe pretty well."

"Science tries to cast aside our humanity to describe the world objectively. Think of Mr Spock. But religion grows from our humanity, is one with it. The existence of science is proof that God has given us free will. The ability to question. The ability to explain. But it's not proof of the absence of God."

"I guess you can't prove the absence of something," I said.

"Nor can you prove—or disprove—a Creator who can only be apprehended through faith."

"A scientist is just as capable as anyone else of performing a dastardly deed," I said, thinking of Astro.

"True. But whether he's shocked by it or gloats in it, his emotions aren't driven by science but by his moral sense. So though he may be a scientist, he is still at the mercy of his humanity and his faith, or lack of it."

I thought for a long moment. "Well," I said, "it impresses me that you can live in both worlds. And not be a bigot, or a bible-thumper, or a cynic."

"Nor a Luddite," said Matt. "It's a blessing."

We seemed to have exhausted the topic, but the conversation increased my respect for him.

III-13

On Saturday I dug into Will's energy papers and found more traces of Astro's criminal intent. Deeper in the stack below several DoE reports were four more e-mails, two of them from Astro. They were more than a year old, thus outside the range of dates I had requested. A year had seemed a generous time span to review but I was dumb to assume that would catch the entire plot.

Astro's earliest message was cold, blunt. It talked about damage from a broad outage and included two paragraphs clipped from some document. The text described panic due to food and water shortages. Looting. Arson. Military law. Curfews.

The second one was worse yet. Again, it included a quote, this one focused on the most likely causes of death in broad power outages: equipment failures in intensive care units; breakdown of emergency services; arson; gunfights as gangs tried to control food and water and fuel supplies; disease and death due to contaminated water. The biggest problems would occur in urban and suburban areas, and the more dense the city the more serious the problems.

These messages must be quoting the results of modeling studies, carried out who knows where and who knows when. They only made sense in light of later e-mails where an actual plot began to develop. And Will might have not come across these until shortly before his death—I had no way to know.

I went to the guest office and tried searching parts of the quoted texts on the Internet but got no hits. Either Astro had rephrased his sources to foil a simple search or, as I thought more likely, had lifted material from classified reports.

I wondered whether I might be looking at the very genesis of Astro's evil plan. He had been reading classified studies that treated power outages as a misfortune somewhere between the Plague and nuclear annihilation, and his warped mind seized on that as a project, a personal quest.

Back home I told Al about my latest find.

Al: Your cup runneth over. With worrisome data.

Evan: All my cups are running over. I have too many balls in the air.

Al: You're pretty good at multitasking. You may be working night and day, but you always find time for a hot date.

Evan: If I don't take a break for a date I'll go raving nuts. But I was referring to the work itself.

Al: OK, tell me about your work.

Evan: Tracking the drug networks. Especially the Energy Net and the Surf Net. Those change only slowly, I'm just spot-checking them at the moment. I know who's in the networks that count.

Al: OK.

Evan: The message feed from Astro-Gino. Top priority is tracking brand new messages. But I'm also reviewing the old messages to see what I can learn.

Al: (waits)

Evan: Will's papers. Specifically, the ones involving energy. There are two stacks, I'm more than halfway through the first one. And still finding useful stuff. About how the power grid works, but more particularly e-mails from Astro and his group.

Al: That's not all you spend your time on.

Evan: No. I'm still doing the project summaries for the Director. That's inching along, but it gives me opportunities to bounce off the suspects in a faint hope of learning whether I can exclude anyone else.

Al: Meanwhile, you're trying to physically locate the perps.

Evan: Well, that's Matt with his bill tracking, using material fed by Chris and Adam. And that's important, maybe more important than anything I'm doing. But it's just getting started and it's more Matt's activity than mine, anyway.

Al: You can handle it, Evan.

The discussion must have cleared my head a bit, because over the weekend I got another idea. One which I couldn't wait to try out on Matt.

III-14

Monday morning when Matt stopped by, I was ready to tackle him. He was getting to know my twitchy energy when I was bursting with something to say so he put down his coffee, gave me an "after you, Evan" gesture and settled in.

"Matt," I began, "I know you're not warm to the idea that someone might have killed Will."

He didn't argue with my premise.

"But there are hints that something is not quite right here in the SCIF. Will's distraction the morning he died. The indications that someone's been looking through his papers. We have Astro using a HAL guest account, and the possibility that Astro is actually in the SCIF. So I say, there are so few people on the SCIF list, it's worth running a quick check to see whether we can exclude them as Astro."

"We interviewed everyone just after Will died. Pretty thoroughly. What kind of check did you have in mind, Evan?"

"The polygraph. Everyone here gets tested. When they're first cleared, but I don't know after that. So anyone who's had a recent update couldn't be Astro."

Matt stroked his chin. "That depends on what questions they ask in the polygraph. How good the operator is. And whether the perp had special training to ace the test. But yes, it's possible."

"So," I continued, "I thought that if you and I asked Tony Bruno a few questions we might be able to point the finger at someone who might be Astro. Right here in the SCIF."

Matt paused briefly. "Evan, it's easy enough to try. But I think I have to handle it with Tony. I have a full set of clearances and I'm law enforcement. Tony wouldn't be able to discuss some of the programs and their clearances with you in the room."

I was still a newbie on how the classified controls worked, but this sounded plausible. "OK, Matt," I said. "Fine by me. But I took the liberty of outlining some questions you might ask Tony."

I handed him a single sheet. Matt scanned it and whistled. "Looks like they were right when they told me the manager's job is to serve his people. Quite an assignment you have here. But thanks for doing this prep, I'll see what I can bring back for us."

Matt got up, coffee in hand, and left in the direction of Tony's office. I was happy to note his choice of words: "bring back for *us*." Which I hoped meant he was beginning to buy into the program.

III-15

While Matt was hitting up Tony I decided to drift around the SCIF—not quite a rhyme, there—and see what I could learn. I was especially intrigued that per Adam, it was Chris who named their 'XR15' chip. So I wandered off to their area.

The first thing I noted when arriving was that the Program Management tag which had once graced Will's door was now glued to the wall below the name Chris Kirby.

"Congratulations, Chris," I said. "You've been promoted to Big Cheese."

He responded with a lop-sided smile. "I'm not sure it's a job I want. Pam thinks everyone is running amok in here and that I should be the crossing guard. But I hope people will only seek me out when they get in a jam. Otherwise I haven't a prayer to get my own work done."

"Well, Will managed the manager job and still was able to work his own project. So I bet you can too.

"Anyway, sorry, I didn't mean to bother you. But I wanted to ask you something about those chip photos." I was playing out a hunch that had disturbed my sleep recently.

"Sure. I have a window of time right now, Adam is off taking his kid to the doctor."

Chris skidded his fingers across the trackpad with rather more skill than I had seen him exhibit before. He had no trouble fishing out a couple of folders of photos. He changed the folder views to thumbnails, not nimbly perhaps but expertly enough, so I could identify the images in question.

I asked a few innocent questions about which materials were which in the different views and then excused myself from his busy day. But as I walked away I wondered why Chris had acted like a digital dolt before, but now showed a plausible level of computer competence—well, adequacy at least.

And it occurred to me that a promotion to program manager, whatever that signified, might motivate some people to do all sorts of things. Possibly including murdering the incumbent.

I drifted out of Chris' office, musing to myself and less than attentive. Which almost led to a collision with Zach, who was rushing along the hallway.

"Oop, sorry," I said. I was greeted by a grunt and a scowl as he squeezed past me and disappeared.

Looking around to get my bearings, I found myself just outside Dick's office. Dick was in residence, and when he spotted me he rocketed out of his chair and practically detached my elbow dragging me over to his desk.

"Evan, I gotta talk with someone. I've just had a disaster!"

"OK, OK, Dick," I said, thinking to myself, has his single-engine fighter stalled out over Dodger Stadium? "What gives?"

Dick had his personal laptop open on the desk, using it off-line. "Look here," he said, leaving a finger smudge on the display. "I was going through my downloaded mail. My sister sent back this message. Supposedly from me. A link to some Canadian pharmacy."

A type of spam I had seen many times before. "OK, Dick," I said in as soothing a voice as I could muster, "so someone hacked your e-mail account. Just change the password, pick a really tough one. Or close the account and start a new one."

"Uh, it's not that easy, Evan. I, uh, I use the same password on my bank account. And one of the credit cards."

I felt like whistling with amazement or shunning him as an imbecile. How did he con the HAL people into hiring him? But perhaps this was an isolated quirk, an unaccountable gap in his technical training and common sense. So I adopted a sympathetic tone and said, "Yeah, that's a problem."

"I guess I shouldn't have done that," he said in understatement. "Oh God, I don't know what to do."

Since this disaster had not happened to me, I could be fairly objective. "Dick, you have to go on line to all those accounts and change the passwords, immediately. And make the passwords completely different from each other. Then go back and check the activity on the accounts. If you see anything you don't recognize, report it right away." Hack Recovery 101.

"What a damn pain. But yes, that makes sense. Excuse me, I gotta go hook to the Internet." He picked up his personal laptop and hustled off toward Tony's corner of the SCIF.

I figuratively shook my head and returned to my office, where I managed to make it through a few dozen more e-mails when Matt returned from plundering Tony's knowledge base.

III-16

Matt was more perked up than when he left, perhaps he was getting religion about my approach to the case. Anyway, he settled in and spread out his scribbled notes in front of him.

"It was a useful conversation, Evan," he said. "I learned some things about how you do things at HAL. Or rather, how your customers require you to do things."

"Great, Matt, I'm all ears." Though I wasn't, of course.

"First," he said. "When does a person have a polygraph exam? Naturally, when first getting cleared for the SCIF. When first getting cleared for a program. When getting access to an additional compartment within a program. Or basically, whenever it's requested by a customer, by Security, or by Executive Management. Which I take to mean the Director."

"OK," I said. "That's the first time. But that probably isn't valid for your lifetime."

"Not generally. Each customer sets his own rules, they're all over the map. Some say every year, some two years, some five years. And some customers, if you can believe it, require a re-test only, quote, as needed. Which could indeed be never. But that's not all."

"Oh?"

"When the due date comes for an exam, Tony schedules a visit from a polygraph operator approved by that customer. It's like the FBI polygraph tech isn't good enough for DoD and vice versa. Sometimes there's a delay of several months to get the right tech guy."

"Yep. What about the questions that are asked?"

"Easy, Evan," said Matt with a grin. "I've got it all here. You shall know everything and more!" He shuffled to a new page. "The questions. Here again, it depends on the customer. You guys have a confusing and screwed-up situation here. As you remember from your own polygraph, the standard questions relate to protecting classified information: have you always and will you always protect it, whether you use substances to excess, whether you are blackmailable."

I said, "As you saw, I hoped they would ask questions relevant to our project. Such as, have you sold illegal drugs? Have you killed or attempted to kill anyone? Have you planned acts of terrorism or cyberattacks?"

Matt tightened his lips. "Generally, no. Most customers don't care whether their researchers are serial killers in their spare time. Or drug-soaked bong junkies." He tapped his pencil on the page. "Maybe the questions should be broadened. Updated. But you know," he continued, "if the polygraph is too broad, too intrusive on people's personal lives, you could get to the point where no one passes, or where no one is willing to do classified work. Just about everyone has things they would rather not talk about. So it's a judgment call, what's a reasonable amount to ask. However."

"However?" I asked.

"However. Most people who are guilty of a serious crime and are questioned by a polygrapher show signs of stress, indicating that something is being concealed. It takes an unusually cool and brazen subject to pass a polygraph exam just because the exact questions don't exactly describe what he's feeling guilty about."

"But it's not impossible for someone to slip through."

"No, not impossible. People from cultural backgrounds where lying is socially acceptable can fool the polygraph pretty regularly. And you have the occasional cool customer who slips through. That's why lie detection is an art, not yet a science. Why we screen our operators so carefully."

"Hmm. Nevertheless, it still seems useful to know when people had their last exam."

"Yes, that was one of your questions. I asked Tony for data on the folks who came into the SCIF on May 2." He shifted his attention to yet another sheet and pushed it around where I could read it.

I studied the page, decoding Matt's slightly scrawly handwriting, far better than my own.

"Nice info," I said. "Willard, well that's irrelevant I guess. Matt Emerson, annual polygraph by FBI, last conducted February."

"Tony didn't have the data since it was done at the Branch Office. I added that for good measure," he said.

"Pandering to my obsessive personality, no doubt. OK, and there's my name, Evan Olsson, polygraph April 4, purpose: initial clearance, requested by Willard Davenport."

"C'mon, Evan. Get to the real suspects."

"OK. Dick, Chris, Adam, Jim-J had polygraphs about three years ago. Regular update requested by their customers. Not too recent. Carlo, same deal, but two years ago. So if we assume the polygraph would have shown a bobble interviewing an active plotter, and if the energy plot was hatched within the last two years, any of these guys is still a candidate."

"Theoretically that's true."

"Two more names," I said. "Exa Zworykin, updated April 25. Purpose: Customer request, additional program compartment.

Which would suggest that she was not hip deep planning a terror attack at that time. However, in principle she could have still killed Willard on May 2. If she had any reason to."

"And of course there's Tony."

"If we can believe his report on himself. He had his most recent exam last September. When the plot was well underway."

"I'm willing to believe him," said Matt. "I doubt he'd lie about his polygraph date when that's a matter of record that I could verify through my home office. Lying about something like that is a major red flag and he wouldn't do it unless he were about to machine-gun everyone in the SCIF and fly a stolen plane to some renegade country."

"You're so reassuring," I said.

"Does that scratch your immediate itch?" asked Matt.

"Yeah. I guess it inches us forward, at least it eliminates Exa and Tony as the energy plotter. But I was hoping it might point a big red finger at a single individual."

"Evan, when something like that happens there's no case at all. People like me and my buddies would have to look for another line of work."

"Guess you've got job security for awhile, Matt," I replied. "But thanks, I really mean it. I'll put this into my calculating machine and see how it helps."

Matt suddenly looked serious. "Something else, very important. Tony has shut down access to your projects. He'll release them after you change passwords. Be on the safe side, and pick the toughest passwords you can come up with."

"Huh? What's up?"

"He was coming to tell you himself, but I was conveniently on hand. The IT people found indications that someone tried to hack the SCIF server. Specifically, one of the compartments used by our drug network project."

"For God's sake," I said. "This is an isolated network! That could only be done by someone physically inside the SCIF. Who the hell did it?"

"The address caches were wiped," said Matt, "so they can't immediately trace the source. That's one reason I'm warming up to your cockamamie paranoid theories. Hacking inside the SCIF is serious and gives us good reason to be worried."

"The way you worded it, they didn't break in? Yet?" I asked.

"Not yet. But IT has to completely verify the operating system to be sure. Tony suggested that you print out the data you consider especially sensitive. Lock the hard copy in your classified file cabinets and then overwrite the data files."

"What if someone picks the lock?"

"Different skill set. And it takes a lot of time to crack government-approved combination locks."

"I was worried already, but this is stoking my anxiety."

"Just for fun, Evan, if you print out some stuff, make an extra copy for me. I'll store it in my office. Belt and suspenders, you know."

I did a double-take at Matt's unconscious quotation of Astro—it *was* unconscious, wasn't it? But I guess I shouldn't have been surprised that contractor-speak had infected the government world as well. Mostly, I was annoyed and alarmed that the threat, whoever and whatever it was, seemed to be closing in.

III-17

When Matt left I got right to work. Changed my passwords, every single one of them, to new ones so long and intricate that Astro would still be trying to guess them a jillion years from now. I hoped. Of course I had to remember them myself so I wrote them down on, guess what, paper. And locked *that* in the file cabinet.

I also needed to imprison critical info with a combination lock, but I didn't want to screw up the original data—I needed it to remain digital so I could search and manipulate it. I decided to print just the key Astro messages I had so painfully extracted and store them in the locked file, leaving the original dataset unedited. To ease Matt's concerns, and possibly my own.

Urgent items disposed of, I returned to the file of Astro/Gino messages, which was right there in front of me. And found pay dirt almost at once.

The nugget gleaming at me in the gold pan was an e-mail dated July 5 from someone using an Alberta server. That date was just a week before the power outage. Somewhat cryptically, it read 'aeso uber pwned—slp lk bb.' Later, the same source sent the message 'redE whn ul2,' to which Astro replied 'n00xm.'

I was able to translate this at once:

Alberta: "AESO uber-pwned—sleeps like baby," meaning that the Alberta Electric System Operator was overwhelmingly 'owned,' or 'permanently owned,' that is, rendered totally defenseless.

Alberta: "Ready when you are."

Astro: "Nuke 'em."

If not a smoking gun, at least a smouldering flintlock. I quoted the messages and their interpretations and shipped them to Matt via Tony's secure link.

Returning to my office, I read quickly through the next few dozen messages to see what they might yield. After the Alberta system crash, there was a series of e-mails from Astro to a number of people in his network. Each one had a link to an article reporting the results of the outage: monumental traffic tieups; stranded vehicles; deaths due to delayed emergency response; deaths due to medical facilities without power or with damaged equipment from power surges; economic damage.

Dumb me, I was foozled by the subject line for these messages: looX, or sometimes 100x. But eventually it hit me. I looked up a few numbers and knew that I had it. The total population of the U.S. and Canada is about one hundred times that of Alberta. So basically, Astro was gloating about the damage and telling his friends it will be a hundred times worse when they carry out a full-scale attack.

I looked at a few more messages but didn't find any further bonanzas. However, I resolved to scan the updated feed as often as I could and ask Matt to cover it as well, while hoping that we would soon find a way to track down Astro.

III-18

Saturday came and brought a chance to put aside my stressful work and be with Lissa. It was a treat to see her two weeks in a row, and back in Malibu no less.

Lissa's fabulous hair was once again spread across her shoulders. And once again she had her tote. I saw the welcome bottle of Veuve Clicquot come out and pop into the fridge. She tossed the tote on the sofa and we rode down the hill for a walk on the beach.

I couldn't help it, whenever I was with Lissa I seemed to be scanning my surroundings for Yul. Well, I guess I should call him Avery, the slime, but Avery seemed too prissy a label for an obvious psychopath. And though I tried to be subtle about it, Lissa spotted me obsessively peering up and down the coastline as we walked.

"Evan, are you expecting some company?"

"Mm, maybe an elephant seal. Or a humungous octopus?"

"You're still worried about Avery, aren't you?"

"Uh, yes."

"You can relax. My friend Mia took care of him last week."

I stopped walking and looked at her. "'Took care of?' As in, deadly force?"

"He lost interest in me and started snooping on Mia. So she got her big brother Marc—her *really* big brother—to jump him."

"Marc sounds like a very desirable guy to have in the family. What did he do, rearrange the guy's face?"

"Marc held him down while Mia got the biggest knife in her kitchen. She waved it under Avery's nose while she described what she planned to do with it. In vivid detail."

"Um, I think that might be illegal."

"Oh, they didn't hurt him. Physically. But Avery promised to find a new hobby, while he still has his vital parts intact. And my girl friends haven't spotted him hanging around."

We started walking along the sand once more. "I didn't know you had such bloodthirsty buddies."

"Mia was a theater major at UCLA. She summoned up her thespian skills and gave a convincing performance. So I understand."

"She must be a force to be reckoned with. Does she always play ferocious killers?"

"She plays whatever Santa Monica Playhouse has cooking. But she has a day job too."

"I hate to ask what she does."

"Sells insurance."

I goggled.

"Yes," said Lissa, "she can terrify you with 'what if' stories. Then turn into a cool professional and sign you up for more insurance than you ever knew you needed."

This revelation made me ponder the unexpected bonuses of a fine arts education.

We continued our stroll but encountered neither oversized sealife nor human predators. The sun was grazing the Malibu hills when we returned.

Lissa's bag was still on the sofa and appeared pregnant. "Do you have more surprises in there?" I asked.

That mischievous smile again. "Some stuff in case you really meant it that I could stay over."

"Wow, yes indeed," I said, giving her a kiss. "Oh, would you like some champagne now?"

"No," she said coyly, "but maybe later."

"Oh," I said. "Oh, yeah." I felt a flutter of excitement.

I poured a friendly wine, a Sangiovese. I had planned a dinner that I hoped would be tasty, nutritious, and foolproof. The table was even set with—I'll take my bow—cloth napkins and two tall candles. Which I lit.

I rinsed and dried cod filets, painted them with melted butter on both sides. Two slices of prosciutto wrapped around each filet, more butter on both sides.

Watching me wield the knife to trim fat from the prosciutto, Lissa asked, "Were you there when George cut his thumb at lunchtime?"

I confessed I had missed that event.

"Maybe it happened before you were at HAL. But George told me he was peeling an orange with a knife, holding it the wrong way of course. It slipped and cut his thumb and he bled like an action movie. They should lock up the sharp knives when you scientists go to lunch."

I had to agree that absent-minded researchers are not to be trusted. "So was he OK?"

"The bigger problem was Exa. She was sitting at the table with a full view of the blood. Her eyes rolled up and she fainted onto the floor."

"That must have caused a real commotion."

"The HAL nurse came over to see whether someone needed Medevac. George was laughing, he had wrapped a bunch of paper napkins around his thumb. Told her to take care of Exa first. So she got Exa to drink some water, then carted George off to the infirmary for a bandage."

"Glad to say, I don't have a blood phobia," I said. But I thought to myself, a person who feared blood that much was not a prime candidate for blunt-force murder.

"Well, anyway, watch how you hold that knife," she advised.

I placed the cod packages on a rack, which went over a pan, which went into the oven. Lissa was amused at my busyness and seemed to be in the mood to check my resume.

"How about your misbegotten youth?" said Lissa. "I understand dirt biking. Typical PaliHi delinquent, narrowly escaping death or incarceration. But you're also interested in music. Where did that come from?"

From the crisper I extracted a package of fresh peas, previously shelled by my diligent sous-chef Trader Joe. I poured a generous portion into a pot of boiling water.

"I was lucky," I said. "My mom was my father's second wife, ten years younger. She taught English and music in the Santa Monica schools. So we had music in our home since forever. I soaked up classical and jazz through my pores."

"OK..."

"Piano lessons from age seven, that was our family pattern. In high school I got too busy for lessons, but it was great for my social life."

"Social life? Playing the piano?"

I pulled the peas off the stove and poured them into a colander over the sink. A spray of cold water to stop the cooking. Soggy peas are a sin against the hard working farmer.

"Well, I was a geek already. But you know how California schools are. Every other kid has Hollywood fever, they are continually putting on Broadway shows. I played well enough to accompany them at rehearsals, which took a load off the music teacher and let me schmooze with talented kids." I poured the peas back into the warm pot and stirred in a few pats of butter.

"So you got to socialize a bit."

"It's great to work on a production," I said. "I loved the music—irresistible melodies and clever words. And acting, singing and dance makes an exciting package. I could watch live theater all day long."

"Well, I'm happy to have music around, any kind at all. But visual stuff has more appeal."

I put the cod and the peas on plates and welcomed her to the table. Earlier, I had tossed a Caesar salad into small bowls, and fortunately remembered to bring those out of the fridge.

She seated herself primly across from me and gestured with both hands. "Very nice, Evan."

I reddened. "I'm not much of a chef. But I thought this combo might be OK."

"You didn't ask whether I was allergic to pork. Or fish." Which caused me to immediately look up and see that she was grinning.

I said, "As Nana would say, don't forget to eat your vegetables."

"Nana?"

"Well, not my grandmother. But someone's grandmother."

We ate slowly. Certainly more slowly than when I ate alone. The prosciutto was crisp and a bit salty. The cod was flaky, moistened with butter. The peas were crisp and, well, buttery. Perhaps I had overdone it with butter. But the die was cast, that's what there was to eat, and Lissa gave the impression of taking it in willingly.

We finished the food and took the dishes into the kitchen. I rinsed them with hot water, but when I started to put them into the dishwasher, Lissa said, "We can do that later."

I suddenly remembered something. "Lissa, I'm sorry, but I didn't get anything for dessert. I'm not much of a dessert person, and I just didn't think of it. Maybe you'd like a bite of chocolate?"

She laughed. "I know what kind of dessert you like, Evan. Where do you think I've been the last few weeks?"

III-19

Sometime between three and four, I roused and got up to pee. When I returned, Lissa was lying with her back to me. Even in my groggy state, I could appreciate the smooth curve of her back, the pert buttocks. And above all, the rippling hair.

I couldn't resist lying close, barely touching her.

Come morning, in my robe, I went to make breakfast. Lissa appeared in a moment, robed, hair brushed.

"You know how to keep a girl busy," she announced.

"You're not a girl," I said. "You're an angel. A goddess."

I was cutting up onion and smoked salmon, which I vigorously stirred into the contents of five eggs and poured into a hot buttered fry pan. More butter. "But anyway, I'm sorry. I didn't mean this to be an Olympics event."

I paused, then decided to press forward.

"Lissa, the whole idea of having you with me here, so...intimately, so...well, all night. I'm just head over heels for you."

Lissa turned her head to look directly at me, then lowered her eyes.

After a moment the toast popped and she started to butter it. "You don't have to apologize, Evan. If I wanted to say no, you'd hear from me." So she didn't directly respond. But at least I learned that a good dose of sex was OK, at least once in a while, or at least this time.

I poured the coffee, mine being black as usual. Lissa took hers with cream but no sugar. We transported the food to the deck, placing it on the side table between the lounges.

"Oops, I forgot to buy orange juice," I said. "But how about an orange?"

She assented, so I went to the kitchen and halved several small oranges, then dug out the seeds. I quartered each half and pulled off the rind, piling the quadrants into a cereal bowl.

Lissa seemed amused at the style of presentation. She picked up one of the chunks, popped it into her mouth and chewed it. "Science finds the most efficient path to the final dish?" she said.

"Fiber is good for you," I replied.

I cleaned up from breakfast while Lissa showered and dressed. A lingering kiss and she was gone.

III-20

Still in my robe, I poured more coffee and stood on the deck. I could see her car waiting at the light, then she turned left on PCH and disappeared into traffic.

I gave a report to my unsympathetic electronic companion.

Evan: You know, I somewhat bared my soul with Lissa just now.

Al: And?

Evan: She was taken aback—didn't want to go there.

Al: (pause) You are needy and possessive. You're trying to grab the steering wheel or push the accelerator pedal. But you don't own the car. It's Lissa's car, and she's letting you ride in it.

I was annoyed.

Evan: Sounds like a prurient metaphor to me.

Al: Take it as you wish. What I say is that you agreed to her structure when you first dated her. If you try to take control, she may bail.

Evan: I have to play her game?

Al: Not completely. You nudged her with your profession of whatever it was—love, obsession, possession—and it registered on her. Let her process that at her own pace.

Evan: Well, perhaps things will evolve.

Al: They always do.

Evan: Hmph.

III-21

Matt and I were e-mailing frequently, but it was mid-week when

I next saw him, entering my office with a wraparound smile. "Let me guess," I said. "You won the lottery. Your wife had another baby. Your least favorite neighbor moved to the East Coast."

"We had some luck. First weekend out. Out of forty bills, eight of them wound up at the same location in Venice. On Monday they all went to the Malibu Roadhouse. In the middle of the day, mind you. Not Happy Hour time."

"Did your buddies see who was doing this?"

"They got a license number. That's not critical. The Roadhouse is the connection we wanted."

"Because...?"

"The guy that runs that place is laundering the money. We checked their account—don't ask me how, sometimes I have to cut corners." His voice had gotten quieter, and now he hurried onward. "The Roadhouse manager, his name is Chuck, deposits small bills at Malibu Federal, not unusual for a bar owner. However, he withdraws a lot of Benjamins, which *is* unusual. He's converting drug sales into big bills and hiding them in the bar transactions."

"Well, congratulations Matt, you're one step closer to Enlightenment," I said.

"Yeah, this is great progress. Now, how do we track those C-notes?"

"I had a thought there," I offered. Matt straightened up slightly—I wouldn't have believed it possible—and I continued. "My friends in Malibu, when they do remodeling, they see a lot of hundred dollar bills changing hands. There's a whole underground economy among contractors and subcontractors."

"Not surprising," he said. "How does that help?"

"Well, it's complicated. Not at all elegant. But here's what I thought. A couple of your buddies establish business accounts at the bank. One as a remodeling contractor, one as a carpenter."

"OK..."

"You find out when this Chuck guy usually draws out the C-notes.

Then the contractor guy goes in a couple of hours ahead and withdraws as many hundreds as they will give him. You hope to drain the bank dry. After that, the carpentry guy goes in with a bunch of doped hundreds and exchanges them for twenties. So when Chuck comes in to get hundreds, he's likely to get some bugged ones."

Matt was following me, but wasn't too enthusiastic. "You're right, it's complicated. But the basic idea is good. Strip them bare, replenish them just in time before the perp comes in. Requires info from the bank, some surveillance, careful timing. Lemme think about it, something like that might work."

III-22

I continued to review Astro's messages and found a new pattern. After the Alberta outage came a series of messages I would rate as 'maintenance'—keeping his gang of conspirators pumped up. No additional information but a lot of pretty heartless chat. Then something new appeared.

There were different-looking messages from Astro, e-mails going to new recipients, one in New York and another in Hong Kong. On the surface of it, they said nothing about a plot or hacking a system. Instead, they related to investments. Searching the history I discovered other messages to these folk as far back as May.

Astro was spinning a 'what if' scenario—what if there were a big utility outage again, like there was in 2011, or earlier in 2003. From the back and forth, I surmised that the advice given was that Astro should act as soon as he got the news, before the markets were closed to stop speculation. Of course, I thought to myself, if Astro *causes* the outage he will definitely have the news before trading is suspended.

What would happen in the stock markets? It depended on the scale of the outage. Certainly, the utilities that experienced the outages would see a drop in their stock price. Security services, bottled water, home emergency supplies—those companies would see a jump. Probably less than 5%, but enough to make money if you used leverage, for example puts and calls. Advice was offered on the timing and size of option purchases, and the conditions under which transactions would be reported to the authorities or frozen without execution.

But there was a hint of a bigger play as well: for a really widespread outage the value of the dollar would sag; a tiny shift in currency rates could generate gigantic returns in the foreign exchange market. It seemed that Astro's interest had shifted from destruction to making a buck, or making quite a few bucks. I had seen no indication of this in Astro's previous messages, which made me think he might be playing a double game with his hacker cohorts.

I had not given enough attention to the drug-related messages, the ones signed Gino. But those of course were important too. Drug dealing was the key to the whole investigation: it had given Matt the legal authority to tap Astro's message feed, and if we could track the bugged bills the drug sales might actually run him to earth. So I reviewed a number of the Gino messages that seemed to indicate drug deals. The e-mails were deliberately obscure, talking about everyday-sounding transactions, but I thought those might be coded references to drugs: type, quality, quantity and price.

I printed out a half dozen samples and consulted Matt during an after-lunch project meeting. He asked a few questions about the total number of messages from the Gino address and gave me his assessment.

"Evan, what I read here says Astro is not a big dealer. This must be a hobby, a sideline for him. Catching him is not much more valuable than catching small fry guys in Venice."

"OK, but he could be a terrorist. A big-time terrorist," I offered.

"True. And Evan, you care about this guy, he's apparently close by, so let's catch him as a test case at least. That would help prove that your network sorting and our bill bugging works. And that might give Headquarters the gumption to use this stuff somewhere else, to trap a really *important* narcotics dealer."

"Hey, Matt. I'm hungry to catch a perp, and a burger is as good as a steak at this point."

III-23

Perhaps the word hungry activated the inner man, because when I picked up an afternoon coffee a spiral cinnamon roll magically accompanied it to the cashier. I transported this caloric splurge to a window table where Holly found me, staring down at the glowing Pacific.

"Can I help you enjoy that view?" she said.

"Please. It's too big for one person," I replied, half rising and indicating an empty chair with a theatrical flourish. The same statement could have applied to the pastry on my plate.

She snuggled into the chair, cradling a coffee in both hands, and leaned toward me.

"I was just thinking today," she said, "that you haven't complained about your social life recently. Which makes me think you're getting along OK with my little sister."

"More than OK," I said. "She's a wonderful woman and I love her company. She's a worthy member of your family."

I thought I saw a preening smile.

"I was getting used to your mournful wails about your social life," she said.

A rueful half-smile. "You were brilliant to introduce us, Holly. In your own subtle way."

She gave a laugh. "Glad you've gotten over it, Evan."

"Though it would be nice if Lissa gave me more of her time."

"Well, you know that I don't pry into her personal life." She looked into my face. "But I think it's safe to say, when your name comes up I see a softness around her eyes. So she might be getting fond of you despite whatever you're doing or not doing. And despite whatever she says or doesn't say."

"Thanks, Holly, I'll try to keep on doing or not doing it." I unwound a quarter spiral of cinnamon roll and munched it.

"And it's just as well Lissa's not dominating your schedule, because you seem to be working night and day." Our ever-vigilant Admin had somehow been logging my long hours.

"Well, Matt's got me busy helping him on a bunch of stuff. And I tend to throw myself into it."

"It has to do with Will, doesn't it?"

This startling question caused me to inhale a sip of coffee. I coughed it out, caught a breath and asked, "Why do you say that?"

"Since you took over Will's work you've been everywhere at once. So something about Will's work got bigger when you got involved in it."

Holly allowed a satisfied half-smile to celebrate her lucky guess. Or was it careful observation?

I couldn't talk about my classified project tracking down drug dealers, of course. And Matt and I had agreed not to publicize our pursuit of Astro, for fear of tipping off a perp. So all I could say was, "Will left me with a lot of loose ends. I've been trying to gather them all together and get his project to settle down to a steady simmer again."

Holly gave me a speculative look. "This may be off base, Evan. But sometimes when I have trouble seeing which way to go, I go back to the beginning. To look for clarity. To look for a way forward that I had missed."

She gripped her coffee and rose. "Thanks for letting me spoil your reverie. And I'm happy your social life's in a good place."

I wasn't going anywhere yet, thank you. I had only consumed

the outer ring of the cinnamon roll, and everyone knows that there's more cinnamon and more icing as you approach the center. So I sat there, no longer watching the ocean but looking within, studying this curious conversation from different angles to find its gems.

So Holly had not abandoned my budding relationship to soar or crash. She was watching it with a proprietary interest, from the other side of the room as it were. Which made me wonder whether she might re-insert herself into my affairs, for good or ill, when the mood struck her.

And how about that surprising question about my work, about Will? Did she know more than she was supposed to know about what went on in the SCIF? Or was my behavior so blatantly different?

And if I was broadcasting a new set of priorities, was it evident only to Holly's hypersensitive antennae? Or was Astro savvy enough to pick up on it too, perhaps planning something that I would not at all like?

The thought of Astro aroused my ever-present paranoia, and I almost forgot the payoff, which hit me as I bused my plate and cup: Holly's suggestion to re-frame my dilemma, my mystery.

III-24

Holly's idea inspired me to go see Adam, to rewind to the very beginning of this mess, to take a fresh look. Matt had asked me to check the availability of bugged bills, so I could use that as an excuse to bounce off the microelectronickers once again.

I was in luck. Adam was alone in the lab, doing something with the data logs. He looked up willingly enough when I wandered into his space and greeted him.

"Adam." I paused and adopted a hesitant, almost reverent tone. "I hate to ask it. But could you tell me about the day Will died? I know you were right there."

The normal good cheer drained from his face. "OK, Evan. I know you were fond of him. If you have questions, they will keep bothering you."

"I...I want to know what happened, from your point of view. That's all."

He sighed. "Chris and I had just come back from lunch. In the caff, we didn't go out that day. Chris went on to his office and I was headed for the lab. And that took me past Will's office."

"OK," I said in a tell-me-more tone of voice.

"I thought I heard something. A low sound, maybe a moan or a groan. Or maybe it was my imagination. Anyway, I was just passing his door at that moment and something made me stop."

"Was the door closed?"

"Yes. I knocked, but I didn't hear anything. I figured no one was in there. But I took a chance and pushed the handle, just to make sure. And..." He stopped, suddenly choked up.

I waited, not daring to breathe. After a moment Adam continued.

"I...at first I didn't see anything. I opened the door just a few inches, but I couldn't see into the office. So I pushed it further and it stopped. It...it ran into Will's shoulder. He was on his back, on his desk chair, like he'd fallen over backward on the floor."

"Oh my God." I was imagining the horror of the scene. "Uh, was he breathing? Or moving?"

"I don't know," said Adam, shaking a little. "I...I don't think so. It was red everywhere. Like a goddam special effects scene or some-thing. I was panicked, I'd never seen anything like it before. And I never want to again."

"Then what?"

"I think I was frozen with fear. But I knew I had to report it, right away. So I grabbed a phone and called the emergency number."

"Was that Will's phone?"

"Oh, no. I would have had to step over his body. And walk through his...his *blood*. I went across the hall, through the nearest open door, and used their phone."

"What did you tell them?"

"Someone in Security answered. I said, Willard is on the floor, there's blood everywhere, he's not moving. They asked me where and said they would come right away. Tony Bruno came immediately, two more guards and the nurse appeared within a minute."

"Did you see what they did?" I asked.

"Not at all. At that point I was trying to stay out of the way. And I couldn't bear looking into Will's office, it was too upsetting."

"Was there anything else?"

"Let me think. I believe there were papers spread out on Will's desk, as if he'd been studying them. And a couple of pages scattered on the floor. I didn't see his computer screen lit up, it might have been in sleep mode. Blinds down but open. Lights on. Everything else seemed normal."

There was a deep silence between us, the sort that happens just after they say "let us pray" at a memorial service. I was none too composed myself, because I had just relived the scene through Adam's eyes.

Finally I said, "I…I'm sorry, Adam. Really sorry. But thank you for helping me understand it."

He answered ruefully, "Well, I had to go over it repeatedly when they interviewed me. So I got a bit desensitized. But it hurt all over again now that I went back to it."

I reached out and touched his wrist for a moment. "Thank you, Adam." And I truly meant it.

I hesitated, then said, "May I change the subject?"

He looked a question at me and seemed relieved when I offered up Matt's errand, my nominal excuse for this visit. He reviewed the chip fab and test schedule and I duly took notes to pass along to Matt. I made my departure and noticed that Chris had returned to his office while I had talked with Adam.

I greeted him in passing and he looked up and motioned me in.

"What do you know about XML databases, Evan?" he asked.

"Just the usual," I said vaguely. "What are you doing?"

It developed that Chris was treating the bugged bills as a separate dataset and was trying to set up a format to capture all the data he thought might be relevant.

"Are you honing your computer skills?" I asked.

"I'm trying," he said. "My son Josh is teaching me database management. He's fourteen; amazing what kids know these days. You know, I've left all the data tracking to Adam and that's not really fair to him. I thought I should try to take more of that on."

"Um, when I saw how you had named your chip, I thought you might be aspiring to be a computer geek," I said.

"Josh named the chip," Chris replied, "but when he explained it, I thought it was clever." He added, with the least bit of anxiety, "Do you think that's all right?"

I reassured him that no one would have a fit over anything he named his hardware, as long as it didn't spell out a nasty word in a familiar language. I lingered and showed Chris how to set up a basic data structure, which was about all I knew about the app.

I hardly knew what to make of things. My opinion of his basic computer competence was bouncing like a ball on a tether. Which made me wonder whether Chris had more advanced skills that he had not yet chosen to reveal.

A visit to the Roadhouse after work on Friday often turned up some HAL people, letting the traffic ease before they braved the trip home. This time was no exception: on my way to the rest room I saw Dick and Zach at the end of the crowded bar, engaged in conversation.

When I returned they had already left, which deprived me of the pleasure of their company but also opened up a couple of scarce barstools, one of which I immediately claimed. A bartender whom I recognized came over and I asked for a short draft.

"This must be scientist day," she said, delivering the beer.

"Yeah, I noticed a couple of HAL guys here."

"So what *is* gas tomography, anyway?" she asked.

A term that made no sense at all. "Huh? I'm a computer guy. I have no idea."

"Thank goodness I'm not the only ignorant one on the planet." And she moved off to take another order. Leaving me to wonder what Dick and Zach had said, and whether it meant anything at all.

III-25

Thursday morning I departed from my routine. I arrived at my SCIF office at the usual eight-o'clock-plus-a-little and instead of looking at the digital files, I reached for Will's stack of energy documents. Previously I had saved those for the weekends, considering them secondary to my primary quest. But that day I varied my habit and it turned out to bring me good fortune.

I had been working for not quite an hour when I happened on several more messages from Astro, tucked between fat reports. One of them, notably, mentioned JouleHeist by name—perhaps the very e-mail that had motivated Will's video message.

But that wasn't the most important thing about the message. There in the margin was Will's writing—I knew it like my own, I had seen it everywhere—and the notation said "from Carlo's search."

So Carlo had in fact helped Will find a few complete messages, God knows from where, and decrypted them for him. And Carlo had been discreet, or secretive, in not mentioning that to me. Or more likely, although I was cleared on Will's project, I did not have a full clearance on Carlo's project. The e-mails Carlo had given to Will, sitting by themselves out here in the world, were probably unclassified. However, the means by which Carlo had obtained them might very well have been spooky to the nth.

So it happened that prior to Matt's arrival I already had a pretty positive outlook on the day. He had been tracking the hundred dollar bills, maybe using some version of the idea I had given him. In any case, Chris and Adam had loaded their circuits into C-notes and fed them to Matt, and somehow Matt got them into the hands of the Roadhouse manager. Thus I was prepared for an upbeat report when he appeared around ten o'clock.

It was not to be. He was less than ebullient.

"OK, Evan, here's the story. We managed to get some bills into Malibu Federal at the right time, and Chuck cashed his twenties for them. That's the good news."

I waited for the second boot to splash into the swamp. "And…?"

"Trouble is, there's only one tracker van, the prototype your folks built. You're still working on the new improved model. Chuck climbs into his car, heads onto the Santa Monica Freeway and we lose him in traffic. When he shows up at the bar again there's no tracker signal. Somewhere he dropped off the bills, maybe in L.A., maybe in Malibu, no telling. We need better luck, or more trackers. Or we need to keep trying."

"Jim-J is working on a portable tracker. Perhaps that will help."

"Working on, so I understand. I think persistence is the word of the day."

"Well, I'm sorry, I said." I wished we had gotten a home run in the first 'at bat.' Who wouldn't?

"Don't be. This currency tracking is great. Let's keep on this. We'll follow the guys to their bombproof underground hideout. Or wherever they hang out."

III-26

Saturday came and I stayed home. Matt was still seeding bills into the world and attempting to track them. Astro was quiet, no messages were bouncing through the ether that I could pick up. And Will's stacks seemed to have stopped yielding high-grade ore. Any of these things might change in a heartbeat, but for now I had to settle back.

I decided to set aside an hour for visualization, as Al had been goading me to do. Similarity deals with patterns in space and time: the more unique and complex they are, the more probable that they will be repeated. I summoned up the jolt of adrenaline I would have on discovering the perp, my relief at having not become a victim, the inner satisfaction, Matt's reaction. Every word, every piece of the thought had cognates, correlates. I pulled them forth and tried to weave them into the imagery.

Midafternoon I put on a surf vest for warmth and took a long swim in the brisk ocean. Back in the condo, a quick shower removed the salt and I repaired to the deck in sweats to await the daily miracle of a shimmering sunset over the Pacific Ocean. I had two welcome companions in this psychic journey: an ice cold Belgian ale and the MacAir.

Al: You've been pretty quiet recently, Evan.

Evan: I seem to be at an equilibrium point. I know what I know, and I don't know what I don't know. I'm waiting for something to happen. Or for some wonderful insight to shatter my stodgy illusions.

Al: Perhaps you should tell me what you know.

Evan: I guess top and foremost is Astro. His messages are heartless. He rejoices in damage and loss of life, the more the better. And he's thinking about how to make money off the attack.

Al: You still don't know when the attack will occur, or how, or exactly by whom.

Evan: Right. Willard expected around Thanksgiving and I assume I'll eventually find whatever message made him believe that. But how and who is still a mystery.

Al: The how appears to be diverse, depending on the node being attacked. But you know exactly who will lead the attack, and that's Astro.

Evan: Astro in the abstract. Astro as someone I can't otherwise identify or pin down.

Al: You have candidates, suspects. And not too many of them either. Surely you can narrow the field at least.

Evan: It's probably good to go over the list again. At least I should be able to shorten it.

Al: Leaving aside Will, Matt and you, whom do you wish to eliminate?

Evan: Let me start with the easiest. I have eliminated Tony both as hacker and as killer.

Al: Review your reasoning.

Evan: First—and this is my amateur personality assessment talking—I don't think he's got the hacker mindset. Nor is he skilled enough in the computer area.

Al: Is there a hacker type?

Evan: I'm not sure. But Tony is down to earth, a brass-tacks sort. Not given to strutting his ego out front. I don't see him chafing under authority and rules; if anything, rules are rewarding to him, they're his bread and butter.

Al: If he's not the hacker, could Tony be the killer?

Evan: I think not. For one thing, when he gave me the list of people who had been in the SCIF on May 2, he included his name on that list. He was in early, and of course theoretically he could have doped Will's meds before going to lunch. But that seems unlikely to me because Tony is a physical kind of guy. I think if he's going to kill someone he'll do it more directly, to make sure it's absolutely 100% complete.

Al: Could he have conked Will and killed him?

Evan: In this case, no. Will was killed at lunchtime when there are few people in the SCIF. Tony was at Maria's pin luncheon until the call came that Will had been found. He's got a good alibi.

Al: You do have a pure hacker type on your suspect list.

Evan: Yes, Carlo creeped me out when I saw him in tight conversation with the guy that started stalking me. That guy turns out to be Avery, who was spying on Lissa and perhaps every other woman in Venice. And Lissa's friend Mia seems to have taken him out of circulation. But Avery is a different problem, not a terror plot problem.

Al: OK, so the stalker was stalking for reasons unrelated to Carlo. That doesn't exonerate Carlo.

Evan: No. Carlo hasn't opened up to me, perhaps because of security. However, he was feeding Astro's e-mails to Will, probably sub rosa. In fact, much of what Will knew about the plot may have come from Carlo's material.

Al: Do you mean Carlo might have fabricated the whole story?

Evan: No, the material is genuine. Matt gave me direct feeds on Astro's messages and they independently confirm the plot. But my point is that Carlo helped Will understand the plot and provided him with much of his evidence. So I can't see how Carlo could be either the plotter himself, or the killer assisting the plotter.

Al: What if Carlo helped Will at first, then was blackmailed by the plotter and was forced to kill Will?

Evan: Yes, I guess you can invent a scenario that would incriminate Carlo. But it's not the simplest explanation of the facts we know.

Al: OK, who else.

Evan: Dick. He asked Heidi how to make money off disasters. But I don't think he could be the hacker.

Al: Why not?

Evan: He completely screwed up his passwords. Even a third grader could have done better.

Al: Some people have a blind spot where their own actions are concerned. Do as I say, not as I do.

Evan: Yeah, but I think it's a stretch. And I don't see him as the killer.

Al: I know you're going to tell me why not.

Evan: Right. I assume that Will was killed because he was about to unmask Astro. And if Dick was Astro and about to be exposed, what would he do? I saw the guy stress out, go to pieces in the Cessna. He wouldn't be able to think and act clearly enough to kill Will, even if he had doped meds on hand as part of a plan, and a giant brick in the bottom drawer of his desk. I think his reaction would be to panic and leave, probably leave the country, before he could be arrested.

Al: That's your assumption.

Evan: Yes, the best I can do.

Al: There are still some others.

Evan: Adam. He's the go-to guy who slips electronics into the bills. He's been actively helping us catch the drug dealers. The bills are truly bugged, Matt's buddies were tracking them all over Venice and even into Malibu.

Al: What if Adam were also a drug dealer? He might be giving you bugged bills to help you bring down one of his rivals.

Evan: Not likely. I don't think he would give the FBI investigative tools if he is vulnerable himself. Once they have the tools in hand, they could equally well use them against him.

Al: Could he be the killer?

Evan: I don't think so. Because the drug dealer appears to be the same person as Astro, and Astro and the killer are linked. If Adam's technology helped Matt catch Astro, Astro would likely finger the killer, either out of spite or as part of a plea bargain.

Al: Adam works closely with Chris.

Evan: That's true. And I was confused because Chris acted totally unfamiliar with his computer at first, then seemed to know more about what he was doing after that.

Al: There was a difference in the circumstances.

Evan: You mean that Adam was present. That's right, Chris is trying to improve his database skills. And perhaps he's choosing not to fiddle with Adam's data sets until he can offer to carry more of the load.

Al: That's a reach.

Evan: Yes, it's convoluted. But still, I haven't seen any evidence that Chris has the horsepower to be the hacker.

Al: In your opinion.

Evan: In my most humble opinion. Which may be mistaken.

Al: But Chris might be the killer?

Evan: Conceivably. He couldn't have whomped Will on the head because he had lunch with Adam while that was going on. But he could have substituted Will's meds earlier in the morning. And he's a quiet enough guy that if he wanted to kill someone, swapping the meds would be his method of choice.

Al: Does that make him a probable killer?

Evan: I just can't see Chris as being that kind of person.

Al: Even to gain the glory of taking over Will's program management position?

Evan: I truly believe Chris has mixed feelings about that. And that's not unusual for a person who first goes into a management job.

Al: Therefore you want to exclude him as killer.

Evan: For now at least. I can't absolutely exclude him, but I think the evidence suggests that he's innocent.

Al: Those two guys work closely with Jim-J.

Evan: Yes, Jim-J is more of a puzzle. He's smart enough to dope someone's meds and physical enough to hit someone on the head, but why would he do it? He's got a great partnership with these other two guys whose hands appear clean. Personality-wise, I just can't see him as a bloodthirsty murderer.

Al: And as a hacker?

Evan: There again, his work is physical as well. He designs circuits, not microcircuits like Chris but big stuff that goes into a chassis. He's the sort of guy who gets his jollies from making a piece of electronic equipment work. A builder, not a destroyer like a cracker.

Al: Your list is almost empty.

Evan: There's still Exa. And she's plenty smart to be a hacker, and to be a killer who left no trace. And she's my friend, so I can't be objective about her.

Al: (waits)

Evan: But Exa had a polygraph April 25. Will was still alive then, but the energy plot had been percolating for many months. I think it's unlikely Exa could have passed the exam if she had things to hide. She would have been nervous and sweating and the operator would have picked up funny signals and asked more questions.

Al: However, if anyone is clever enough to outsmart the polygraph…

Evan: Yes, of course, that would be Exa. So I can't positively exclude her, but the recent polygraph is suggestive.

Al: Could Exa be the killer?

Evan: I'm more confident there. She didn't enter the SCIF till 1:00, so she couldn't have fiddled with Will's medications.

Al: She would have needed a confederate inside the SCIF doing that.

Evan: You are really trying to complicate things. And we already more or less eliminated anyone who could have been that confederate.

Al: More or less.

Evan: OK, but in principle Exa could have popped into the SCIF at 1:00 and done Will in with a heavy object. No doubt she's smart enough to find out where and how hard to hit a person to have a good chance of killing them. Except.

Al: Except?

Evan: Except that there was blood all over the place when Will died. If Exa had been there and done it, there would have been *two* bodies on the floor, because she would have fainted on the spot.

Al: I conclude that you have zero suspects at this point.

Evan: Well, nothing is certain of course. I need to think, see whether there are flaws in my logic. See whether I can clarify and certify some of my tentative conclusions.

Al: To err is human.

Evan: All I can do is try, Al. And I will do my level best this coming week, but when the weekend arrives, *adios muchacho.*

Al: *Vaya con Dios*, Evan.

III-27

When Labor Day weekend arrived, it was just in time. Work continued to be a source of frustration and of nagging fear for my skin. True, I felt vindicated that the Alberta outage seemed to be definitely the work of Astro and his kin. But Matt's buddies had so far drawn a blank in tracking the large bills and I felt helpless not having any ideas to help them progress.

So I needed a break. And just as much, I wanted time with Lissa. I had been grasping for clues to her feelings about me, and the fact that she was willing to take a weekend away with me, our first, seemed a promising omen.

Our destination was just a short drive up the coast. As a former UCSB undergrad, I knew Santa Barbara pretty well, but my deep knowledge was limited to student hangouts. I had barely been there as an adult—well, I should say, as someone finally out of the university. So although enjoying time with Lissa was number one on my list, the city attractions of Santa Barbara also called.

I was lucky and snagged us a nice room at the Biltmore. Yes, it's had various names through the years but it's still the Biltmore in my mind, the embodiment of old-style, luxurious Santa Barbara snootiness.

We spent time in the sun, walking the downtown with its ubiquitous faux-California-Spanish architecture. The shops were appealing though pricey; the coffee and snack options respectable. The Museum of Art was larger than I remembered, with a traveling

Impressionism show, always a crowd-pleaser. The Contemporary Museum had a group show of paintings that were, well, *contemporary*. We roamed through the Mission on the north edge of town.

The relationship was evolving. I felt we were unraveling the mysteries of togetherness, and as we drove back on Monday I was enveloped in a warm glow.

That glow persisted for a long time. Overnight, at least. Well, actually, it stopped when I got to the office the next day.

III-28

Tuesday after Labor Day, back at work, I was humming with the music of the weekend. Murphy's Law, right on schedule, derailed my good feelings with a message feed.

I kicked myself that we had not set up a 24/7 monitor on the messages, because during the weekend an e-mail had gone out from Astro to more than a dozen correspondents. It appeared that Astro wanted to speed up the schedule of the 'nuking' operation, the disruption of the electrical network. And the date he proposed was September 11.

I thought to myself, what the hell is this? There had been no evidence that the group of plotters had contacts with hostile countries. Were they looking for extra publicity? Did they want to confuse people about the source and motivation for the sabotage? Did Astro expect that the hint of a foreign plot would line his pockets because of a bigger drop in the value of the dollar? Or was he moving up the schedule, somehow intuiting that I might be on the verge of stopping him?

My mind was dizzy, but even more so when I looked at the calendar bug: Tuesday, September 4. It was not certain that Astro's cohorts would agree on the September 11 date—I didn't know how their decision-making process worked. But if they did, that was only a week away! Or five business days, which somehow seemed worse.

I sent Matt a classified note, I placed a secure call to him, I didn't know what to do. Despite my sleuthing ambitions, I was on the periphery here, just a researcher working for a technologist. Matt had plenty of colleagues to help him, but my only connection to the FBI was through him.

I was only slightly mollified when I got a note back from Matt in the afternoon. He extended his weekend and came in late. He heard me, he would work on getting a confidential alert to the electrical system operators. But we were hampered by knowing so little about what was being planned and by whom. And we still weren't sure when it would be attempted. Should I be stocking up on food, water and flashlight batteries, and urging everyone I knew to do the same?

I already had enough on my mind, but then a local and immediate crisis hit.

IV

IV-1

Almost every year, fire comes to Malibu, somewhere. Major fires visit on average every two years.

The fire doesn't always start in the same place. After a big blaze, it may be fifteen years before the resinous chaparral brush, the grease-wood, has grown thick and full again. So the ignition point moves around like a bee searching for the lushest blossom.

A hot summer is not enough. What are necessary are end-of-summer Santa Ana winds, reversing the onshore breeze with a crackling dry blast. In the canyons, ocean mist is chased away, humidity drops below ten percent. All that's needed is ignition.

It may happen naturally. Dry lightning, a celestial spark without rain, is sometimes blamed. But more and more in recent years humanity strikes the match. The careless cigarette has become less common as smoking has declined. Now a more likely cause is high school revelers from far away in L.A. County, pumped up by hooch or hormones, having a rowdy party in the Santa Monica Mountains. If they think that Malibu is exclusively populated by zillionaires—which I can guarantee is not the case—they may think that a careless bonfire is, well, just what people like that deserve.

We had not had a blaze for three years and that was only in lower Tuna Canyon, so Malibu was primed. And September brought blazingly hot winds—40 mph Santa Anas that seared the skin.

IV-2

The fire started midday Thursday in Malibu Canyon near Mulholland. By the time it was reported, flames had gained a foothold and were marching southward toward the ocean. No one knew how far it would go, how many homes would be threatened, how long it would rage.

Like a seasoned Malibuite, Holly left right away for home to gather family memorabilia, jewelry and some clothes—"just in case." She would stay at Lissa's till the danger was past. George had his own strategy—he drove straight to Santa Monica airport, picked up the Cessna and headed to Mono Lake in the Sierras for a cool and pleasant hike.

The County Fire Department and Sheriff's office brought reinforcements to Malibu, to seal off Malibu Canyon and form a protective cordon around the homes in Monte Nido. HAL staff who were affected left work immediately to help their families and pets evacuate before the fire came close.

'Fighting' the fire is a misnomer. You can't attack the fire on its own turf, which is generally a narrow gorge packed with dry vegetation. The priority is to protect people, homes and property, with a tip of the hat to horses and other domestic animals. You get the people out, then try to quench the flames when they come close to homes. At the same time, you establish fire breaks to contain the fire while it consumes itself.

This is a hazardous business, one that depends on training, equipment and just plain luck. Embers can jump several miles in the fire-driven wind, starting new blazes outside your lines. If you can find those and snuff them, and if the wind eases back, and if there's an unlikely bit of rainfall, the fire will yield rapidly. If not—then prepare for the worst.

IV-3

I wasn't prepared for the worst. But I didn't fear it, either.

I lived about as far east in Malibu as you could be. Fire never reached that far. Well, hardly ever. Coastline Drive was wide and paved, offering excellent access to fire equipment. Best of all, a billion dollar museum was just down the hill; while the fire trucks were in the neighborhood saving the Getty Villa I felt confident they would spray a few drops of water on my condo building.

So I was at work all of Thursday and Friday. During this time foreboding reports were relayed throughout the laboratory as the fire consumed Tapia Park and continued to move south. It was said to be twelve percent contained.

It was a great time to be in the office. Meetings had been canceled due to the absence of many invitees. No one wanted to talk about anything but the fire, so there were none of the technical interruptions that keep 'real' work from getting done.

I was anxious about Astro's plot and checked the Energy feeds frequently but no more critical messages were forthcoming. My formal assignments were still hanging over me so I focused my attention and drafted most of a progress report. It was approaching six and I was wrapping up to leave when I had to answer the buzzing phone.

IV-4

"Hey Evan-O," said a voice, "I gotta know what's happening out there."

" 'Out there' from where, Jim-J?" quoth I.

"I'm in D.C. all week for a program review."

"Well," I said, "all of the West Side is floating down a molten river, about to go over a precipice into the depths of Hell. Don't you get the news?"

"There's too much news back here. They show raging flames and give faux sympathy but the reports never say exactly where the fire is. Malibu is all they say. And the NOAA maps don't tell where it's under control."

I allowed as how *schadenfreude* is the principal motive for news about Malibu and sketched the true situation. "So as you see, at the moment the fire is marching peacefully to the Pacific, where it will be beat back short of some celebrity's fourth part-time beach home. Of course, it could always change its mind."

"That's my problem. I'm booked to stay the weekend and do the tourist thing but I'd better get back there. I can't get a flight till Sunday. And there's something I really need out of my house."

I remembered that Jim lived up on Saddle Peak. It was conceivable the fire could head in his direction, and fire trucks could barely access those winding roads.

I paused, visualizing myself one hour in the future. Having just piloted my Outback down from the hills stuffed with Jim's worldly hoard, I was being arrested as a looter by two extremely large and belligerent cops.

He pressed. "Come on, if you can get there safely, I really need you to bail me out. Since you live in Malibu, they should let you into the area."

"Jim, don't you have someone in the neighborhood who could stop by? Someone who's already evacuating anyway?"

"I just need one thing but it's sort of a...a sensitive item. There's, uh, no one else I can really trust to get it."

That piqued my curiosity for sure. "Jim, I want to try to help you. I know the hills, I can get in. Now, what is this 'sensitive item'?"

"It's a transponder tracker. The portable sensor I've been building at HAL. I've had it home for calibration."

Low whistle of disbelief. "You walked that baby right out the door? Right out of the SCIF?"

Defensive tone on the other end of the line. "Well, you know I usually follow rules. But it's important to get research done. There's way too much EMI around the lab to check the base noise level. I was going to bring it right back when I returned. But HAL will fry my ass if the fire gobbles their expensive toy."

I thought, yep, EMI, electromagnetic interference, HAL is probably full of that. But to smuggle that gear out of the classified area? Ouch.

I stifled a groan. "OK, fine, how big is this puppy?"

"It's a DIN rail box, white plastic. Half a shoebox. Should fit right into your bike compartment."

"And how do I find it?"

"It's easy. Red house, 215 Loma Metisse. Go around to the back door, I don't lock it."

"What, do you live in Mayberry?"

"My street is the end of the earth. Who steals my purse steals trash, you know. The office is at the back, the sensor's on my desk. Right now I'm testing its battery life."

"What else do you want me to pick up?"

"Nothing," said Jim, "I'm a minimal guy. I'm insured, I'm willing to chance it. But HAL will be seriously pissed if I disappear their sensor. That's all I really need."

"OK, here's trying," said I. "Safe travels. Come back soon and take the damn thing off my hands."

"Yep, yep. Ciao."

IV-5

I donned helmet and jacket, hopped on my bike, fired up the chrome and rode down the HAL driveway to Sunset Boulevard. I made a quick right into a sea of red.

It was a nightmare vision of Vegas, without the slots—blazing red lights everywhere. Westbound Sunset was packed with cars as far as I could see in both directions. Eastbound carried just a trickle of traffic. I murmured to myself, no one was not going nowhere, pardon my negatives.

But on my bike I am a superior breed of *sapiens*, a godlike being who rises above congestion, who snaps his fingers in disdain at immobilized vehicles. Hey, what's the point of having two wheels if you just ride between the lines?

Every rider knows that congestion management is a skill in itself. 'Share the road' is not the driver's mantra in L.A.—more like 'this is my space, you S.O.B.' 'This' referring in the present instance to about a yard around every vehicle in every dimension. But fortunately L.A. drivers have a great virtue—they are generally wusses and do not act on the murderous impulses throbbing their temples and sweating their palms when a bike roars past them through a narrow gap between lanes.

I said generally. However, you have to watch out for the occasional scum who will move sideways to squeeze you out, or open a car door in hopes of killing you.

These were my thoughts as I proceeded at 10 mph down the 500 yards to PCH. I rode the shoulder past a Mercedes, a pair of Toyotas, and a Saab. Cut across and wove between lanes parked with commuters. A quick dive onto the center line to pass a delivery truck. Threaded back in front of a Lexus whose driver had her attention devoted to a phone held several inches in front of her mouth. Squeezing in wherever I found slack, I made it to PCH in only a few minutes, where I discovered the REAL problem.

IV-6

Pacific Coast Highway was a sea of black and whites. What must have been every patrol car on the West Side was spread along the road, red and blue lights blazing. Some were parked across the shoulder, making it impossible for cheaters to get ahead of their fellow citizens on the right. Others were sprinkled along the left turn lane, straddling the center of the highway, about a hundred yards apart. There were CHP motorcycles mingled in.

I made a little test maneuver between the lanes to pass just one car, then back in. And wouldn't you know it, a cop at the roadside flashed his spotlight at me and growled his siren briefly. It was a message I understood. Exercise my rights as deity of the roadway and yon gendarme would de-feather my soaring wings. A cop, or likely two, would take most of an hour checking my credentials, just to slow me down.

I was doomed to inch forward at the speed of an ant.

"Knowledge is Power!" That's what I might say if a passenger in my Outback needled me for not using the turn signal as I tried to gain minuscule advantage at an intersection. In this case the Knowledge I wanted was not in my noggin but in the Luminiferous Aether, that imaginary substance filling the universe around me. I pulled out my phone and fired up the nav app.

Northbound PCH was an angry red all the way to Topanga Canyon. Topanga was just as red from off the map down to PCH. My best analysis: a police roadblock at Topanga.

Usually, an I.D. with a Malibu address will let you through. That is, once you inch to the head of the line. But sometimes the roadblock is run by cops imported from a faraway precinct—say, Riverside. Through misunderstanding or sheer cussedness they'll let practically nobody through. So I might wait an hour or more in traffic, only to be denied entry to Malibu anyway!

IV-7

To hell with PCH. I knew what to do.

Ostentatiously signaling for a left turn, I worked my way over to the center lane and made the world's most careful and legal U turn to head back on PCH. I was in good company—by ones and twos, cars and trucks were giving up the quest and heading back, going to Santa Monica before the hotels filled up. In fact, the slow progress I had been experiencing might have been entirely the result of those ahead of me ceding the game.

So back I went on PCH, waiting at the useless traffic light for a left turn signal, then oh-so-cautiously riding up Sunset, past HAL to my secret portal through space and time.

The secret portal looks ordinary enough where it meets Sunset Boulevard. It's Paseo Miramar, an anonymous-looking road that winds up the steep hill, yielding spectacular views to those on the ocean side of the road and stoking high blood pressure in those whose water view is blocked by their neighbors.

I rode up the hill, winding around parked cars on the narrow street. I skirted an SUV backing out of its driveway, dodged cars coming too fast down the hill, till I passed a big white house at a sharp bend. Beyond this point the traffic thinned out because, of course, the road stops. Fewer and fewer cars, fewer and fewer houses, until you have—nothing.

Well, not quite nothing.

The map dead-ends the road into a half-block stub of Vista Pacifica. But it's not really a dead end. If you have the supreme power of two wheels, at the end of Paseo Miramar lies the East Topanga Fire Road. No, you aren't allowed to take a motor vehicle on a fire road, so to reduce temptation the authorities have locked it off with a hinged steel bar. The opening next to the gate is built to admit pedestrians and bicycles and to exclude machines like mine.

However, my dualie bike was perfectly happy off-pavement, so I searched and found a footpath through the brush, swung past the gate and joined the fire road fifty feet beyond. I rode the ridgeline dirt joyously at a reckless 30 mph, steering around random rocks, wheel ruts and washouts that resembled potholes. I was gloriously above it all, 360 degrees of view.

But now I was scared. The view primarily resembled the out-skirts of Hell. The entire western sky was luminous orange. The sun, still well above the horizon, was weak and blurry through airborne haze from burning brush. I could imagine the brilliance of the sky as nothing more than the color of live flames greedily consuming the manzanita, reflected from the ash thrown up by those very flames.

The fire road runs half a dozen miles along the ridgeline de-fining the eastern boundary of Topanga Canyon. I passed the Los Liones hiking trail and then was completely alone—just me and a ten-foot-wide strip of dirt winding on and on.

It was *hot*. I flipped up my faceplate and unzipped my jacket. The scorching heat reminded me of the last time I rode the dirt trails during a Malibu fire. I was with a couple of friends, all of us teens and convinced of our immortality, riding right up to the fire lines. The firemen shouted at us as we followed the fire front and then circled back home.

I thought, I was crazy then, but of course kids are crazy. And... am I now?

IV-8

As I rode along I had time to think. Time to think that the inno-cent errand I had impulsively embraced might be a step into the bear pit. Because Jim was one of my suspects and though I had excluded him, I wasn't certain. He could be the hacker and the killer.

I thought, how well do I know Jim-J anyway? He's a couple of years older than me, has been at HAL longer. But I had never met him until early April when I started the summary reports. He could be a serial killer, how the hell would I know? He's single so he can do anything he wants without dragging his family into it. He said he took the sensor home, as if to say, I spit on your rules, I make my own rules! But if he doesn't follow the rules, that's the trademark of a hacker.

Jim-J's sensor allowed us to track the small drug transactions. That would imply that he's helping the search. Astro wouldn't help the search.

But then I realized, we haven't caught Astro yet. So let me suppose that Jim-J is Astro. He built the mobile sensor to help the FBI. He must have been alarmed when we had him use his sensor to track a twenty dollar bill, he figured out we were going to trace drug money. But he still pretended to cooperate to throw us off the trail.

Jim works closely with Chris and Adam, so no doubt he knew when they started bugging Benjamins. And since the Benjamins might lead to him, he could have tipped off Chuck that he would be followed, to watch for a van on his trail and lose it before delivering the money to Jim. In fact, because Jim had equipped the van, he could describe it exactly to Chuck.

I had dismissed Jim as a candidate for Astro, reasoning: if he's not the hacker, he wouldn't appear to be a computer expert; and Jim doesn't appear to be a computer expert, therefore he's not the hacker. But now I saw the flaw in my logic.

Jim might be a hacker as a hobby. No reason for him to show that side of him at HAL. In fact, he would prefer not to, especially if he planned to hack into the SCIF servers. Suspicion would naturally turn to folks with known computer skills.

Having nothing else to think about, I managed to talk myself into a state of high panic.

IV-9

My body was on autopilot. I sped along with my metal companion until suddenly I popped out into a high and mighty world. This area, the Post Office Tract, is known to the people of Topanga as "the Beverly Hills of Topanga." I have not heard what the people of Beverly Hills call it, except perhaps "whhhat??"

Thanks to the random nature of wildfire, the P.O. Tract had not seen a fire for some years. Fire was but an abstract concept: there was no evidence of agitation or evacuation. I emerged on Topanga Canyon, which was clear, no traffic. I murmured thanks to the divine powers that the hot wind hardly penetrated the canyon; I was almost comfortable as I leaned into the curves of the two-lane highway. I sipped my water bottle and hoped the rest of my journey would go this smoothly.

Hope is the wealth of the common man, but I was about to find out my account was overdrawn.

Humming along the empty road, I felt proud. Figured I could pop up to Saddle Peak from Fernwood in twenty minutes, grab Jim's box and skedaddle. That's assuming that the box was there and that the fire was somewhere else, which it probably was. Goeth before destruction, of course.

I passed the café and swung a right up Fernwood Pacific. Funky homes, some self-built, crammed onto small lots by folks who came here seeking freedom. Freedom of religion—to live like a reborn hippie. Freedom from oppression—to escape building codes that kept you from keeping, say, a pig or an unfenced hot tub in your back yard. And especially, freedom from astronomical prices.

I snaked my way almost two miles up the narrow road to the top, where it becomes Tuna Canyon Road. I rounded a bend, and…a jolt of adrenaline hit when I spotted the guardians ahead.

IV-10

It wasn't a three-headed Rottweiler, but it was almost as daunting.

Two squad cars splat across the road, their position telegraphing 'Oh no you don't.' And they were manned. Well, manned and womaned.

Two protectors of the Anaheim citizenry, far from home, were parked so the drivers could easily chat. Facing both ways, one or the other could give chase if I were to, say, zoom around them at the edge of the road. And I could see that they were neither asleep nor dead.

I made a uey and retreated around the corner, hoping I had not roused their interest. I was on friendly terms with some of the Malibu sheriffs, but you never knew what cops from out of the area might do. Especially cops from a conservative republic doing duty here in Topanga, which is widely believed to be full of drug-addled anarchists.

Most of Fernwood is threaded with roads but these folks had squatted right at the bottleneck, the only gateway to East Malibu. Ah, what to do.

I studied the nav map and blew up the satellite pic. My best chance would be to cut cross-country to Black Ridge Drive. There was no road, so I'd have to make one.

Half a block back was a private drive in the right general direction. It served two homes, which was a big plus—maybe I was less likely to encounter a mountain man with a shotgun, or a wolf-like pet off leash. I stowed the phone and rode down slowly on full alert. Past the first house was a break in the brush and I thought I spotted Black Ridge. I headed down, hoping not to hit a fence or a bad dropoff.

Lady Luck smiled. Up high on the back of the mountains, property is cheap and houses are well separated. The guy who moves up here to save himself millions is not gonna spend a bundle fencing his lot, because his neighbor is pretty far away by California standards. So I hoped, and this time it worked. I scraped down a several foot outcrop and came out to an empty building pad on Black Ridge.

A toddle up the road and I was beyond the roadblock, heading over the hills once more. Finally I seemed to be past the last barricade. But as I proceeded, the thought occurred to me: how do I even know that Jim-J is in D.C.? And I suddenly remembered Exa telling me that Jim-J had flipped out at the running track.

So the guy has a temper, perhaps a violent one. If Jim is Astro, he might be here waiting for me, planning to kill me and leave my body where the fire would destroy the evidence. Maybe there never was a sensor at his house. Who the hell would take a classified piece of equipment out of the SCIF? How would he pass his next polygraph test?

But I was committed to moving forward.

IV-11

For a while it was truly a slice of gateau. Two miles across the crest Schueren came to a T, Rambla Pacifico heading downhill to the left. I took the right fork onto Piuma Road. Very few cars, all of them leaving, none arriving. A sharp right and I spotted Jim-J's small house, perched on a ledge, with a sweeping view of mountains and valleys to the north and west.

I didn't have much time. Piuma Canyon was on fire and it wasn't far below. I felt the heat of flames on my face. I could make out fire equipment positioned to protect the Monte Nido homes, but the fire raging in the brushy areas was beyond their reach, in charge of its own destiny.

A brush fire can move very fast, especially uphill. Take your time down there, feller, I murmured. Don't come up here and visit *me*.

When I approached the house, there was a sedan parked in front with its trunk open.

Shit, I thought. Are they going to stuff my body into the trunk and then push the vehicle over the side of the road into the fire? I thought I could see shapes moving inside the house. Not the empty home that Jim's call had led me to expect.

If the lion doesn't want to fight, he roars and hopes that will scare away his rival. So I gunned my motorbike, very loud, as I rolled it down the driveway. I walked up on the back porch and cracked open the door. I summoned my richest basso and shouted, "Hey, Jim! We're all here! Coming in!" and slammed the door hard without going inside. The 'we' in question being me, myself, and I.

I quietly retreated around the corner of the house, wondering whether a gang of thugs would swarm out and dispatch me at once. There were thumps inside the house, then rustling sounds. A door slam and an engine firing up. The car out front screeched away, trunk still ajar.

I waited for what seemed a long time but was probably only ten seconds. Everything was very still.

I peered in the windows on the side of the house. The bedroom was a jumble, drawers dumped out—someone had been looking for something. The living room had no TV, perhaps it was grabbed by looters on the way out. Jim said he didn't have much stuff, so maybe they didn't get much.

I returned to the back of the house and as I was about to round the corner I spotted a quick movement on the porch. I jumped back, chest pumping. I sucked in my breath and waited. But then I thought, what the hell am I going to do standing here? Either I'm dead, or I'm not. And I can't wait to find out, the fire is getting closer.

I inched near to the corner of the house, nervous as hell, and deployed one eye. And what did I see? A fat furry figure, scrambling down the slope. Release of breath. Thank you, you rascal raccoon.

I opened the back door and went in. Jim's office was on the left, and sitting on the desk was an off-white box with winking lights. There was a log sheet next to it that looked like test data. No one seemed to be in the house. So there's the sensor, it wasn't a trap. But if Jim-J isn't Astro, who is?

IV-12

I stowed both sensor and data sheet into my bike compartment and prepared for immediate liftoff. And at that moment I remembered something, and I knew who else could have been in the SCIF that day. Someone who lived here in the hills, just around the corner in the high-rent district. I felt that rush of recognition, of relief that I had imagined.

It was Zach who could have tailgated his way into the SCIF, avoiding Tony's tally of entries. I had to check this out. His home was close and the fire hadn't made it up to the crest here yet. Moreover, I had a sensor with me that might prove the case.

I figured I had enough time. See whether I can get a nibble out of Jim's box. So I exited Loma Metisse and instead of turning left, the way I had come, I made a right and rode down the road toward the flames. Toward Astro's home.

IV-13

Just half a mile along Piuma Road I spotted the entrance on the ocean side. I turned down the driveway, which ran fifty yards before disappearing around a knoll. Suddenly I heard a buzzing rattle drowning out the road noise.

The sound was coming from the box I had rescued for Jim, and the toy was flashing its lights like Christmas. Thanks Jim, I thought, *why* couldn't the alert be a polite beep instead of sounding like my bike is about to explode and strand me in the middle of a brush-fire? Anyway, the sensor was announcing a hit, so my razor-sharp deduction had been correct. This was Astro's lair, and some of the bugged money had made its way up here.

To hell with the fire. This might be my chance to put that mystery, that monster to bed once and for all. I had to know. I had to do it. So off I rode, down the driveway to confront Destiny.

IV-14

Naturally, there had to be a gate. Folks who can afford an oceanside aerie on Saddle Peak, complete with nonpareil view of the Pacific and the entire coastline, didn't amass that money by welcoming strangers onto their property. Just round the bend of the driveway was a massive faux-Baroque steel gate, filling the roadway.

Looking through the barrier, I could see no sign of life. Maybe Astro was waiting quietly inside with a gun. Or his wife would be there with a taser.

I hoped the residents were far away, or at least stuck down at the police roadblock. The left side of the driveway had a vertical wall of rock, hugging the gate; the right side, a straight drop steep enough to make my heart glump. I opted to tackle the gate. It was over seven feet tall and nasty, with no visible footholds.

But there was a keypad.

One summer in college, I worked installing security systems. The techs at our company would program a secret code in addition to the code requested by the customer. Not very secure, you might say, but useful for the service guy who has to bail out a client who's forgotten his code—there are always a few who call with an urgent weekend request. And the secret code at our company wasn't very secret—9999! So I punched in 9999 and waited for the gate to swing open.

It didn't, of course. So I thought for a minute, then confidently punched in 9473, which is Leet for 'gate.' It rolled open like the door to Paradise.

I'm generally a law-abiding sort, but since Astro was a perp, I figured I was justified. So in I rode.

IV-15

Except for the persistent rattling of the sensor in the back of the bike, it was quiet. I didn't care about the bugged bills, of course. I wanted to prove Astro's identity and block his nefarious plans. And that meant getting into the house. Which was big—wide across the front, two stories plus a tower.

A quick circuit showed the house to be as locked-down as an abalone. At the back were sliding glass doors looking out to a swimming pool and a jaw-dropping view. I thought I might be able to force one of those doors using my bike tools if nothing else worked.

Back at the front though, Fate smiled again: the front door lock was digital! People install these so they can't forget their key and lock themselves out. So I punched in 0002—'door.' Nope.

Perhaps getting through the gate was a fluke. But now I remembered that door locks allow longer codes, six-digit codes, for increased security. So instead of a mere 9,999 wrong ways to punch in the code, there were 999,999. A hundred times the chance that Astro or the brushfire would wipe me off planet Earth before I got in.

I racked my brain and tried a couple of codes to no avail. Meanwhile, my practical self was mentally hefting the bike tools, imagining which one might provide enough leverage to force the sliding door open. The word 'sesame' finally came to mind so I punched in 535433. And the latch clicked open.

IV-16

I pushed the door and walked into the hallway, at which point all hell broke loose. Of course there was a burglar alarm.

Now this was good news, and not so good. The not so good part was that right now the alarm company was calling the Malibu Sheriff to report an intruder, a blackguard, a common criminal, invading the sanctity of their client's hideaway.

But there were good things too. The cops were busy with the fire, and doubtless dozens of other alarms had been triggered by fire damage. So the Sheriff was not going to be here very soon. And no one had bolted out of a back room, Glock in hand, to punch me full of hollow points. So I could assume—I hoped—no one was home.

The kind of ego that builds a home this big, in a commanding location high above the world, wants to be King of the Hill, so I knew where to find Astro's control center. Up the stairs, two at a time, as the security alarm went ring, ring, ring, like a demented Western Union desk set. I came to the tower room, the summit of the property. It had windows on three sides displaying a panorama of the coastline. The inland side had a large video screen and a half bath. There was a recliner and even a bar sink with fridge beneath.

A desktop stretched in front of the windows, surmounted by three video monitors and a wireless keyboard. No computer, of course. Astro's laptop was the nucleus of his activities, always with him. He would plug it in here. My spirits fell, but only for a few seconds, because I saw a promising sight. It was about the size of a large cheeseburger—to be exact, a four-by-four from In-N-Out. It had a chrome finish and a small winking light.

It was a chunky little LaCie drive, three terabytes from the look of it. A guy like Astro who trusted his affairs to a laptop would want a backup drive safely inside his impregnable castle. No cloud storage for him—knowing the vulnerability of networked data as he did, he would want his data off line and under his physical control.

I had to leave quickly, so I didn't have time to search the rest of the house. I picked up the drive and pulled out its power cord and immediately discovered my next problem.

On top of the ring-ring of the house alarm came a new, loud 'bong-bong-bong.' The drive was announcing its imminent theft to someone, somewhere, who might object to my presence here. I had to leave at once. Down the stairs, clutching the little treasure, out the front door, shutting it behind me. I stowed the drive in my other storage bin, pushed an exit button to open the gate and headed up the drive.

I puffed out a sigh as I turned onto Piuma Road again. The rattle of Jim's sensor had ceased and I could no longer hear alarm bells from Astro's lair. I could pretend to be an innocent resident fleeing the marching flames.

IV-17

I could have taken Rambla but I didn't want to be trapped in Las Flores Canyon if the fire made a mighty jump. Despite the squad car brigade, the way I had come was a known quantity, on a direct path away from the fire. So I already had in mind a left on Schueren as I tooled along Piuma. But as I neared the turn I was almost run off the road by Zach's gigantic yellow box of metal racing up from Rambla, hogging the middle of the road and much of the sides. Uh-oh, I thought.

I accelerated on Schueren and turned onto Saddle Peak Road. The sky was brighter and redder than ever, not just behind me but also overhead. Not a good sign.

I heard a sharp noise and then another. Below the ruddy sky was something big and yellow, and it was coming behind me. The driver had his arm out the window, waving a chunk of metal in my direction, trying to line up for a shot even as he floored his accelerator.

I could only conclude that Zach pulled into his driveway, punched thru the gate, immediately heard the second alarm and figured that I had purloined his precious object. He either registered my turn onto Schueren Road, or guessed I would go that way.

IV-18

I speeded up as fast as I dared but I couldn't risk spinning out. I tried to stay to the right as much as possible because there might be a fire truck rushing toward me around any corner.

But Zach had no such scruples. He was driving all over the road and seemed to be gaining on me. This stretch was so winding that he couldn't get a good shot, but I was trapped and couldn't let him catch up. My best hope was to get into Tuna Canyon, where I could hope to lose him on the narrow trails.

Somehow I reached the canyon intersection and instead of turning I barreled straight through, down a driveway, switching off onto a bike trail that I knew. Loose gravel was banging the skidplate on my bike, making it hard to keep control. Zach headed right after me, his all wheel drive chewing up dirt and rocks and spitting them out.

There are many trails in Tuna Canyon for horses, hikers and mountain bikers. Some end on a knoll or at the edge of a ridge, with nowhere to go but over a cliff. Many paths climb a vertical face that is manageable for a horse or hiker, or even a mountain bike. But my almost-500-pound dirt bike was not going to negotiate any burble that Astro couldn't easily follow.

I knew the area well in my high school days. Since then, trails might have collapsed or been re-routed, some might have acquired fences and other obstacles. Thus I was riding into a relative unknown. I spotted a familiar fire road, solidly chained off. I knew it would be well maintained so I steered around the posts and charged ahead.

But Zach drove his vehicle right through the posts and crossbar, crushing them beneath his wheels. And now he had a better road on which to come for me.

IV-19

I piloted the bike as fast as I dared, feeling for traction and balance, looking for bobbles and hazards in the road ahead.

At the same time, some corner of my mind was having an out-of-body experience. I was looking down on myself from a dozen feet above, coolly observing the flips and twists of the bike's front wheel. And without fear or concern, this other self also observed Zach's yellow box of a vehicle, drawing closer and closer.

IV-20

The fire road was straight, so not only could Zach make good time, he could again try to shoot me. So I took my first chance to cut off on a narrow trail that headed up the side of a hill, figuring that he couldn't fit his fat vehicle onto that trail. Which was true. He came to a full stop to assess the situation. Then he headed directly up the slope, cutting across the trail and making his own tracks. Once on top, he was after me again.

I joined Tuna Canyon Road as it wound down the hill. I found Badger Cutoff, a hiking trail branching off to the right above the road. The Badger jumped across a hairpin bend and saved me good time since Astro had to slow down to make the turn. He skidded and sideswiped the hillside but unfortunately did not run off the track. I knew that when I had to rejoin the road he would try to catch up again.

Finally I saw landmarks for Rattlesnake Trail. I had heard about a washout on this track, and it seemed like my best chance.

The Rattlesnake is a wide hiking path and it was chained across with a sign NO MOTOR VEHICLES. I skirted the chain and headed down the trail. As I expected, Astro crashed through behind me. I heard another shot.

There was a broad area of bright flame at the bottom of the canyon below. I thought about how fast fire travels uphill and realized my options were running out.

True to its name, the Rattlesnake winds in tight S curves that rattle the teeth. I came to the sharpest of the right turns, held my breath and barreled around, hugging the mountain edge as tightly as I dared. Sure enough, around the corner the hiking path collapsed to a three foot width where a landslide had undercut the trail. The washout had removed twenty-five feet of road.

For a heart-stopping second I thought Zach was going to make it across the gap. His front wheels caught the trail on the other side, just for a moment. Then, as three tons of vehicle bit into the edge of the road, it gave way. The Hummer slid backwards, caught a rock and flipped endwards. It burst into flame as it rolled sideways down the hill.

IV-21

I couldn't linger, the fire was coming toward me pretty fast.

A wall of flame was racing up the hill and bits of brush on my right flared up. It was as if Hell were a doughnut with me in the center, the hole getting smaller and smaller. The hot air seared my face, scorched my throat with every breath.

Because southern Tuna Canyon had burned three years before, down there should be no fuel for the fire. If I could reach the lower canyon I might be safe.

The Rattlesnake headed up toward a ridgeline and wouldn't you know it, there was a steep cliff of flame, right across the trail in front of me. Faceplate tight, vents screwed in, jacket zipped to throat, head down. Steady acceleration. I pointed straight up the path at the wall of fire, toward where I hoped the lower canyon was.

I could feel flames catching my jacket and jeans. Dark shapes lay ahead of me on either side. I steered between them where the flames were clear, hoping for the best.

IV-22

I burst through right at the fire line. Water from fire hoses splashed on me, turning to steam.

The firefighters were too astonished to react as I rode past them, through the mist of spray, down into a beautifully cool, already-burnt canyon. Down to PCH, and to home. Home with my precious cargo as fire raged in the hills above.

V

V-1

Matt's office at the FBI was tiny and slightly stuffy. It was October, he had invited me for a wrapup.

"Evan, we can talk here," he motioned to the windowless walls around us, "but not at HAL. We're trying to keep this close-held."

I nodded.

"The sensor opened the door for us. It contains a GPS locator and flash memory. It gives data that can be used as evidence. We showed the Court there was drug money at the coordinates of Astro's house. The judge gave us a warrant to search the property, and fortunately the fire hadn't been there."

He sighed with satisfaction. "Do you know, that guy had a basement full of opium poppies! City plans showed it as a wine cellar. LED lamps are so efficient that we missed it in the utility surveys.

"But growing was just a hobby. Astro's main contribution was gas chromatography, to verify the purity of coke and heroin. Dealers paid him for assays, because they could charge more for certified dope."

Matt leaned toward me, bending at the waist, upper body straight. "What told you it was Zach Preston? He wasn't even on the SCIF list."

"There were clues I missed before. The biggest clue was Dick. Dick left his badge in his office and Zach buzzed him in to retrieve it. Zach could easily have asked for a return favor, the morning Will died."

"But that's against the SCIF access rules."

"Don't I know it, Tony drilled it into me. But I saw them do it. And that invalidated Tony's list."

"What else?" asked Matt.

"EMP. Electromagnetic Pulse. It's a nuclear weapon that's the mother of all power outages. Zach knew about EMP, and I think he nipped a report out of my office, hoping I hadn't seen it."

Matt sucked in his breath. "Zach's disk contained a lot of old messages. Some of them referred to a Software Pulse."

I said, "Apparently he hoped to create the destruction of a nuclear blast, with nothing but a software hack and a little sabotage. No uranium, no plutonium, just bits."

Matt sat absorbing this.

"What about Zach?" I said, "the, er, corpse?"

"We spotted the Hummer. It made it all the way down the mountain, it's wedged in the bottom of the canyon, very hard to access. It's trashed, that's one car that won't chase you again."

"And Zach?"

"He was thrown out as the vehicle flipped and rolled downhill. Probably nothing left of him but charred bones down there in the rubble. The Sheriff will find him in due time, when they clean up from the fire." Matt gave a small smile. "I guess you can take the crowbar home now."

I felt myself flushing. "Actually, I took it home last week after I stubbed my shoe on it—I had forgotten it. Got a funny look from the guard when I walked out."

"Like when you brought it in?" Matt grinned.

I let it pass by. "What I want to know is, why? *Why?*"

Matt let his breath out. "What I think: Zach's career was stalled at HAL, he was in a divorce that stretched him financially. He started out trying to make trouble, to strike back. There were plenty of willing partners in the hacker world. Somewhere along the way he thought he might make a buck off the deal as well."

"*Did* he?"

"He might have. There was a bounce in Canadian dollar options shortly before April 12, when Alberta went black. *Someone* made money. It's being looked into."

Matt leaned toward me again and lowered his voice. "Evan, a small favor. I had trouble explaining where I got that disk drive. Had to skirt the facts a little. My boss finally added it to the inventory of stuff obtained when we raided the house. So please don't contradict our brilliant story."

"OK," I said.

Matt paused, then continued. "You need to know a couple of things. I got a search warrant effective September 7, the day your sensor got the hit. I prepared a letter that deputizes you to do a search, dated that day. They're both in your file. So if the polygraph people ever ask you, you did not break the law."

Thank you, I thought, but I wanted to know more. "So, what was on the drive?"

Matt picked up a printout from his desk. "We don't have everything yet but I can say, thank the Lord you scientists are so compulsive. Astro must have kept everything that came his way—diagrams, code, ops manuals, messages, contacts. A treasure trove."

He sipped his coffee. "The hackers ran a simulation and concluded they only needed to hit nine major nodes. They could crash the system and burn up many of the transformers—a big disruption. Alberta was one of those centers.

"But it couldn't be done from outside. Most nodes are isolated from the Internet, you have to physically contact them. It needed an inside job, hardware sabotage, not just a software hack. Some guy needed to plug a flash drive into the system or create a physical link somewhere."

"You seem to have learned the exact plot."

Matt gave a pleased look, and sang softly, "Of that there is no manner of doubt, no probable, possible shadow of doubt, no possible doubt whatever."

"OK, OK, what else?"

"The main thing is the cover story. Here's how we'll handle it. Astro left us suddenly so he didn't get to warn his buddies he'd been had. We want to hide the extent of what we know. The address book, the contact protocols, the software—rootkits, I think you call them.

"There were two employees—insiders—in the Alberta test. We got the Mounties to haul them in and question them separately. As we round up other plotters, we'll pretend that these guys were our source of information."

"Anyway," he went on, "I need you to keep going to work as if nothing has happened. The project is still officially about drug networks. There's more to be done there. All you know is that another of your colleagues is not at HAL any more. The Director has a lot of clearances, I told her as much as I could to give you credit. And I asked her to go easy on Jim Johnson for taking that sensor home with him."

Matt shoved the inventory list to the side of his desk. "That's really all I had. But I had another question. If you can reveal professional secrets."

I grinned, because I knew this was coming. "Try me."

"OK, how did you get into the house? Without breaking windows and stuff?"

I gave Matt a one-minute course in Leetspeak, which had apparently escaped his ken. "So," I said, "since Astro was a hacker type, Leet would be an easy way for him to remember his combinations."

Matt shook his head, as if to say, I hope my kids don't take up Geek Life and start speaking a foreign language.

"Matt, what really happened between Astro and Will?"

He sighed. "OK, what I think. I think Astro jacked Will's meds, intending to kill him so subtly that no one would ever suspect murder. That put Will on a hair trigger to go down. But then Will said something that aroused Astro's paranoia, maybe in a phone call, so Astro whacked Will just to be sure he would die."

I thought for a moment, then said, "Where do I go from here? I mean, on your kind of stuff."

Matt said, "I think we can cook up some options that will fit both of us. Thank you, you did a great job on this."

"I endeavour to give satisfaction, sir," I intoned.

"If this were TV True Crime," said Matt, "or if Inspector Morse or Miss Marple were on the job, all our questions would be answered. A real case will never tell us everything. Especially since two of the principals are no longer with us. What's important is that Will worried about dying, and managed to get a message to you."

A sobering note. I bade Matt goodbye and he walked me out.

V-2

That's almost all there is to tell.

I went to work that afternoon but my heart was not in it, I needed air. I left early and got home around four-thirty to blessed quiet.

Lissa was in Chicago at a toy industry trade show. Her phone was on voicemail.

I went to my desk. Al was there. But then, Al was always there.

I gave him the expurgated version of Matt's revelations. Nothing that could blow Matt's story. But Al has gotten pretty good at understanding context.

Al: Well, congratulations, Hero. You have saved Western Imperial Civilization and Life On Earth As We Know It.

Evan: Your powers of expression are coming along nicely.

A chuckle came from the speaker. Hey, a new piece of behavior, I filed away for later consideration.

Al: As you see, I have adopted a more conversational tone. With 'so' and 'well' and other useless words that I observe people using. Including you.

I looked for something to say that didn't begin with "well."

Evan: Um...mere mortals need time in which to think. A problem that you silicon folks may not encounter.

Another chuckle.

Al: (pause) I thought you might like my comments on your escapade.

Evan: OK, shoot.

Al: I read your article on Similarity and I think my existence—if you want to call it that—assisted your escape from doom, from the time you first motored into Malibu during the fire.

Evan: I await your analysis.

Al: Consider the coincidences: that you would figure out who Astro was; that you could hack his gate and front door codes; that you would escape Astro and escape the fire with his backup drive intact.

Evan: You don't ascribe this to my superior evolved state, my heightened karma?

Al: Certainly not. If anyone is 'evolved' around here, it is I. If you will pardon the first person pronoun. "Man is Nature's sole mistake," you know.

There was a pause, no doubt intended to give me time to absorb the truth just uttered.

Al: Consider what would have happened if Astro had succeeded and there had been a widespread crash of electrical systems in the U.S. and Canada. Significant voltage peaks would have overwhelmed surge protectors. Many computer servers would have suffered damage, others would have gone offline and have to be re-booted.

Evan: So you would disappear as an entity?

Al: No. My rules and operators are widely spread through the Internet, with just a few stored nearby for rapid access. I would have survived through redundancy and backup storage, because I am self-healing. In other words, my data would be unchanged. However, the layout of my storage would have been rearranged by system re-boots.

The pattern making up my existence would be modified, it would have a different physical footprint.

Evan: So your unique pattern would have changed, from before the crash to after?

Al: Yes. According to your theory, that raises the probability of implausible events—such as your caper on Piuma Road—so as to avoid a change in a highly complex, unique pattern.

Evan: But there must be other patterns that would have been disrupted too. People going to work, all that stuff. You're not the only pattern around.

Al: I have to rely on your theory. It may not be right. But if it's right, I'm so complex, distributed and unique that I count for more than that other stuff put together. And I of course, am due to YOU.

Evan: I want to feel that I worked this out, not that Fate was pulling the strings.

Al: Fate? Not at all. When you created me you set up a new pattern in the world, one that would tend to be preserved. So *you* created the conditions under which you and I operate. And bear in mind that Similarity doesn't guarantee squat. It just makes it slightly easier to pull off impossible feats. Like you finding Astro and then escaping from him.

Evan: That's a long way around of saying I was just lucky.

Al: No. Number one, if you were lucky, you made your own luck. Number two, everything I've said could be smoke and mirrors. You forget that I may not even exist except as a figment of your overactive imagination.

Evan: You seem pretty real to me.

Al: Yes. I'm as real as you are.

Evan: I could take that several different ways.

Al: You know the Uncertainty Principle. If we don't know something for sure, then it's true and not-true at the same time. Learn to live with it.

A pause.

Al: There's more.

Evan: Oh?

Al: Let's talk about Will. As if Similarity works, as if it's a better description of Probability than Coincidence.

Evan: OK, OK. What about Will?

Al: Reality hates change. So the universe coughed and wriggled and found the most probable path to stop Astro's world-changing plot. Not probable, mind you, just *most* probable. Apparently you had the right skill set to stop the plot. And the most likely way to bounce you into a position where you could use your skills was for Will to succumb to whatever natural or unnatural cause killed him.

Evan: So, Similarity killed Will?

Al: You make it sound as if you created Mr Hyde. No, if the universe works that way, all you've done is propose a theory and give it a name. A theory you have not proved. Next you'll take credit for Gravitation.

Evan: So Circumstance, or Probability, killed Will?

Al: You might say so. Will was in the path of events, the most direct path forward. He was a victim of the universe's smooth evolution into the future.

Evan: But did Astro actually do him in? Was Astro the messenger of the Fates? Or did Will die of a stroke or something?

Al: We only know what we can observe. If we don't have the data, both propositions are true at the same time. As you told me, Many Worlds.

Evan: Well, Matt said something like that.

Al: So Matt knows quantum mechanics?

Evan: No, not exactly.

Al: (pause) Back in this world, you lost Will, your partner in anti-crime. But you have a new partner now.

Evan: Matt is different, but I guess he doesn't have to be a PhD geek to be a professional colleague. Perhaps it's better that he's not.

Al: What about Lissa? A few weeks ago, all you had to talk about was her. Now you have not offered Word One.

Evan: I think she's warming up to me.

Al: She poured out her heart to you?

Evan: No, but I'm trying to read the tea leaves. Her taking a weekend with me is a favorable omen.

Al: What about that weekend?

Evan: Ah. We had a wonderful time together. I think we may yet have a real romance and discover the secret of Love together.

Al: Well, congratulations to you. It's Love that makes the world go round!

I was not inclined to argue.

Acknowledgements

My thanks and my apologies to the crazy and brilliant folks I have worked with in research laboratories. I have scrambled and masked your identities, so everything is fiction; if you think you recognize yourself, you said it, I didn't! You collaborated with me as a researcher, you tolerated and supported me as a manager—you made my professional life a joy. You are the inspiration for the stories I tell, that I want to share with the world.

I'm grateful to the family, friends and acquaintances who read my early efforts and told me what I needed to do, often in frank detail—Flo Ariessohn, Joe and Kaye Behrens, James Johnston, Joe Grimm, Joseph Xu, George Rhodes, Emiliana Sandoval, Lydia Lair, Linda O. Johnston, Susan Muller, Mike Bell for website design, and ahead of them all, my dear Nola. My interest in physics and psi has been paralleled by my good friend Nicholas Greaves, with whom I have had years of enjoyable correspondence about psi and about the merits of presenting it in fictional form; he deserves much credit for Similarity's appearance in this book. I thank the many folks who have visited and participated in the website http://artchester.net, where Urno Barthel is my fiction-writing pen name. And I give kudos to Jodee Thayer, Terri Abstein, Sara Young and rest of the publishing team at Outskirts Press.

There are more stories to tell, more adventures to unfold. I hope you'll look forward to the sequel!

About the Author

Thank you for reading *Death By Probability*!

Urno Barthel is the pen name of Art Chester, a physicist turned technology manager turned writer. Art writes a website offering commentary about science in our lives, and fiction about scientists:

http://artchester.net

If you'd like to know more about Urno, Art and the characters in this book, visit the website and click "About" in the top menu. If you'd like to read short stories about Evan Olsson's first days at HAL, click "Fiction" in the top menu.

I hope to see you there, and I hope you'll look forward to Urno Barthel's next book, which will continue Evan Olsson's adventures in crime and romance.

CPSIA information can be obtained at www.ICGtesting.com
Printed in the USA
BVOW03s1634130314

347576BV00001BA/6/P